KINO and the KING

Jen Angeli

Paperback ISBN: 978-1-62747-063-6
eBook ISBN: 978-1-62747-065-0

This book is dedicated to the keikis (children) throughout Hawaii
and the world, and to the keiki in you, dear reader.

To my children Leah, Alixandria, Brielle, Patrick, and Lianna,
and my grandbabies Madeline, Carter, Dominic, and Sofia ~

May you live the life you dream of.
Dream big.

For

"My Fada" Frank C Ramos.
Hope you have a nice "espatula" to use in Heaven's kitchen.

Special Acknowledgements:

My "Tribe," Jonni Adaniya, Joanne Godley, and Troy Tahara – for keeping me on track on the final stretch. My "editors" of Hemet and Pearl City Writing Groups, Jim Hitt, Vicki Hitt, Howard Fishbaum, Melissa Eiselein, Judy Howard, Doris Chu, Maya Mendoza, and Daniel Johnson. My Hawaiian language consultant Pomaikai'i Akiona. Sam Ohu Gon III for giving me some ideas for authenticity of Hawaiian lore. Jeff Chung for doing my photos. Masters Jang, Park, and Cat of Body and Brain Yoga/Tai Chi Hawaii for helping me find myself and teaching me to heal with energy. Mrs. Edna Sullivan, my English Teacher at St. Francis High School for developing my writing skills. Liz Wright for giving the mean girls a voice. Dr. and Mrs. Warner Johnson, for your support in honing my craft. My parents Frank and Nathalie Ramos, for blessing me with a great education and high standards; and to all my family and friends for the unending love and faith in me. And last, but not least, my best friend Kino Shigekane who helps me function in life. Thanks for letting me borrow your name.

Oahu, 1964

A gentle drizzle fell outside the jalousie windows of a small bedroom, scenting the air with rain. Inside, the single-paneled wooden walls held pictures of dark-haired, smiling faces, and a scenic oil painting of Diamond Head surrounded by deep-blue water.

"You look just as beautiful as your mother did in this dress on her wedding day," an old woman said as she fastened a small spray of white flowers around the base of a young woman's hair bun. The old woman's shiny black hair, slicked back from her face with coconut oil, glowed in the soft light.

"Thank you, Tutu. I wish she could be here," said the young woman. Her brown eyes met her grandmother's in the oval, koa-wood mirror in front of them. The very same-shaped eyes, though creased with deep wrinkles, smiled back at her.

"She is with us, and she is very proud of you. She watches you every day from heaven." The older woman pulled a small, woven box from the top drawer of the dresser in front of them. "Since her dress is old, you still need the new, borrowed, and blue items." She placed the box on her granddaughter's lap.

As she lifted the lid, the bride gasped. Inside, on a bed of white-satin material, lay a gold bracelet bearing intricate, black-enamel calligraphic letters spelling the name, "Wahinenohopono," surrounded by an elaborate etched design of waves and flowers. Next to the bracelet laid a two-inch, shimmery blue-green stone.

"It's beautiful! Mahalo nui, mahalo nui." She slipped the bracelet onto her slender, tan wrist then looked down at the rock for a moment before picking it up.

"That is not for you to keep, but you can borrow it. It belongs to someone not yet born. Your granddaughter."

The younger woman's eyes widened as she peered at the stone. When she touched it, she swore she felt a slight vibrational hum, and the ribbon of gold throughout it seemed to flow like a stream.

"This is a sacred hopena pōhaku – a stone of destiny. It has been passed down from my great-great-grandma for generations. It is important to give it to her on the day she turns twelve."

"Granddaughter? I haven't even thought of becoming a mom," said the young woman.

"Like me, you will be the mother of one daughter, and she will have only one daughter – the chosen one. She will bear your Hawaiian name." The old woman covered the box and returned it to the drawer. "She must receive the stone. The future of all your descendants depends on it."

A knock, followed by a man's deep voice, called from the other side of the door, "It's time to head to the church. Everyone in the car."

"Promise me you will give it to her." The old woman folded the younger woman's fingers over the stone.

The bride nodded. "I promise."

1

'Ekahi

Oahu, 2016

"How do you say your Hawaiian name again, Gramma?" Kino Kahele rotated the gold bangle so that the black enamel letters faced her. She knew that the Hawaiian language called for each letter in a word to be pronounced, and she mouthed the sounds as her grandma said them.

"Wa-hee-neh no-ho po-no," her grandmother called over her shoulder. "And you need to practice saying it, since it's your Hawaiian name too – and one day that bracelet will be yours."

"What does it mean again?" Kino pulled the bangle over her skinny hand and watched it drop to her elbow.

"It means 'Woman of strength and character,' which is what you are." Her grandmother placed a hand on the back of Kino's chair and leaned forward. "Breakfast is ready." She set a platter of eggs and Portuguese sausage in the center of the table and sat down. "I hope you're hungry!"

Kino surrendered the bracelet to her grandmother and watched her slip it on her plump wrist. She loved how her grandma always looked festive in bright floral dresses, with flowers either tucked behind her ear or at the base of her salt-and-pepper hair bun, and how she always smelled like coconut oil.

"Before you eat, close your eyes and open your hands!" Gramma pressed something hard onto Kino's upturned palms. "This may not

1

look like much, but long ago, my kupuna – your great-great grandmother – gave it to me, and I had to promise that I would give it to my granddaughter on her twelfth birthday."

Kino opened her eyes and looked at the three-inch, square, brown wooden box. The wood bore intricate designs on its sides, and a honu, a Hawaiian sea turtle, carved on the lid.

Bummer. She was hoping for a cell phone or a tablet.

"Thanks, Gramma, I'll cherish it forever." Kino tried not to sound disappointed as she placed the box on the table.

"No, silly girl, look inside." Her grandmother pushed the box toward her. Kino giggled and felt like a dork. She lifted the lid and poured out its contents onto her hand.

What the heck? A rock?

Then her eyes started to marvel at the glistening deep-green and blue hues of the stone. A hairline ribbon of gold flowed in a random pattern throughout the rock, which shimmered as the light hit it.

The stone was two inches wide, oval, with a flat bottom like a skipping stone. The center had a slight indentation, which made a perfect place to hold it between her thumb and index finger. She held it that way, and swore she felt a gentle humming vibration.

"My grandmother said that this hopena pōhaku is sacred, and that it's filled with mana, the life force of the islands." Gramma put a weathered hand under Kino's open palm. "It will help you find your destiny."

Gramma Momi, like most native islanders, was descended from generations of blended nationalities. She spoke with a mix of proper English and Pidgin, the dialect of the islands. Her Hawaiian ancestry taught her spirituality in nature. Animals, plants, and things from the earth itself held a lot of meaning for her.

"What do you mean?" Kino held the rock inches away from her face and examined it.

"It means that you are destined for something special," said Gramma. "It's up to you to believe in yourself enough to follow it."

"How am I supposed to know when I have found my destiny?" Kino put the stone on her open palm and poked it. The shiny flecks glittered as it rolled over.

"You will know." Gramma patted Kino's knee. "Keep the Aloha spirit in your heart, and trust your ancestors to guide you."

"Did it help you find your destiny?"

"No. This pōhaku belongs only to you. It is special, and so are you."

"I still don't get it, but thank you." Kino wondered if her grandma found the rock outside and gave her it to her because they didn't have money to spend on a store-bought present. She returned the stone to the box and closed the lid.

"Put the stone in your pocket and keep it on you, always," her grandmother instructed. "Use the box for something else. I got it at the swap meet."

Kino smiled. "Okay, Gramma. I'll change into something with pockets, and carry it with me today." She was still hoping for an iPad.

"Happy Birthday, Babygirl!" Her mom Paula placed a stack of pancakes with a single lit candle in front of Kino. The two women sang the "Happy Birthday" song as Kino watched a solo drop of melted wax pool and dribble down the candle.

Mom held her cell phone out. "Smile!" Kino made a face at the camera and then blew out the flame. "Did you make a wish?" her mom asked.

Kino murmured, "Mmhmmm…" as she pulled out the candle, reached for the butter, and hoped her mom wouldn't ask what it was. She didn't want to tell her that she wished they were back in California, in their old house, with her old friends.

Pushing those thoughts to the side, Kino dug into her breakfast. Chocolate macadamia nut pancakes with bits of banana in it, drizzled with sweet, warm coconut syrup, her favorite. Kino flashed her mom a smile and said, "It's just so good!" which sounded like, "Ufsufsogoo," with her mouth full.

Gramma chuckled. "Slow down, the food not going run away."

The doorbell rang.

"I'll get it." Gramma went into the living room. Kino poured herself more juice. Gramma returned with an envelope.

"Who was that?" asked Mom.

"The mailman, he dropped off this. I think it's certified. I had to sign something."

She handed her daughter, Paula, the envelope. "Can you read it? My glasses are in my purse. Ki, honey, hand me my bag."

Kino retrieved her grandmother's beige leather handbag and returned to the table with it.

Mom read the front of the envelope and a look of concern washed over her face. "It's a letter from an attorney." She slid a butter knife across the envelope's edge and pulled out a tri-folded sheet of white paper.

Kino couldn't see the letter from where she sat, but she could see a faint emblem through the paper, and it looked official.

Mom continued reading in silence. "This can't be right. Ma, don't you own this house fee simple?"

Kino asked, "What's fee simple?"

"It's a real estate term that means you own the land your home is on," said Gramma. Turning toward Paula, she replied, "No, we could afford this house and the biggest lot after we got married because it wasn't fee simple. And your father knew the guy who owned the land, so he gave us a good discount on our lease."

"This letter says that the land and the surrounding lots have been purchased by a corporation that terminated your lease." Mom handed her the note. "This is a sixty-day notice to vacate."

"Auwe! What do you mean 'vacate'?" Gramma dug into her purse, retrieved her glasses, put them on, and peered at the letter. "Sixty days to find a new home and move? How we going pay for that? You dad's insurance no can cover all of his hospital bills as it is." She sat down hard on the chair opposite Kino.

"I'll give them a call right now to find out what this is about. Ki, we're leaving in twenty." Mom left the room with the letter in one hand and her cellphone in the other.

"I'm sorry, Kitten, I'm not feeling well. I think I have to go lie down." Gramma offered her granddaughter a weak smile.

Kino didn't understand what was going on, but she knew better than to ask any questions. "It's okay, Gramma." She stood up, went over and put her arms around her grandmother's shoulders. "I love you."

"I love you more." Gramma hugged her tight.

Kino placed the small box on her dresser before changing into teal denim shorts. It was the only clean pair she had with pockets. Glancing in the mirror, she pouted at her reflection. Her clothes still looked like they belonged on an eleven-year-old kid. She didn't look different – and she definitely did not feel different – much to her disappointment.

Some of her friends at school changed when they turned twelve. Alix Tanaka started wearing deodorant and Lianna Lawrence got braces on their twelfth birthdays. She sniffed her armpits. No smell. She examined her teeth in the mirror. They were naturally straight and really white. Her mom seldom let her have sodas or candy. She opened her mouth to see if her wisdom teeth were coming in. Nope. Nothing. She twisted her chestnut-brown hair into a single braid. After only five weeks in Hawaii, her shoulder-length mane was streaked with gold highlights from the sun.

Mom called from the living room, "Let's go! I'll meet you in the car."

Kino sighed then grabbed her backpack that hung between posters of Pat Benatar and some band called Loverboy on the wall next to her dresser. Her grandparents had never changed her mom's room since 1984. This time capsule was now Kino's room, a fraction of the size of her old room in California. Grandpa's illness had prompted their sudden move, and Mom was adamant about getting rid of everything, to avoid the cost of shipping any of it to Hawaii. Anything that Kino wanted to keep had to all fit inside her backpack, suitcase, and one moving box, leaving little room for personal decor.

The turtle on the wooden box caught her eye. She opened its lid and stared at the rock. It was a random and unusual gift, but it seemed so special and important to Gramma that Kino figured she could at least humor her elder.

Oh, what the heck.

She stuck it into the pocket of her shorts, and walked out.

2

'Elua

"Gross," Kino muttered under her breath, as she pulled the sticky, white trash bag of cans from the trunk. It swung and bumped her thigh, leaving a wet spot on her shorts. She held the bag straight out in front of her and nearly thrust it into the hands of the recycling attendant.

Despite the overcast, cloudy sky, the lack of wind made the air humid and hot. Moist heat emanated from the glass, plastic, and can-filled rubber bins that lined the path to the metal shipping container. Sweat dripped down her temples. She wiped her forehead with the sleeve on her upper arm before retrieving the second bag. All along, Kino resented the effort they were going through, just for a little extra money.

Mom's almost-daily mantra was, "It's too expensive to live in Hawaii." That's probably the reason she had let her black roots grow out on her normally honey-highlighted hair. Mom had not had her hair done since they arrived. Although she was no fashion plate, she always managed to look groomed and styled. That is, until the move. Since then, she had given up on simple luxuries that were not a big thing on the mainland, such as having her eyebrows waxed, and she'd even forgone her monthly mani/pedi.

By the time they'd driven into the Bishop Museum's parking lot, several luxury cars were idling at the curb, waiting to let their passengers out. Mom pulled in behind the last one. Their red 1998 Hyundai with its missing hubcap, splotchy rust patches, and a slight ding in the driver's door looked like a sad caboose on a train made up of Mercedes and BMWs.

Kino watched as the other kids stepped out of their expensive rides. They all looked to be around her age, some maybe a year or two older. Several of them recognized each other and walked in as a group.

A girl with shiny black hair stepped out of the white Jaguar sedan in front of them. In an instant, Kino recognized Maylani Cho, her rich, snobby classmate from school.

"Great," Kino muttered under her breath.

The girl gave her a "stink-eye" look as she hoisted a Louis Vuitton backpack out of the car and onto her shoulders. Kino dropped her gaze to the plain, purple nylon backpack at her own feet. Mom had bought the backpack from Target at the beginning of the school year. Seven months and two states later, it looked dirty and worn. The hole that the point of her math compass had made on the first day of school caught her attention. She hated that hole and had tried to cover it up with stickers. None of them stayed on. They just left a gummy, gray residue, making the bag look extra dirty.

At least her shoes were new, an early birthday present from Mom. Kino had managed to keep them spotless for the last few days, and she intended on keeping them as clean as possible for as long as she could.

"Do I HAVE to go to this class?" she asked, knowing full well what the answer was.

"Your understanding of your Hawaiian roots means a lot to your grandparents. We're lucky I could get you in at the last minute." Mom glanced in the rear view mirror. "Even with my school employee discount it was still expensive. Besides, you'll get to meet kids from other private schools on the island."

Great. That meant more kids she had nothing in common with.

Mom said, "Kawika will be there; his uncle is teaching the class."

They rolled forward until it was Kino's turn to get out. Slinging her old backpack over one shoulder, she threaded her other arm through a strap before hoisting it onto her back as she climbed up the steps toward the entrance. She caught her reflection in a mirror as she entered the gift shop. Some of the hair in her braid had come undone at the recycling center. After pulling off her rubber band, she loosened up her remaining brown coils and put it all into a ponytail. It felt icky touching her hair with dirty fingers, but she couldn't walk in looking as if she had just rolled out of bed.

She went to wipe her hands on the front of her shorts, only to discover that one of the juice cans she'd handled earlier had dripped its sticky remnants down her leg. With not enough time to wash up in the restroom, she bent over, licked her index finger and tried to erase the juice streak on her thigh. Too busy licking and wiping, she failed to notice when someone walked up behind her.

"Look, girls, Kino is so poor, she has to give herself a spit bath."

Kino looked up at Maylani speaking to her clique, Cyan, Tiffany and Chanel. The four snobby girls ruled the sixth grade at Trinity Prep Academy, a prestigious all girls' school in Honolulu. Mom taught there, allowing Kino to attend the school for free. Otherwise, her family could never ever afford the costly tuition.

"What are *you* doing here?" Maylani sounded inconvenienced and annoyed. She and her groupies stood with their hands on their hips. Kino thought they looked like a magazine ad for The Gap.

"Uhh, trying to clean the juice that dripped..." Kino answered slowly.

Maylani fiddled with the gold plumeria pendant around her neck that matched the other girls' necklaces. "Ugh. I don't mean here, right now." She scoffed and rolled her eyes. "I mean, like, here, in this program. You don't look like you belong here."

She said what Kino had thought the first time she saw the other kids in their expensive rides, mall store clothes, and stylish gear. Most of the clothes Kino had brought from California were too heavy to wear in the island heat. She wore uniforms to school, so Mom just replenished her wardrobe with t-shirts and shorts from the swap meet when they arrived. The only designer clothes she owned was a pair of Tommy Hilfiger jeans and a Burberry top, but those had come from their last visit to the Salvation Army.

Before Kino could say anything, Chanel walked up, flipped her black hair back and said, "She's probably only here because the school has to look like they're doing something to help the disadvantaged."

Cyan came over with her pendant in her mouth, and eyed Kino up and down. She let it drop and asked, "Where did you get your clothes? Goodwill?"

Kino glanced down. Today's outfit came from the latest Walmart collection, another place Mom and Gramma frequently shopped at.

Before she could think of a rebuttal, she heard a familiar voice.

"Hey, Kino!"

She turned around. Kawika, her dark-haired, thirteen-year-old neighbor, walked towards the group.

The girls whispered among themselves and stared at his tall, athletic frame and tanned complexion.

Ignoring Maylani, Kino headed toward him.

Cyan stuck her polished foot out as Kino passed, causing her to stumble. Thankfully she didn't fall. The four girls laughed at her.

Maylani smiled and said in a cloyingly sweet tone, "Hi, Kawika."

The other girls giggled.

"Hey," he answered, then turned his focus on Kino. "I wondered if you were coming. Oh, and happy birthday by the way."

"Thanks," she smiled. She was surprised he'd remembered.

"We'd better hurry – class is about to start."

He led the way to a classroom with no chairs or tables. A beige, woven lauhala mat covered most of the wooden floor. Kino recognized the type of mat it was since her class at school had just woven a similar one, with the dried, inch-wide leaves of the lauhala tree.

A whiteboard hung on the wall in front of the room. Large letters on it said:

Please Remove Your Shoes

Kawika slipped out of his Vans and put them along the wall with the toes facing out. Kino set her shoes against the wall, a few inches away from Kawika's, then went and sat down on the mat near the front. Kawika sat down next to her.

Other kids showed up and took their places on the ground nearby. Kino counted sixteen of them, including herself. Maylani and her friends entered and sat down on the other side of Kawika. Kino noticed that Maylani made it a point to sit the closest to him.

A heavy-set Hawaiian man in a bright blue-and-white aloha shirt entered and greeted the class with a warm smile and a loud "Aloha!" He stretched out the "o" sound a bit longer than the other letters.

Only some of the kids returned the greeting.

The man shook his head and said, "Let's try this again. Al-Ohhh-ha!"

This time the class answered in unison, "Al-Ohhh-ha!"

The man grinned. "My name is Kumu Alika Lokepa. I will be your teacher for da next few weeks." Although he spoke proper English, he said the words with a thick Pidgin inflection. "In this interactive class, you will learn about da Hawaiian culture through language, crafts, food, and hula. But, first things first. Let us start with da basic sounds of da Hawaiian alphabet."

He erased the words on the whiteboard, then wrote the vowels A, E, I, O, U in their place. Under that he wrote: H, K, L, M, N, P, W, a backwards apostrophe he called an 'okina, and a dash he called a kahakō that changed the sound of vowels when written over them.

They spent a half hour going over proper pronunciation and basic words. Even though everything was pronounced phonetically, Kino still struggled to get the hang of it.

Kumu Alika introduced the class to the Kumulipo, a complicated Hawaiian chant made up of two thousand lines of verse, broken into sixteen time periods of ancient Hawaii. It summarized the natural creation of the islands and the gods that had made it possible. "You will need to partner up, learn the English translation, and be able to recite a part of it to the class."

As soon as he mentioned that they would be working in pairs, several whispers came from behind Kino. As Kumu continued explaining their assignment, Maylani inched toward Kawika.

On impulse Kino leaned in close to his head and blurted out, "Wanna be my partner?" The words came out louder than she expected.

He looked startled then smiled and said, "I was going to ask you."

Maylani stopped and shot daggers at Kino with her eyes.

Kumu then told the class that the partners needed to pair with another couple to form a group of four.

A boy and girl in front of them turned around and offered to team up. They introduced themselves as Madison Watanabe and Tyler Lee. Both were twelve and attended 'Iolani. Kino admired Madison's long, jet-black hair and almond-shaped green eyes. The product of a Caucasian mom and Japanese dad, Madison reminded her of an exotic cat.

"So, how do you guys want to do this?" Tyler asked, staring at the paper in his hand. His black-framed glasses slipped. He looked up and pushed them back up against his nose.

They all looked down at their sheets.

"How about Tyler and I memorize the first half," Madison suggested, "and you guys do the second part, starting with verse nine."

"Sounds fine with me," Kawika said. "Kino, is that okay with you?"

"Sure." Kino nodded in agreement.

At the end of class, Kino and Kawika stood up to put their shoes on. Kawika's shoes still sat neatly against the wall. Kino's were buried under a pile of girls' sandals. She immediately recognized them as belonging to Maylani and the three other mean girls.

Bending over, she pushed the sandals off then picked up her shoes. The once-spotless tops and laces were now marred with dirt and black scuff marks. She wanted to cry.

She heard giggling and looked over. The four girls whispered to each other while glancing at Kino. Chanel covered her smile with her hand and turned away, while Maylani looked at her squarely and smirked. The other two girls just sneered behind their leader like backup dancers with bad attitudes.

Not wanting to give them the satisfaction of seeing her upset, Kino took a deep breath and dropped her shoes at her feet before slipping them on.

Kawika crouched on the ground next to her, tying a bow on his left shoe. He looked up when she put her feet into her sneakers and said, "Want me to tie them? I can if you want."

Kino hesitated, unsure what to do. It was a weird offer. She looked at the gaggle of girls, silenced by Kawika's proposition.

She smiled inwardly. "Sure!" She placed a palm against the wall for balance then stuck her right foot out in front of him.

Kawika tied tight, firm bows on both shoes, then stood up and said, "There you go, Cinderella!"

Kino giggled and took a step. He cinched the first knot so tight that the tops of her feet felt choked. It hurt a little, but she grinned at him and said, "Thanks!"

She could feel the four girls' hard stares. She smiled at the ground.

"Do you have time to go over the chant?" Kawika asked as they headed for the exit. "I have to wait for my uncle, who is getting everything ready for tomorrow's class, so he'll be a while.

"No, sorry," she shook her head. "My mom is coming to get me."

Kawika walked her out to the parking lot. "We're going first thing in the morning to pick up fresh malasadas before class. You should come."

"I have to ask my mom."

"Okay." He shoved his hands into his pockets and looked at her. "So what did you get for your birthday?"

"A rock."

"A what?"

The faded red Hyundai pulled up to the curb.

"A rock. I'll show it to you tomorrow," Kino said, and climbed into the car.

Mom lowered the passenger-side window down and yelled, "Hi, Kawika, do you need a ride?"

The boy crouched down and answered, "Hi, Ms. Kahele. No, thank you, my uncle will take me home. I told Kino she could ride with us tomorrow."

She leaned her head next to Kino's and called out, "That would be great. Have your mom call me tonight, okay?"

"I will," he waved, and stood up. Looking back at Kino, Kawika smiled again and said, "Happy Birthday."

"Thanks!"

She couldn't help but smile back. It hadn't been a great birthday, but it was nice that someone other than her family members remembered.

13

*****

Kino had just finished helping Gramma clean up after dinner when she heard her mom curse, followed by a loud crash that sounded like a dish falling and breaking. Mom had been sorting through boxes of files, looking for financial and real estate records. Both Kino and Gramma hurried into the room.

Mom was hunched over on her knees with her back facing the door.

"Mom! Are you okay?" Kino rushed over.

"I'm okay, sweetie." Mom stood up. "I wish I could say the same about this poor thing." She held out colorful broken ceramic pieces in one hand and a round cork disc in the other.

Kino recognized it in an instant. It was a clay bank she had made in kindergarten with "Kino $" crudely carved on the side. The dollar sign was backwards.

"I'm really sorry about your bank," Mom said, as she dropped the pieces and the cork into the trash can. "I didn't see it when I pulled that box out from the top shelf."

Kino looked in the direction that her mom was pointing. A small paper scroll lay next to the box. "What's that?" she asked.

Mom went over, picked it up, and unrolled it.

"Oh my! It's a ten-thousand-dollar savings bond with your name on it."

Kino had no idea what a savings bond was, but she understood the part about a ten thousand dollars.

"Oh yeah," Gramma said. "We bought that when she was born. For college."

"If you bought it that long ago, we could probably get face value for the bond. That should cover moving costs, and the first month's rent and security deposit on a new place," Mom said. "I'm sure Kino understands that it's for a good cause."

Kino nodded in agreement.

Gramma shook her head. "No. That's Kino's money so she can get her degree. It may not be a lot, but it should help get her started."

"It's okay, Gramma," said Kino. "This is way more important right now."

"I said no. It took us a long time to save all that money. We want you to get a good education, so you won't have to struggle like me and Grandpa did. He only finished the tenth grade. He had to drop out and get a job to help his mom and seven brothers, since he was the oldest." She put a hand on Kino's shoulder. "So, me and Grandpa saved up to give our future generations a chance at a better life, and that starts with you. We'll figure out something else."

Kino wasn't sure what to say, so she went over and hugged her grandmother. Her mom joined in for a group hug. Both Mom and Gramma were crying.

Mom wiped her tears off her cheeks and said, "We'll get through this. I spoke to Mrs. Tanaka across the street. She said that everyone on the block received the same letter. Rumor has it, GRANDAGRA wants to rezone the land for agriculture."

Gramma let out a sound of frustration that sounded like a cross between a growl and a sigh. She let her arms drop. The group hug was clearly over.

"It's always the same story. Some big company comes in and takes land that belongs to the people." She walked out shaking her head.

"Do we really have to move again?" Kino asked, once her grandmother was out of earshot.

"Let's not worry about that right now," Mom said softly, as she cupped Kino's chin in her hand. "Mrs. Tanaka's daughter is a real estate attorney who promised to get to the bottom of this."

The phone rang. Gramma picked it up in the kitchen then called out to say that Kawika's mom was on the line. As Mom picked up the receiver in the bedroom, Kino went to watch the science fiction channel in the living room until bedtime.

At eight o'clock she brushed her teeth and climbed into bed. Just as she pulled the covers over her legs, Mom knocked on the doorframe. Kino didn't like sleeping with the door closed yet. The room still didn't feel like hers.

"I came in to say goodnight," Mom said gently, as she walked in. "Kawika should be here at eight-thirty, so be ready." She pulled the blanket up to Kino's chest and gave her a kiss on her forehead. "Sweet dreams. Don't forget to say your prayers." She turned off the lamp next to the bed and walked out.

Kino sighed and rolled over to face the wall. She was not looking forward to another challenging class at the museum, and another inevitable run-in with Maylani and her crew. Unfortunately, it was only the first day of a six-week program that met daily. It was bad enough that Kino had to deal with them at school. Now they had the weekends to bully her, too.

3

'Ekolu

The class spent the morning going over the Kumulipo as a group. After the break, Kino, Kawika, Madison and Tyler went to the cafe to study.

Even though Kino only needed to recite the English version and not the original Hawaiian one, some parts always tripped her up. Kawika helped by coaching her on the words and phrases. She made it through the ninth and tenth era with no trouble remembering, and almost made it through the eleventh.

"Born was Pola'a

Born was rough weather, born the current

Born the booming of the sea, the breaking of foam

Born the roaring, advancing, and receding of waves, the rumbling sound, the earthquake

The sea rages, rises over the beach

Rises silently…"

"Ummm…" Kino tapped her forehead and did her best to remember. Nothing came to her.

Kawika finished the verse, "To the inhabited places… Rises gradually up over the land."

"How do you know this already?" she asked.

"I have four older sisters who all took this class. I've heard it every year since I turned eight."

Kino laughed. Kawika just smiled.

"Can you help me too?" Maylani walked toward the pair. When she reached the table, she put her hand on the edge and turned her body sideways to face Kawika, her elbow mere inches away from Kino's face.

"Uh, maybe later? I am practicing with Kino," Kawika replied politely. "I can see if Kumu Alika can help you. If you want."

Maylani rolled her eyes. "Ughh. Never mind." She spun around and glared at the rest of the girls, who all pretended to be suddenly busy. Chanel tapped at the screen on her iPhone, Tiffany reapplied lip-gloss over the glob already on her lips, and Cyan picked at the polish on her nails. Maylani walked back to her seat with a disgusted look on her face, as if she smelled something rotten.

Kino smashed her lips together to stifle a smile and stared hard at the sheet of paper with the chant on it. She had to admit it tickled her how hard Maylani always tried to get Kawika's attention – and he barely noticed her.

By the time their break ended, Kino had memorized a good chunk of her part. She and Kawika agreed that she should be the one to recite it, and that he would jump in if she ran into trouble.

When class resumed, Kumu announced, "It has come to my attention that several of you are having a hard time remembering the intricate verses. So, I've decided to give everyone more time to learn the chant."

Several of the kids sighed in relief.

"Instead, we are going to go to another room, so you can see what you'll be painting for Kamehameha Day." He walked over to the lecture stand and pulled out a white cardboard poster holder. "Follow me."

Kumu led the class to another part of the museum. He pushed open the double doors, revealing a large backdrop panel that stretched fifteen feet wide and twelve feet tall. Outlines, as well as color swatches indicating what hue to paint each section, were the only things on the canvas. Positioned in the very center was the outline of a shield, with the shapes of an inverted triangle on a stick between two crossed canoe paddles – the design for the Kanaka Maoli, the original emblem of the native Hawaiians. It was dabbed with yellow, red, and green spots of paint, flanked by horizontal and diagonal lines, that were to be painted into strips of red, white, and blue like the Hawaii state flag.

"This is how it's going to look when we're done with it." Kumu uncapped the cardboard tube, pulled out the artist's rendering of the mural, unfurled it, and held it up.

"Wow," exclaimed many of the students; and others let out soft gasps, filling the room. Someone said, "Cool." The end design was a giant Hawaiian flag with the Kanaka Maoli flag in the center of it. Above that lay outlines of the island chain.

They returned to their classroom and received a sheet of paper that the group went over together. The upcoming schedule for the next few weeks: field trips to sites like Makapuʻu tide pools, ʻIolani Palace, and Waimea Falls on weekends. Crafts, language, and history would be covered during the week. A brief description next to each topic elaborated the details.

Kumu picked up a stack of bright-blue paper, divided it into smaller stacks and handed them out to the kids in the front row. They each took a sheet and passed the papers to the kids behind them. Kawika ended up with two and handed Kino one.

"This is about a contest to write a story about old Hawaii, and you must include specific details from that time period," said Kumu. "The rules and application are online."

Murmurs of excitement and simultaneous groans from the crowd followed.

He collected the extra handouts. "I strongly encourage all of you to enter. The grand prize is a first-year scholarship to the University of Hawaii."

Kino looked at the blue sheet of paper in her hand. It didn't sound the least bit interesting. But if she won the scholarship, her family could use the savings bond to help pay moving expenses and some of Grandpa's hospital bills. She had won school writing awards before, but never for something this big. She owed it to her family to enter.

At the end of class, Kino and Kawika walked out to the great lawn to wait for Kumu Alika to give them a ride home.

"Now let's see this birthday rock," Kawika said, as he sat on the grass beside her. Kino reached into her pocket and pulled out the greenish-blue stone. Kawika's eyes widened. "Can I see it?" he extended an open hand. Kino placed the rock in his palm. The ribbon of gold shimmered in the sun. "It's nice," he observed, "but it's a pretty random present."

"I know, right? It's supposed to help me in life or something."

Kawika looked at her and raised an eyebrow.

"It's been in my family for many generations," she said. "And it's supposed to help me find my destiny, whatever that means."

Kawika handed it back to her. "Cool. I like it."

She turned it over between her fingers. "Yeah. Me too."

Kumu Alika walked up and asked Kawika to help him carry some boxes to the car. Kino offered to help, but Kumu said, "No need." Kawika told her he'd be right back and walked off with his uncle.

She sat there with her stone in her hand. Holding it up to the sunlight, she marveled at the way the gold flecks sparkled when she turned it in any direction.

"Aww, Kino is so poor she has to play with a rock," said a familiar, spiteful voice from behind her. Kino knew, without having to look, that it belonged to Maylani.

"Let me see it," her highness demanded, and sauntered toward her.

Kino pocketed the rock before standing up. Her heart beat faster. By now, all four girls stood in front of her.

Maylani clenched her teeth. "I SAID, let me see it!" She held out her palm.

The other three girls took their places behind and on either side of her. Chanel and Cyan crossed their arms and Tiffany put her hands on her hips.

Kino crossed her arms and stood her ground.

Just then, she heard her name. She turned and saw Kawika wave as he headed toward them.

Maylani said, "This isn't over." She dropped her hand, whipping her hair as she spun around and walked off. Her crew turned in unison to follow their leader, right as Kawika reached her.

"What's that about?" he asked as he watched them walk away.

"Nothing." Her heart had not slowed to normal yet. Taking a deep breath, she put her head down and stuck her hand into her pocket. As soon as her fingertips felt the cool, hard surface of the stone, she exhaled and felt calmer. Its soft vibration comforted her.

"We're ready to go. Uncle said he'll take us to get shave ice on the way home!" Kawika's eyes shone with excitement. He picked up Kino's backpack and slung it over his shoulder as they headed to the car.

Kino sat silent in the back seat during the ride. Kawika and Kumu discussed what flavors they wanted on their shave ice, as well as what other ingredients they'd add. Kino's thoughts lay elsewhere. She slid her hand into her pocket and brought the rock out.

She had never been able to stand up to Maylani like that before. No one in school ever said no to her or any of her crew. That's how Kylie Ashton's Hello Kitty key ring ended up on Maylani's Louis Vuitton backpack, and Chelsea Arakawa's butterfly bracelet ended up on Maylani's wrist. It was also how Kino had lost her favorite hair clip. Maylani wore it for a week, then gave it to Cyan, who wore it a couple of times after that. Kino had not seen it since.

But with her newfound courage, she promised herself that things were going to change. Maylani had stolen her dignity one too many times already. Kino wasn't going to let her get her hands on her precious stone.

*****

During dinner, Mom filled the family in on the latest news about the house situation. Their neighbor's daughter, the real estate attorney, was able to get a stay on the eviction, meaning they didn't have to move right away. Gramma nodded and said that the delay would give them time to at least get money from their tax returns, whatever that meant.

"I have good news," Gramma announced. "Grandpa's condition is getting better enough to move out of ICU, and into a regular hospital room, pretty soon."

"Yay!" Kino clapped.

Mom said, "Thank God. Do you know when?"

Gramma shook her head, "No, only that it could be in the next few days."

The news made Kino ecstatic. She missed Grandpa dearly and couldn't wait to see him. "Why is he in the hospital again?"

Gramma said, "Your grandpa came down with a really high fever several months ago. Shortly after that, boils went appear all over his body." She shook her head and looked at the table, as if recalling a sad memory.

Kino frowned. "I don't know what boils are, but they sound painful and gross."

"They're like big bubbles on the skin. The boils turned into blisters that never healed. Only got worse. Anyway, we can go visit once he's moved."

Kino grinned and said, "I hope it's soon." She decided to put together a scrapbook of the different topics she was learning about in the museum's program. Grandpa would love it.

After the meal, she helped with the dishes then went into the office. On the bottom of the bookshelf was a photo album she had started last summer, with intentions of documenting her annual visits. It already had some seashells glued on the cover.

Gathering the museum pamphlets, postcards, and some of her drawings, she went back to her room and sat on the floor. Armed with a bottle of glue and pair of scissors, she went to work. When she was done, it wasn't enough to fill more than four pages, but she liked what she had put together so far.

4

'Ehā

The next two weeks flew by. Kino was enjoying her after-school class, and couldn't wait to get to the museum every day. Even though she still resented their abrupt move, she was really beginning to appreciate the beauty and history of Hawaii.

One day, when her grandma came to pick her up after the class, Kino noticed she was wearing lipstick. Her grandma seldom wore any makeup.

"We're going to visit Grandpa!" Gramma declared, once Kino had kissed her hello and buckled her seat belt.

"Can we stop by the house to pick up the scrapbook I made for him? I want to show Grandpa what I've learned so far."

"I got it already. I figured you wanted to give it to him." She patted Kino's hand and put the car into gear.

"Awesome!" Kino reached back to grab the book. She opened it up to admire her handiwork. Among the decorations and souvenirs she had placed in the album, she'd also included pictures of herself at the different places her Hawaiian group visited, as well as pictures of the things she'd crafted.

Her mom didn't have a digital camera, so she bought a disposable wind-up one for Kino to use instead. Maylani and her friends always made snide remarks and laughed every time Kino brought it out, and she cringed every time she wound it because of the loud *skritch-skritch* noise. Despite Kino's embarrassment and her low-end camera, the beauty of the islands looked amazing on film and filled her scrapbook with vivid colors.

When they arrived at her grandfather's room, she hesitated before going in. She had never visited anyone in a hospital before, and prayed that he wouldn't be hooked up to big, scary machines with pumps, wires and noises, like the hospitals on TV.

"There is nothing to be afraid of, Kitten – it's just Grandpa." Gramma placed a gentle hand on Kino's shoulder.

Kino swallowed hard and entered the room.

"There she is – my favorite granddaughter!" Grandpa grinned. It was a running joke, considering Mom was an only child, and so was she.

His voice was raspy and hoarse, as though he had not spoken in days. He sat semi-reclined at a forty-degree angle on his bed. There were no pumps or big machines, but he did have a needle taped to the back of his hand, which was attached to a tube fed by a bag of clear liquid, that hung on a pole next to the bed. A few wires poked out from the sleeves of his hospital gown, leading to a small machine that monitored his heart rate, and an oxygen tube that stretched across his face.

"Hi, Grandpa!" Kino said, as she rushed to his side and gave him a gentle kiss on the cheek. That's when she noticed that his arms were wrapped in gauze bandages from his shoulders to his wrists.

"Wow, look at you! You got so big!" He struggled to sit up. Gramma picked up a big remote that was wired to the bed. With a press of a button, the upper half of the mattress rose higher until he was sitting nearly upright.

Kino clutched the bedrail as she watched him settle in.

"How you been? How is school?" Grandpa asked. He looked tired, and skinnier than she remembered, but she pretended not to notice.

"Good, everything is fine," she said, smiling. Hugging the book, she exclaimed, "I made you something, Grandpa!"

She put the scrapbook onto his lap, and he winced in pain. Gramma quickly lifted the book up, and put it on the bedside table.

Kino put her hands in the air. "I'm so sorry, Grandpa! Did I hurt you?"

He smiled, but she could see the pain in his watery eyes. "No, it's okay. There are just some parts of my body that are worse than others. Mostly my arms and legs."

Kino lowered her hands and silently scolded herself for being careless. "Have the doctors said anything about when you can come home?"

"No," he answered, "not until they can figure out what is happening to me," as he held out his bandaged arms. "The swelling is all gone, but the sores are spreading."

Kino looked at her grandfather's body. A sheet covered his lower half, leaving her no clues to his ailment.

"The doctors don't know what's wrong?" She picked up the scrapbook.

Her grandfather shook his head. "No. At first they thought it was a serious form of a skin bacteria called MRSA, but none of the medicine or treatments they used worked. So now they have to do more tests…"

Gramma interrupted. "That's 'cause he needs a different kind of healing. Something more traditional."

Before Kino could ask what she meant, a tall, dark-skinned Hawaiian man with snowy white hair walked in.

"Aloha," the man said, "you must be John, and you must be Kino. My name is Andrew Kaleopapa." He extended his right hand and shook Grandpa's.

"Kahu Kaleopapa is a kahuna la'au lapa'au. He is an expert in the ancient art of natural healing," Gramma said. "I asked him to come today and take a look at your wounds." She glanced at Kino, "Let's go to see what they got at the cafeteria so Grandpa them can talk in private."

Disappointed that she was unable to show her grandfather the scrapbook, Kino put the album back onto the table then followed her grandmother out.

After eating a chocolate chip cookie and drinking a glass of milk, Kino and her grandmother returned to the room. The kahuna finished re-wrapping Grandpa's bandages just as they walked in.

"Can you do anything for him?" Gramma asked.

The man slowly shook his head. "I have never seen sores like this before, although I have heard of them." He spoke with a slight pidgin inflection.

"What do you mean?" Gramma moved closer to the bed. Kino followed.

"I come from a long line of kahuna la'au lapa'au. Traditional healers," said Kaleopapa. "Going all the way back to the days before Kamehameha. When I was just a boy, my kupuna told me a story his grandfather told him about a mad woman who traveled the countryside going to people's homes and demanding food. If you gave her some she would leave and not come back. But if you didn't, she would curse you and your future generations. At the time no one really knew what the curse did, since word of the woman travelled faster than she did – as most rumors do. Then one day a neighbor asked my ancestor to visit a man with raw, open sores covering his body.

"Like yours," he acknowledged Grandpa John, "the man's wounds seemed to be devouring his skin. He told my ancestor that an old lady had come by asking for food. He didn't have enough to feed his family, so he said he could not help her. She became angry, and cursed him and all his future generations of sons.

"Of course he told her she was crazy and to get off his property. The next day he woke up with lesions on his arms and legs. Over time, they got so bad he could barely move. Painful, weeping blisters covered his whole body. He grew weaker by the day.

"So my ancestor went out to pick the different herbs to soothe the man's skin, but as soon as he started to apply the medicine, the man started screaming in pain. He stopped treatment right away and told the man to come back the next day, so Kahu would have time to figure out a new mixture.

"That night he had a dream. A vision of a beautiful young woman, dressed in white, and carrying the center coil of the golden hapu'u fern. She held up the rare fern and told him that it could remove any sickness caused by a curse. Then she dropped it into a bowl of black round berries and blue flowers, and mashed it all with a big black rock in one strike.

"When he awoke, he remembered that he had seen a grove of golden ferns at the top of a mountain. It took all day to climb it to get the plant. Then he made a remedy using all the items from his dream and cured the man."

"Great!" Kino said, "all we have to do is find one of these ferns and you can make the medicine to heal Grandpa."

"Unfortunately," Kahu Kaleopapa said, "the golden hapuʻu fern is now extinct. Wiped out sometime in the forties, when the US military cleared land to set up bunkers and radio towers in the mountains."

"Just great," Kino replied.

"But I will pray about it, and see if my ancestors will give me a vision to help your grandfather," said the kahuna.

Both her grandparents thanked the man before he left. Kino sat in silence for a few minutes, thinking about the kahuna's tale.

"Do you think that's what happened to you, Grandpa? Did your father have this?" She took the seat next to his bed.

"My father died in an accident when I was a boy, but I don't remember him being sick like this," he shook his head. "My Uncle Henry, his only brother, died in the war. Their father – my grandfather – passed before I was even born. I don't know anything about the generations before. The only thing I know about anyone's health is that my great-great grandfather was missing a hand. Cut off at the wrist in battle."

Kino sat back and thought for a moment, then asked, "Do you think this kahuna can help cure you?"

"We can only hope and pray," said Grandpa. "But let's not worry about that now. What is that book you brought?"

Kino grinned and said, "It's a scrapbook I made for you." She handed her grandfather the album.

Gramma cleared off a tray with the remnants of lunch and wheeled the table to the side of Grandpa's bed. "Here," she pushed the tabletop in front of Grandpa. "You can put the book on top this."

Grandpa opened the book and placed it on the table. Kino moved closer to him so that she could explain each item. It made her happy to see how interested her grandfather was in everything she had put in it. As she recited the part of the Kumulipo chant she'd memorized, her grandfather beamed with happiness.

"I'm so proud of you, Kino! It makes my heart want to burst with joy to see how you are learning about our culture and our Hawaiian heritage." He reached for her hand and held it. "I have something for you. I asked Gramma to bring it so I can give it to you myself."

Kino wondered if it was another rock.

Gramma smiled and opened up the brown grocery bag she had brought with her. She reached in with both hands and brought out an oversized chocolate cupcake with neon-pink frosting in a clear plastic container.

"We cannot light a candle because of the oxygen tanks, but Grandpa wanted to celebrate your birthday with you." She reached into the bag again and pulled out a small, purple-and-gold pinwheel for Kino to blow on instead, and stuck it in the thick coil of frosting.

Kino grinned as her grandparents the birthday song to her in Hawaiian. She giggled before blowing the pinwheel at the end of the song.

Grandpa gave Gramma a nod. Kino watched her grandmother reach into her purse and pull out something round, the size of a pocket watch, with a cord of twine dangling from one end. Gramma gently placed it in Grandpa's free hand. He lifted his palm toward her.

"This belonged to my father. He got it from his father and so on. It's been in the family for generations."

She looked down at a handsome compass, made of a rich, brownish-red wood, with an abalone shell face under a glass crystal. A slender, black, diamond-shaped pointer indicated that north was to her left.

Kino picked it up the by the cord with her free hand, then let go of her grandfather's. She placed the compass on her open palm to examine it closer.

Grandpa said, "Keep it with you always. It will help you find your way home."

Kino couldn't imagine herself carrying a compass around, since she always knew how to get home from the few places she knew how to get to. She did, however, picture herself using the compass on her next hike.

"Thank you, Grandpa. I will." She glanced at the colorful, round prism of light that the glass reflected on the wall. Picking up the compass at its edges, she examined it closer. She loved the pearly luminescent face, and when she ran her fingers over it, she liked how smooth and cool the wood felt.

A blonde nurse peeked her head in the doorway. "Excuse me, it's time for vitals." She pushed a small cart into the room.

"Time to go," said Gramma.

Kino protested. "But we didn't get to eat the cupcake!"

Grandpa smiled at her. "You take it home. Enjoy it for the both of us."

Kino frowned and looked at his tan, wrinkled face. She wasn't ready to leave him.

Grandma leaned over and kissed her husband on the cheek. Kino kissed his other cheek and said, "Bye, Grandpa. I love you."

"I love you too, sweetheart. Take good care of your mom and grandma."

"I will!" Kino blew him a kiss.

Grandpa "caught" the air kiss and put it in his pretend shirt pocket before almost collapsing back on the bed. It pained her to see her grandfather, who was normally so robust, looking so frail.

She and Gramma barely spoke on the car ride home. Kino wondered what this all meant for his future. What if they couldn't find a remedy? What if it got worse? How long would he have to stay in the hospital? Was he doomed to be covered in painful sores for the rest of his life? Was his condition somehow related to an ancient curse? If so, what could help cure him if this special healing plant no longer existed? She wished for answers, or at least options.

That night she couldn't sleep. She lay in bed staring at the dark ceiling while contemplating the day's events. Seeing her grandfather in the hospital really shook her up. The fact that he was there and not at home bothered her, but his strange condition kept running through her mind. She wished she could somehow do something to help him. But what good can a twelve-year-old do that the doctors can't?

Nothing.

She sighed. Reaching under her pillow, Kino felt for the colorful stone she'd been carrying with her daily since her grandma gave it to her. She wouldn't exactly call it a lucky rock, since nothing seemed to be getting better, but she did find it comforting to have it with her all the time.

The urge to check out the odd gifts from her grandparents washed over her. Sitting up, she leaned over and flicked on the lamp next to her bed. Kino stood up and walked to the dresser where the compass lay, its needle aimed at the mirror in front of her. She placed her rock next to it. The compass needle turned and pointed at the blue-green stone. Her eyes widened.

She lifted the rock and put it on the other side of the compass. The needle followed. She picked up the compass and tapped the glass. The needle swiveled slightly, then turned its nose toward the stone. She returned the compass back to the dresser, then moved the rock once more. Again, the needle followed.

Great. Not only did she get another random gift that didn't even slightly resemble an electronic gadget, this one seemed to be broken as well.

She let out a sigh and returned to bed. This time, she didn't even bother putting the stone back under her pillow.

5

'Elima

The next morning, as Kino dressed to go to the museum, the compass caught her eye. She debated whether or not to take it. She had already put the rock into one of her shorts pockets, as she did every day. She decided to bring the compass to at least show Kawika, so she stuck it in her back pocket before pulling on a skirt over her shorts.

Gramma came into the kitchen when Kino sat down for breakfast. After filling her coffee cup, she kissed Kino on the top of her head and sat down.

"Good morning, sweetheart. How did you sleep?"

"Mmfgood," Kino answered, her cheeks stuffed with cereal.

"In all the excitement yesterday, I think you forgot to make your wish." Gramma blew into her cup before taking a sip.

Kino swallowed. "What wish?"

"Did you make a wish when you blew the pinwheel?"

Kino thought about it. It had never occurred to her to make a wish. After all, it wasn't a candle. "No, I guess I didn't."

"Well then, I think you have a wish you still have to make."

Kino gazed at her grandma, uncertain if she was kidding, or instructing her to make one. Without any conscious thought, she heard a voice in her head say, "I wish I could do something to help Grandpa." She felt a vibration buzz her thigh. She reached down and pulled the stone from her pocket. It stopped moving.

Weird. She dropped it back in her shorts.

31

Mom walked in and said, "Put on your slippahs and get in the car, we have to go. We need to drop off the recycling on the way over, then get gas."

Long lines at both places caused Kino to show up late. She found her class already gathered in the room with the giant canvas. Some of the kids were prepping one end while the rest of the group was filling in the various colors on the other. A large sheet of blue tarp lay on the floor, protecting it from spills.

Everyone worked barefoot. Kino didn't see any other bags and figured they had all left them in a different classroom, so she put her backpack on the ground near the door, kicked off her flip flops and walked over to her group.

Kawika was one of the primers on the opposite end. When he saw her, he laid down his paintbrush and hurried over. He always seemed happy to see her. She had to admit, she looked forward to his familiar smile.

He caught her up on the day's game plan. Kumu Alika had divided the areas to paint into groups. Kino's job was to fix the white stripes in between the red and blue ones that Madison and Tyler were working on.

Maylani and her crew were painting right next to Kino's team, forcing her to overhear their pointless conversation. The girls talked about a new TV show and the cute male actors. Kino rolled her eyes every time one of the girls said, "Oh, totally," which was often. She wasn't sure what she found more annoying – the stupid topic or the way Maylani's friends kissed her butt.

Madison had finished her application of red by the time Kino started, which left just her and Tyler, who sat on the ground at her feet, painting the bottom lines. She decided to start at eye level and work her way down.

Taking her time, she dipped her narrow paintbrush into the cup of white paint she held, and started to touch up the overlapped areas. Painting between the lines was more challenging than she had thought, even with a steady hand. Every time she touched her brush to the canvas, she held her breath.

She concentrated so hard that by the time she reached the lower part of the painting, she had tuned out the lame discussion happening next to her. Focusing on not making a mistake, she jumped when she heard a familiar voice say, "Did you bring your lunch?"

Kawika stood a few feet away.

The annoying girls stared at her. She glanced at them, then at Kawika, and said, "Um, no. We were out of bread at home, so my mom just gave me some money for the café."

"My uncle made too much food and we have extra. My aunty was supposed to meet us for lunch but she couldn't make it. You can have hers."

Kino said, "'K. Thanks!"

Kawika told her he'd meet her outside on the lawn at lunchtime.

"Don't you want to eat with us today?" Maylani asked Kino, then shot a coy look at Kawika, her tone syrupy sweet.

The question surprised Kino – until she realized that Maylani had only invited her so that Kawika would join them.

"Um, no, thank you." Kino glanced at Kawika as he walked away.

"You're making a big mistake," Chanel said. "Don't you know how lucky you are to even be invited? There are girls at school who would trade places with you so they can be with us. Some of them want to BE us."

Kino wanted to laugh. "No thanks." She pursed her lips to hide her smile then turned around to fix a streak of red paint that had dripped all the way down to the last red line on the bottom. She could hear the girls whispering behind her. One of them let out a giggle. They returned to their places at the canvas in silence.

Tyler finished his final line and left to wash up. Kino took his spot on the floor. Dabbing white to correct an overlapped spot, she felt something wet hit her hair and dribble down to her shirt. She reached back and touched the thick liquid. When she looked at her fingers, she saw a gob of blue paint. Kino looked up at Maylani, still poised over her, paintbrush in hand.

"Ooops, I dripped some," Maylani announced, as if Kino weren't there. Kino ran the wet strands between her thumb and fingers to squeeze out the paint. It was less than a teaspoon, so she just ignored everyone and continued to work on the canvas.

Seconds later, something thick and goopy hit the top of her head and oozed down the back of her clothes. Kino touched the liquid and glanced at her fingers. Blue paint. A lot more this time. She looked up in time to see Maylani flip her paint cup back upright.

The other three girls giggled. Maylani said, "Oops, sorry. Again." Her tone was far from apologetic.

Kino stood up, and without saying anything, poured the contents of her own paint cup over Maylani's head.

"Oops, I spilled some." Kino countered. She had no idea what had come over her. Normally, she would do anything to avoid conflict. But she'd had enough of Maylani, and she wasn't sorry for pouring paint on her.

They stared at each other for a second as the white paint dribbled down Maylani's hair, down her shirt, and onto the ground. Kino dropped her brush and bolted for the door. She glanced at the spot where she had placed her backpack, but it was gone. Without pause, she ran out of the room and heard Maylani say, "Get her!" and, "Grab the rock!"

Ever since Maylani first saw Kino with the blue green stone, she had made several attempts at getting her hands on it. Kino had even caught Chanel going through her locker at PE. Of course the girl had tried to play it off as if she had the wrong locker. Kino guessed that that's why one of them had taken her backpack this time.

She sprinted across the courtyard and into the Hawaiian Hall. She didn't know where to go. She just knew that she needed to hide. As she ran into main area, she heard the girls coming. It sounded as if the four had split into pairs, and were headed toward her from two different directions.

In the rear of the exhibit hall stood an ancient hale pili, a single room grass hut. She rushed to the back of it, ducked under the security rope and crawled through the hut's small entrance. Once inside, Kino pressed herself against the corner and listened as the girls ran past. She could hear them regroup somewhere nearby, but couldn't make out they were saying.

Her pocket began vibrating. She reached in and pulled out her stone. She could feel the energy from it adding to her adrenaline. Kino clutched it and leaned forward, cautiously peering out from the small doorway.

Cyan stood a few feet away, with her back toward the hut and Kino's backpack slung over her shoulder. She was looking up and scanning the upper floors. Then she lowered her gaze and studied the ground floor. Her eyes panned toward the hut.

Kino sat back into the darkness and debated what to do. She didn't think they were going to actually hurt her. Well, maybe just a little. What she did know was that Maylani would take her precious stone.

Scooting back up toward the wall, her hand touched something hard. She picked it up and recognized it in an instant. Kino was now holding a conch shell, the type that men blew into to signal the start of a hula competition or other traditional Hawaiian ceremony. Next to it was a dried, polished gourd called an ipu.

She came up with a plan: Stash her rock in the shell, so that way, if they caught her, she wouldn't have it on her. Then she could come back after the class and get it.

Taking the rock out of her pocket, she held it next to the shell. The sound of the girls' voices faded, as if they were walking away. Maybe they gave up or got bored. Kino palmed the rock, put the conch shell down and crept toward the door on her hands and knees. Sticking her head out the doorway and seeing no one, she put a tentative foot on the ground outside the hut. Then, keeping her ears perked for voices, she put her other foot on the ground and lifted herself up off the display.

"She's here!" Cyan came running around a pillar.

Kino fell back into the hale, rolled on her stomach and grabbed the conch. Cyan arrived at the entrance. Kino dropped the rock into the shell. A bright flash of light burst from the conch. She shut her eyes tightly and held her breath.

6

'Eono

When Kino opened her eyes, she gasped.

Is that sunlight?

She crawled to the doorway. The daylight pierced her eyes and she paused to refocus. Once her eyes adjusted, she realized that she, and the hut, were in an outdoor compound with several triangular hale pili nearby.

She must be dreaming. Any minute now she'd wake up back in the museum. Scowling, she pinched herself hard on the arm. Nothing happened. Her surroundings remained the same. Squeezing her eyes shut, she pinched herself even harder then opened them. The grass huts were still there.

"What the..." she said under her breath.

The cooling breeze of the trade winds welcomed her. A chicken walked by. She was definitely not in the museum anymore.

How the heck did I get here? And where is "here"?

Reaching into her pocket, she pulled out the compass. It pointed north, as it should. Not much use, though, considering she didn't know where she was to begin with.

On the other side of the compound sat a tall, pointy boulder shaped like a surfboard, centered between two palm trees that crisscrossed like a giant X. She realized that these would be good, solid landmarks to find her way back to the hut if she needed to.

Walking to the edge of the yard, Kino spotted several other thatched houses, and a dirt road, further down the hill. A narrow path led to the lower homes. She decided to follow it, hoping it connected to the road.

As she made her way down the trail, she recognized the high-pitched sound of a nose flute. She noticed a shirtless Hawaiian man, sitting on the ground in front of a grass house, on the other side of a wide ditch.

"Hello!" she waved.

The man put down the flute and called back, "Aloha!"

Kino walked closer and yelled, "I think I'm lost. Can I borrow your phone?"

The man just smiled at her and waved.

She cupped her hands around her mouth. "Your phone?" she asked louder.

The guy raised his eyebrows and threw his head back as if to say, "What's up?"

"Can you hear me? Do you have a…" she pointed her right thumb up toward her right ear and stuck her pinky out, then pointed to that hand with her left one, "you know, phone?"

A broad smile appeared on the guy's face and he gave her the "shaka" or "hang-loose" sign. Kino looked at her right hand and face-palmed herself. Sighing, she shook her head and continued on.

She followed the footpath until it reached a larger trail, wide enough for two people to walk side by side. One direction headed uphill, toward several triangle-shaped thatched hales. The other way went downhill. She opted for the latter.

Vibrant, colorful flowers enriched the landscape. The air was filled with the melodic sounds of various birds, hidden in the trees. A dense wall of dark-green foliage and patches of tall, thick trees flanked the road. Occasionally, their branches stretched and met over the path, giving her fleeting relief from the hot sun and brief, random showers.

Kino smiled to herself, enjoying the curious journey. She was used to being alone, but not used to being lost. Yet, she didn't feel alarmed or frightened, certain she would eventually come across the rest of her class.

By the long shadows of the trees, she guessed it to be sometime in the late afternoon. Her stomach, angry about missing lunch, complained with a loud gurgle. Eager to find food and a phone, she focused on walking and picked up her pace.

Further down the road she came across several dwarf banana trees with ripe bunches. After pulling down as many clusters of the small yellow fruit as she could, Kino headed to a patch of shade trees and sat down. She pulled a banana off its bunch and finished it in two big bites, consuming six of them in a matter of minutes. Cool shade, warm, humid air, and a full stomach made the perfect combination for a nap. She decided to lie down.

I'm just going to rest my eyes for a few minutes.

When she awoke it was dark. Her heart raced. Where was everyone? Why hasn't anyone found her yet?

Does anyone know I'm lost?

Standing up, she dusted off and slowly spun around, scanning her surroundings. The wind rustled the dark leaves in the trees. Her heart now banged in her ears. She felt a pressure grip her chest, making it hard to breathe.

You can do this – just find a house and call home. Everything will be okay.

Taking a deep breath, she held it for ten seconds and then emptied her lungs through her mouth. "Paaa-hhh…" She felt a little better. She slowed down her breathing.

The waxing moon provided good visibility, making it easy to see the trail ahead. She looked up at the night sky. Spotting a shooting star, she closed her eyes and wished for food before opening them again.

What was I thinking? Food? I should have wished I were home where we have food!

Annoyed at herself, her mind drifted to what she was craving… a Spam musubi. Her stomach rumbled in agreement. Consumed by her thoughts of seared Spam and rice wrapped in a sheet of dried seaweed, she didn't pay attention to the road. A flash of brown and white swooped down above her and dropped something, forcing her to stop.

She looked down. The tips of her toes grazed the edge of a shallow hole, not big enough for her to fall into, but wide enough to injure an ankle. A leafless stick lay partially in the hole.

Gazing in the direction that the object had flown, she spotted a large Hawaiian owl, perched in a tree. Kino continued walking until she stood directly below it. Although it was dark, she could make out the pale, v-shaped mark between its unblinking yellow eyes. Its white feathers almost looked like stripes and spots throughout the brown ones. She could have sworn it was waiting for her. It reminded her of her grandpa, and the lifelike owl statue in his yard. He called it his pueo, the Hawaiian word for owl.

The regal bird gazed at her for a moment before taking off down the road – flying ahead, then alighting on a tree branch until she caught up, then heading off again, leading the way forward.

Minutes later, the owl landed on a fallen tree between two paths. When she reached the fork she debated if she should head mauka, towards the mountain, or makai, towards the ocean.

"Any help here?" She looked at the owl. It ignored her, cocking its head sideways as it tuned toward a signal like a small, feathered satellite dish.

Kino headed uphill, but after a few yards she noticed that the owl had not followed. She turned and walked backwards, staring at it while continuing up the road. The owl sat motionless. Curious to see what it would do, she walked back toward it. When she arrived at the fork she called out, "Aloha, pueo!"

The bird unfolded its wings and let out a hoot.

Kino headed makai.

The owl lifted off and took the lead once more.

As she came around a bend, flickering lights in the distance caught her eye. The sound of chanting drifted toward her. Her mind raced. This scenario seemed eerily familiar. Could it be… the deadly warrior spirits she'd heard of? The ones that were called Night Marchers?

Her heart beat faster. She tried to remember what her grandfather had told her to do if she ever saw torches and heard chanting at night.

Stop, drop, and roll? Wait, no, that's in case she was on fire.

The lights weren't moving. As far as she knew, Night Marchers were named not for just who they were but what they did. No longer fearful, she became hopeful.

Finally! Civilization! Maybe they'll have a phone I can use. And food!

A small, grassy field stood between her and the lights. She walked faster, ignoring the pain of occasional rocks jabbing at her soles. Stopping at the edge of the lawn, she debated if she should continue on the road until she reached actual buildings. She scanned the trees and sky, looking for the owl, but it was gone.

Glancing towards the lights again, she decided to take her chances there. She made her way across the field. The blades of calf-high grass made her legs itch. She prayed she wouldn't step on anything gross like a toad. At least she didn't have to worry about snakes in Hawaii.

She soon found herself standing on one side of a really wide wall, made of stones the sizes of bowling balls and softballs, packed tightly together. She climbed up a few rocks to see the other side.

A large group of shirtless, three-foot tall men, with skin the color of chocolate, handed stones similar to the ones in the wall to each other, bucket-brigade style, while singing joyfully in Hawaiian. They wore bright-colored malos, loincloths with a wide panel of fabric in front and back.

Several men at the other end of the pond stood in waist-high water and stacked the rocks on an almost-completed dam. And they were building one heck of a dam!

She watched them work, in awe at their quick and efficient manner.

Why do they seem so familiar? Then it came to her. She gasped. Menehunes!

Menehunes are the leprechauns of Hawaiian folklore. According to legends, they were fine craftsmen who could engineer and build structures such as temples and fishponds in just one night. Toiling from dark until dawn, they had to be unseen by others, or else they would abandon their work.

Kino lost her footing off the rock, and she yelped as she landed hard on her bottom. In her mind she heard a silly nursery rhyme, "Ha na okolele, you broke your oko-lele." It was a singsong way that local island kids teased you when you fell on your butt.

By the time she'd clambered back up, the men were gone, the place deserted. Only moonlight reflected off the water near the completed dam. Disappointed, yet still a bit excited, she turned back to the road.

Kino wondered if these little folks could be the famed menehunes, or something less magical. It was hard to dismiss the fact that the dam was constructed without any special tools or machinery that she could see. Why were these people so short? Most Hawaiians she knew were much taller. The shortest people she ever came across were of Asian ancestry. These people were definitely not from the Far East.

Kino paid no attention to the incline of the road. Her mind was focused only on the small brown men. As she walked on, she entered a canopy of trees that blocked out the moonlight. When she emerged on the other side, she found herself on a plateau, overlooking a dark little town made of wood buildings and scattered thatched houses.

Yards later, the path sloped downhill. On one side of her was the bushy hillside; on the other, a steep drop into a ravine. Clouds passed in front of the moon, making it too dark to see clearly.

Kino slowed down her stride, but she still managed to step on a rock and roll her ankle. She lost her balance, fell into the bushes, and landed hard on her left side. Her ribs and shoulder started throbbing. The sharp branches scratched up her arms and legs in angry red welts. She burst out into tears, feeling sorry for herself.

This strange adventure needed to end. Images of her mom and grandparents flashed through her mind. She wished that one of them were there with her. Then she wished instead to be home with all three of them.

Kino realized that crying in the brush wasn't going to help her situation. Struggling, she hoisted herself up. A thorny branch snagged her skirt and ripped a long slit across the back as she pulled away. She fought the urge to cry again, and wondered what to do next. Since she could not get to the town below, her only option was to spend the night on the side of the road. She didn't want to take any chances of falling off the edge.

The large owl flew past and landed in a tree on the side of the hill. Instinct told her she needed to follow the bird. She grimaced and winced as she limped her way up toward it. When she reached its perch, she looked at the dark owl shape. A pair of golden eyes gazed down at her. It stared at her for a moment before flying away, revealing clusters of small pear shapes. She pulled one down and smelled it. Immediately, she recognized her favorite island fruit, mountain apples. She picked six, sat down, and reclined against the tree.

When Kino bit into one, she savored its delicate, sweet flavor. An image of her grandfather's mountain apple tree flashed in her mind. It comforted her. She ate the rest of them, pausing only seconds between each.

Tossing the seed away from her last piece of fruit, she wiped her hands on her shirt and curled up with her arm under her head. She had never spent the night outdoors before, but she was too tired to think about being scared.

It felt as if she had just closed her eyes, but when she opened them again, it was morning. The sounds of many kinds of birds filled the air. A flock of geese flew in a V formation across a cloudless sky. She wondered if they were pointing the way home. Yawning, she pushed herself up.

Kino picked several mountain apples to eat and set off down the road, intent on getting to the town and finding a phone. She couldn't wait to get home, take a shower, and eat real food.

Just as she finished her last fruit, she arrived at the base of the hill, not far from the edge of town. Nearing the intersection of a much wider dirt road, she noticed a man on horseback galloping in her direction. Dressed in a black suit with a wide-brimmed hat, he leaned forward, almost standing in the stirrups, and whipped his horse as he rushed toward her.

"Excuse me!" Kino called, jumping and waving to get the man's attention. She sprinted to the edge of the road. But it was too late. By the time she had reached it, he was long gone. Sighing, she set out once more toward the buildings.

Grass huts, of different sizes and shapes, dotted the land in no apparent order. Most of them were triangular, and much taller than the rectangular one from the museum. In the distance, men in dark malos stood in calf-high water in a large taro field, tending to the shoots. Half naked, little brown kids laughed and chased each other in a nearby yard.

Stepping onto a cool strip of grass, Kino walked until she reached another dirt intersection. An open-air horse-drawn carriage with wooden spoke wheels and a black-fringed canopy rumbled down the street toward her. The driver wore a long black coat and old-fashioned hat, looking like the rider before, which struck Kino as odd. Were these men in costumes? She waved at him, but his eyes stayed focused on the road.

Undaunted, she continued to wave, hoping the passengers would notice her. A pale woman with brown hair looked down her pointed nose at a book, oblivious to Kino's now-desperate gestures. Next to the woman sat a rosy-cheeked toddler with blonde ringlets. The youngster clutched a porcelain doll that resembled its owner. They wore matching purple dresses with puffy lavender sleeves. The little girl stared and waved back to Kino, but didn't say anything to the woman. Disappointed, Kino sighed and picked up her pace.

7

'Ehiku

Near the edge of the town, a path split away from the road. Kino followed it into a narrow alley between two single-story wooden buildings. The short passageway led to an active street. Carriages and horses awaited passengers along both sides of the road, while pedestrians milled about.

It surprised Kino to see Haoles; the local name for Caucasians, going about their business dressed in clothes from a bygone era. The men wore long pants and dark-colored waistcoats with tails. They reminded her of orchestra conductors, with chin-high collars and big, loose bows tied around their necks. Most wore colored top hats or black wide-brimmed ones. The women's attire consisted of bright-colored long dresses with long tailored sleeves. Some ladies had on colorful, fancy hats while others wore cloth or straw bonnets.

A handful of Hawaiian women sat under a tree, sewing flowers into long strings of leis. They all wore conservative pastel muu muus with long sleeves and tall collars. A pair of younger girls gawked at Kino as they hurried past. They wore traditional dresses called kīkepas, sarongs that wrapped around their bodies under one arm and tied over the shoulder on the opposite arm.

People stared, whispered and stepped out of Kino's path as she walked through the town. She wondered if she had wandered onto some sort of film set. Kino's eyes darted around, scanning the area for cameras, but saw none.

This must be some kind of historical reenactment!

People with crates and cloth sacks emerged out of a dark-brown building across the street. An old man in spectacles and an apron helped another man load burlap bags onto a flatbed wagon.

A store! Hopefully I can use their phone.

She crossed the street and stepped onto the wooden porch. A young, blond woman in a long purple dress, and straw hat, holding a tower of boxes in her arms, bustled out in a rush. She crashed into Kino, knocking her backward onto the road. As Kino's butt landed in a shallow puddle, it splashed mud up her back and hair. Three of the boxes landed near her.

The young woman put the rest of the packages down and rushed over. Kino stood up. Dirty water dripped from her skirt to the ground.

"Heavens!" the woman exclaimed, "Are you all right? I am so sorry!"

"I'm okay," Kino reached back and bunched the bottom of her skirt in her fist, squeezing the water out. "Do you know where I can find a phone? I need to call my mom."

The woman knitted her brows and asked, "My dear child, where are your clothes?"

Kino looked down at her damp, dirty outfit. As far as she was concerned, she was wearing them.

"Why you're practically naked. You'll catch your death of cold. Do you live nearby?"

"No, I am pretty sure I live nowhere near here. I just know that I want to call my mom as soon as possible." She studied the lady and guessed her to be around Mom's age. The woman wore lavender gloves that matched the scarf around her neck. Under her hat peeked red curls.

"Well, I can help you call your mother."

Kino picked up the three boxes. "Great!"

"What is your mother's name?" The woman pulled her gloves up.

"Paula."

"Got it. Paaaulaaa!!!" She cupped her hands on either side of her mouth and yelled even louder. "Paaaaaau-laaaa!"

"What are you doing?" Kino frowned.

The woman dropped her hands. "You said you needed help calling her, so I'm helping you call her."

Kino waited for the lady to laugh and pull out her mobile phone. Instead, she took the packages from Kino's hands and added them to her pile.

"I meant call her on the phone," Kino said, somewhat amused, somewhat perturbed.

"What is a thefone?" the blond woman asked.

"Ha, ha. Seriously ma'am, I would really like to call my mom right now. I'm tired, really hungry, and now, super dirty. I just want to go home."

"Where do you live?" The woman eyed the blue paint streaks in Kino's hair.

" Calif..." Kino almost said. "I mean, Kalihi, not far from Damien Memorial School."

"Damien's Memorial School? Kalihi?"

"Yes, Kalihi," Kino insisted, tired of whatever game this lady was playing.

The woman pulled out a white handkerchief from her ivory-colored purse and held it out. "I have not heard of any of those places, but I haven't been here very long myself. How did you get here?"

Kino took the hankie and wiped her hands.

"That's the problem," Kino handed the dirty cloth back. "I have no idea how I got here or where 'here' even is."

"Well, do you have a horse or did you walk?" The lady removed the lavender scarf from around her neck.

"I walked."

"And where did you walk from?" She picked up the handkerchief by the corner with her gloved thumb and index finger.

"Aside from the grass hut," Kino said, "I don't know." She realized she sounded like an idiot.

The lady stared at Kino for a few seconds before placing the hankie in the middle of the scarf. She folded it and tucked it into her handbag.

"I'm not stupid, or crazy or anything." Kino's anxious voice spiraled up as she explained. "I fell asleep in the hut at the Bishop

Museum. You know, in the Hawaiian Hall. I know it said to keep out, but I was trying to hide from…" Her belly let out a loud rumble. She looked down at it in embarrassment.

"Never mind," the woman smiled. "You don't have to say any more. It's easy to get lost here, especially if you don't know your way around. There's so much change happening all the time." She glanced at Kino's tummy. "It sounds like you could use a good meal. You are welcome to come with me to my house. We can get you cleaned up there."

One thing Kino loved about Hawaii was that most local people were welcoming and hospitable. The islanders helped those in need, even strangers, and food was always offered to guests of a home. It was the "Aloha Spirit" Gramma often spoke of.

The woman handed her three of the boxes. "I guess we should make proper introductions. My name is Sophie Whittaker, what is your name?"

"Kino," she answered. "Kino Kahele."

"Now that's an interesting name, Kino Kino Kahele. It's a pleasure to meet you." Sophie winked, picked up the remaining packages and said, "Follow me."

8

ʻEwalu

As the pair neared the house, Kino spotted a plump, middle-aged Hawaiian woman in a long-sleeved pastel blue muʻu muʻu, hanging clothes on a line in the yard. Behind her stood a simple white wooden house with a thatched roof. Centered between two glass-paned windows was an open door.

"Auwe!" The woman dropped the clothes back into the basket at her feet and hurried toward them. "I help you."

"It's all right, Makani. They barely weigh anything," Sophie said, as the woman reached them. "I brought a guest home who will be joining us for lunch. This is Kino. Kino, meet Makani."

There was something familiar about Makani's eyes. Her black hair, piled on top of her head in a loose bun, reminded Kino of Gramma's, minus her grays.

"Aloha, Kino." Her voice was soft and gentle. The dark-skinned woman stepped forward and cradled Kinoʻs face with both hands. She leaned down, pressed the bridges of their noses together and inhaled.

What the heck? Did she just smell me? Kino then recalled that this was how Hawaiians greeted each other in the distant past.

Sophie said, "She is lost. I invited her here to clean up and eat."

Makani smiled while eyeing Kino's dirty clothes.

Sophie asked, "Will you please fill the tub for our guest? I'll get these packages into the house and start making lunch."

"ʻAe." Makani picked up the basket and walked to the side of the house.

Sophie said, "Makani doesn't speak a whole lot of English but understands it well. Her husband is my husband's navigator. She's been quite helpful in helping me learn about island customs."

Kino followed Sophie into the home. It took a minute for her eyes to adjust from the sunny outdoors to the darkened room. The sun's gradual descent toward the western horizon allowed only dim light into the space from the windows facing east. In the corner stood a small, black iron stove with a single burner. Next to it was a white wooden cabinet with plates and bowls stacked on it. She guessed it was the kitchen, but did not see a refrigerator.

Sophie took off her hat and gloves and placed them on the table. "Don't let the house fool you – we're not rich or anything. My husband's family was nice enough to send the wood for our walls and floors as a wedding present, and my parents sent the windows."

Kino put the parcels she held onto the table and wiped the sweat from her brow.

Sophie picked up a glass pitcher on the table, poured some water into a wooden cup and held it in front of Kino.

"Thanks," Kino smiled, gulping it all down in four big sips. Sophie laughed each time Kino held her cup out for more, but after the third refill, Sophie put the container on the table and said, "Help yourself."

Makani walked in. "Da tub is filled. You ready?"

Kino nodded and followed her outside to the back. A woven three-sided screen enclosed a small area at the rear of the house. In the center of it was a round metal washbasin next to a stool with a wooden bowl on top of it.

"Where is the shower?" Kino asked in surprise.

Makani's eyes widened. "Show-er?"

"Shower, you know, in the bathroom? Where water comes out and gets you clean?" Kino made scrubbing motions on her arm and belly.

"Dis is da room for da bath. Da lumi 'au 'au," Makani picked up the bowl, scooped it into the water and handed it to Kino with a bar of hard white soap. "You need help 'au 'au?"

"Uh, no thanks, I can bathe myself."

"Put dis on when you pau. Hang your clothes deya." The woman chin-pointed at an empty spot on the clothesline before disappearing behind the screen.

Kino examined the bar of soap. It was rough and hard, and it smelled like wax. She set it and the bowl on the stool and removed the compass from her pocket. As she placed it next to the container, it knocked the soap off the cramped surface.

"Ugh."

The old bathroom at Gramma's house, with its peeling paint, mold-stained grout, and minimal counter space was luxurious compared to this.

As she undressed, she felt her pockets.

Where's the stone?

Shoving her hand down till her fingers reached the bottom, she fished around. Nothing. She pulled the pocket inside out.

Did it fall out somewhere on the road? She racked her brain... The last thing she'd done before she woke up in the hale pili was to drop it into the conch shell... At least she knew where she'd left it.

As Kino pushed the vacant pocket back into her shorts, an empty feeling washed over her. She missed the shiny stone and felt incomplete without it. Her grumbling stomach reminded her to hurry.

The clothes Makani gave her looked like a man's white, old-fashioned nightshirt that ended at her knees. She put it on and debated what to do with the compass while her shorts dried. She decided to leave it on the stool, since the shirt had no pockets.

Both women were busy preparing food when Kino stepped through the kitchen doorway. The room was much warmer than when she first entered.

Sophie's face lit up when she saw her. "Well, hello there! Feeling better?" She placed a bowl of sliced mangos on the table, next to a plate of steamed fish.

Before Kino could answer, a sudden gust of wind blew the shirt up. She quickly pushed its hem down. The cool breeze on her butt cheeks was an immediate reminder that she wasn't wearing pants.

"I think I have something that just might fit you," Sophie smiled. "Follow me."

51

She led Kino down the hall to a small, cramped room. A plain wooden dresser stood in the corner. Next to the dresser was an oval full-length mirror on a wooden stand. A narrow, quilt-covered, four-poster bed occupied the space under a window on the far wall.

"Why don't you give this a try?" Sophie gestured toward the bed.

A long, jade-green velvet dress, with gold trim and lace on the collar and sleeves, lay across the quilt.

"It is a bit formal, but it's clean and I can no longer fit into it.

"These," she held up a pair of dark green shoes, "go with that dress." She placed them on the floor.

"Um, thanks." Kino picked up the dress and held it at arm's length. She didn't want to be rude, but she hated long dresses. Having her legs covered make her feel claustrophobic in warm weather. Unfortunately, it was her only option, since her own clothes were a damp mess.

Sophie said, "I would let you borrow my other pair of knickers, but I'm afraid they may still be damp."

Kino pictured the long cotton bloomers that she'd seen on the clothesline when she first arrived.

"That's okay. I'll be fine in this for now." She was glad she had washed her own underwear earlier, and wondered how long it would take to dry.

Sophie walked out and closed the door behind her. Kino held the dress against her body and looked in the mirror. Sophie was at least four inches taller, so the hem draped on the floor.

She undressed, pulled it on, and pushed the sleeves up to her elbows. They were too long. The lace cuffs stopped at her knuckles. Twenty small, round, pearl-covered buttons secured the dress from the front. Even with Kino's thin, nimble fingers, they were difficult to fasten.

The fabric shoes were stiff and uncomfortable, but they fit, for the most part. The two-inch heels and narrow toes were definitely made for a grownup. She backed up to look at herself in the mirror, stepped on her hem, and lost her balance. She caught herself with one of the corner posts of the bed.

"Mental note: be more careful," she said under her breath. She straightened up and looked at her reflection. It was the longest dress and the highest heels she'd ever worn. She gathered up the skirt with both hands and headed back to the kitchen.

Sophie's face brightened when she laid eyes on Kino. "You look better in that dress than I do," she exclaimed, as she clasped her hands together and grinned.

Kino looked down at the pouching bodice, a little too long for her torso. "Thanks," she said, knowing the woman was just being polite.

"Supper is ready – have a seat here." Sophie pointed at the plate with fish and fruit to the left of Kino, before pulling out her own chair and sitting down.

Makani placed a big bowl of poi in the center of the table, family style, and took her seat.

"Let us give thanks." Sophie laced her fingers in prayer and said, "Bless us, oh Lord, and these thy gifts, for which we are about to partake in thy body, through Christ. Amen."

"Amen," said Kino and Makani in unison.

Sophie raised an eyebrow as Kino shoveled a big piece of mango into her mouth and could barely keep her lips closed as she chewed it. Sophie and Makani exchanged looks of amusement as they watched her with reassuring smiles.

Several minutes into the meal, Sophie lifted the cloth napkin off her lap and patted her mouth.

"Well, dear, tell us about yourself. How old are you?"

Kino looked at the folded cloth next to her plate, picked it up and dabbed at her own mouth before answering.

"I'm twelve, and my mom and I just moved in with my grandparents. Oh, and I'm lost."

"Do you remember what road you took to get into town?"

"I know what road I came in from; I just don't know exactly where I started from. I mean I started from the grass hut in the museum…" She picked up the napkin and put it on her lap. "I think I fell asleep, and when I woke up, I was still in the hut but not in the museum."

Sophie put her index and middle fingers together, scooped them into the poi and rotated her wrists and held them up. "I've been practicing." She winked at Makani. "What museum?" The poi disappeared into her mouth.

Kino swallowed her own two fingertips of poi. "You know, the Bishop Museum."

Sophie shook her head and held her napkin to her lips as she chewed.

"I left the hut and just followed roads until I found this place... uh, town." Kino wiped her fingers on her napkin. "Was I supposed to check in somewhere or something?"

The two women stared at her.

Kino continued, "I mean, I haven't seen any of the other kids."

Sophie lowered her eyes. "I cannot have any children, and Makani's daughter lives on a different island."

An odd sensation of confusion and regret came over Kino. Feeling like a jerk for making her hostess feel bad, she bit her lip and fidgeted in her seat.

"By the look on your face," Sophie realized, "I'm guessing that wasn't what you were asking about."

Kino shook her head. "No. I'm sorry. I meant I was looking for my classmates. I haven't seen anyone since I got here. I spent the night in the middle of nowhere, and I don't know what I'm supposed to do next." Her foot tapped out her agitation in rapid staccato.

Sophie frowned. "I haven't the slightest idea what you're talking about, my dear, but it will be dark soon. You're welcome to stay the night, and perhaps tomorrow you can find your group."

It sounded as though another night away from home was in store. Kino gazed at Sophie, waiting to for a change in her expression. "What year is this?"

"Why, it's 1825, of course!" Sophie tilted her head. "What an odd question."

Kino had no idea what had been happening in Hawaiian history during that time, but now she at least knew what era she was experiencing. *What's the harm in playing along? This could be fun.*

"Sorry, I'm just trying to figure out what to expect. So, what's life like?"

Sophie said, "I'm not sure what you mean. It's quiet here. My husband is the captain of a ship, which only comes to port once a year. Thank goodness for Makani, or I wouldn't have a soul to talk to." She put her napkin on her now-empty plate. "Your visit is the first interesting thing that has happened in a long while."

In the short time they sat there, the afternoon faded into early dusk. Makani stood up and retrieved a box of wooden matches. Striking a matchstick against the stove, she lit a white, stubby taper then used it to light the other candles throughout the room.

When she finished, she dipped the flame onto a hardened cascade of dribbled wax until it softened, then stuck the candle into the brass candlestick in the center of the table.

Kino waited until the woman returned to her seat before speaking.

"Umm… my mom and I just moved from Los Angeles, just a couple months ago, when my grandpa got really sick." She took a sip of water.

"Los Angeles? Where is that?" Sophie asked.

Was this a geography quiz? Kino hesitated before speaking. "Uhhh…" As she put her cup down, the back of her hand knocked over a candlestick. The flame caught the fringe of her sleeve, setting the lace cuff ablaze.

Out of nowhere, a big gust of wind blew the door and windows open and snuffed the candles out. Before anyone could move, a brown and white owl flew in and hovered for a second over Kino. The draft from its wings extinguished the flame on her sleeve. It then circled the room and flew out as quickly as it had appeared.

Sophie sprang to her feet, and closed the door and windows. Makani relit the candles around the room.

"Well, that was a lot of commotion!" Sophie said, flopping back on her seat. "I have never seen anything like that happen before! Are you all right, Kino?" She fanned her face with a napkin.

"That looks like the owl I kept seeing earlier!" Kino looked down at her wrist. The lace was gone. The material that the lace had been sewn onto was now scorched and hard, and the flame had singed the edge of the cuff black.

"What was that, dear?" Sophie asked. "What do you mean, you kept seeing that owl?" Her eyes grew larger. "Do you think it's following you?"

"This probably sounds crazy, but I think it might be. I saw it last night. It helped me."

"Ahh," Makani nodded. "Dat must be your 'amakua."

"Her what-a-what-a?" Sophie asked. Kino giggled.

Makani relit the candle on the table. "Her 'amakua, or spirit guardian. All Hawaiian families have dem. Dey help protect and guide us and can take on many forms in nature." She sat down and said, "Some Hawaiians have several 'amakuas to help dem. Dey appear in nature as rocks or animals."

"That makes sense," Kino said. "An owl kept showing up and seemed to direct me to things like fruit trees and what direction to head in!"

"That's fascinating!" Sophie clapped her hands together. "You must tell us more!"

Kino opened her mouth to answer but instead let out a big yawn. She couldn't help it.

"You poor dear," said Sophie, looking at Kino's wearied face. "Why don't you head off to bed? You certainly could use a good night's sleep."

Sophie was right. Despite the sudden excitement, Kino felt exhausted. She thanked the women for the dinner and said goodnight. Before she left, Makani said, "Your 'amakua will always watch over you."

Kino smiled with the little energy she had left then headed to the bedroom. She didn't bother changing back into the nightshirt. Instead, she kicked off her shoes, plopped down face first on the bed and fell asleep on top of the covers.

*****

Makani greeted her with a warm, "Aloha kakahiaka!" as Kino walked into the kitchen the next morning.

"Aloha!" Kino grinned.

"Sit down, eat." Makani motioned at the boiled eggs and fruit on ti leaf-covered wooden dishes.

Kino ate breakfast without pause, eager to get going. As she finished her last bite, Sophie walked in and placed a brown paper-wrapped box on the table.

"You're up! Great! Would you mind taking something into town for me? I promised my sister I would send her some seashells."

Scrawled in fancy longhand calligraphy were the words, "Emily A. Thompson, New England."

"Do you have the address that it's going to?" Kino asked.

"Of course, silly, that's why I wrote it on the package. Now here, take it to the general store in town, and tell Sam he can apply the change to my house account."

She handed Kino a yellowed piece of paper with some printing on it. On it was the number five, and the words, "Elima Kala," as well as other words, written in Hawaiian.

Kino held the bill with both hands. "Cool, is this money?"

"Of course, dear."

Before Kino could ask any more questions, Sophie shooed her out.

"Put it in your pocket so you don't lose it, and please hurry. If it doesn't make it out on today's ship, I'll need to wait an entire month before I can send it again."

That made no sense to Kino, but she didn't want to ask. She put the paper into a pocket on the dress and said, "Thank you so much for everything."

"Aren't you returning?" Sophie asked.

"Probably not. If I can't reach my mom, I'll call my grandma to see if she can come and get me." As Kino headed for the door, her heel caught the bottom of the dress. She lurched forward and grabbed the doorway.

"Oh my, that is a wee bit too long," said Sophie. "If you want, I can hem it."

"No, thanks, it's okay." Kino was anxious to leave. "I can just hold it up." She gathered the skirt and raised it a few inches on one side, but the rest of it still draped on the floor. Using both hands, she lifted it above her ankles. Then she remembered she had to carry something.

Sensing Kino's urgency, Sophie said, "Let's try this out." She picked up the roll of the twine she'd used on the package, and measured it around Kino's waist. Then she cut it, re-wrapped it around Kino, and tied the ends in a double knot. Holding the string with one hand, she pulled at the material above it and pulled the fabric over. It raised the hem of the skirt but made Kino look like she had a flat, big butt.

"Is it okay if I borrow these clothes?" Kino asked, "I can wash them and bring them back next week."

"You may keep everything. But do come back, if you are not able to reach anyone," Sophie followed Kino to the door. "You are welcome to stay here as long as you wish."

"Thank you again for everything," Kino hugged her hostess, "just in case."

"You're welcome," Sophie winked, "just in case."

9

'Eiwa

Kino picked the package up by its string and walked out to the clothesline. After pulling on her shorts, she stuffed the compass into her left pocket and glanced up at her dirt-stained t-shirt and torn skirt. No use taking them with her. Maybe mom can drive her back in a few days to get them.

Within minutes, beads of perspiration trickled down the sides of her face as she reached the road. Uncomfortable in Sophie's heavy dress, she couldn't wait to get home and change.

Entering the town, she headed to the plain wooden structure where she had first run into Sophie. A row of amber bottles, labeled "Dr. Fredrick's Elixir," sat in the dirty store window. Aside from two wooden crates near the door, the outside of the store was empty.

Inside the dark, damp space, it was a different story. Shelves holding miscellaneous jars, bottles and cans lined the walls. Barrels and burlap bags crowded the tight floor space. The stale, musty air smelled like leather, dried fish, and sweat. Behind the front counter, a wrinkled Haole man with white hair stood with his back to the door, rearranging cans on the shelves on the wall.

"Are you Sam?" Kino asked.

"Yes, I am." He pushed a row of glass jars together and turned to face her.

"Sophie Whittaker sent me. She needs this mailed today." Kino placed the package on the counter and pulled out the yellowed paper. "She said to give this to you for the postage and tell you to put the rest toward her house account."

The clerk wiped hands on his apron, "Ah yes, she did mention something about that yesterday." He picked up the slip and walked over to an ornate brass register. "She's one of my best customers. Always pays cash and never asks for credit."

He pressed a button on the machine. A small tab that said NO SALE popped up behind a small glass window on top of it. It made a loud "ding" as the drawer popped open. He deposited the bill and slammed the drawer shut. The NO SALE tab shot back into the machine.

Sam returned for the box and took it over to a big book. Next to it lay a foot-long gray feather. He picked it up and dipped its end into an ink jar. Bending over, he scrunched up his face and began writing in the ledger.

Kino looked around and spotted a thin newspaper at the end of the counter. The headline read, "Creek Indians Sign Treaty with United States."

"I love these old newspapers," she said, touching the corner of the paper.

"I don't know what you mean by old. It's the latest issue from the States. Granted, it takes several weeks to get here."

Kino looked at the paper again. Under "National Gazette" were the words Friday, February 13, 1825. Talk about attention to detail.

She walked back the register and asked, "Can I please borrow your phone?"

He stopped writing and lifted his head. "Sorry, I don't carry that." He dipped the quill into the inkwell and continued scrawling while muttering to himself.

Thinking he misunderstood her question, she waited until he put down the feathered pen. This time she made sure to enunciate her words and spoke a little slower.

"Please sir, I know you have to stick to whatever 'theme,'" she made the air quote sign with her fingers, "this is, but I just want to get home. You must have a phone I can borrow."

"Now look here, young lady. I do not know what you're talking about. I don't know what this 'yourfone,'" he returned the air quote gesture, "or 'afone' is." Again, with the air quotes. "And if I had such things, I certainly would question why I would let you borrow them."

Disappointed, Kino browsed through the items along the counter while inching up on her tiptoes to peek over it.

"Ahem," Sam raised an eyebrow at her. "Is there anything else I can help you with?"

She waited for him to say something like, "You've been pranked! There are cameras there, there, and there." But he did no such thing. He stood staring at her.

She thought she'd take one more stab at asking him.

"Please, Sam. Sir. It's been a crazy past few days. I don't know where I am, and I just want to call my mom. Can I please borrow your telephone?"

He looked at her point blank and said, "Look, child. I don't know how much clearer I can be. I do not have a yourfone. I do not have an a-fone. And I certainly do not have a tele-fone. There are no fones of any kind." He pointed at the back of the store. "We have fans..."

Kino face-palmed herself.

"Is there anywhere in town I might be able to find someone with one?"

"My guess, if it's something expensive, they might have it at the Palace."

"The palace? You mean the 'Iolani Palace?" Finally, a place she recognized.

"King Kamehameha's palace. I don't know if it has a name. We just all call it the Palace." Sam stooped over, picked up a burlap bag then hoisted it onto the counter. Pulling out a pocketknife, he opened the blade, stabbed the bag and tore at the hole. The fabric didn't open, so he wrestled with it for a moment. The stubborn material gave way and tore apart, streaming a slew of dried red beans onto the counter. A few landed on the ground. He let out a sound of frustration and pulled the sides of the bag up quickly.

"I have to say," Kino said, trying to sound casual. "I've learned a lot from this first-hand experience. But can I just call my mom? I just want to go home now."

"I don't see why not," he said, scooping the spilled beans up with his hands. He poured them into the bag. Twice as many fell out. He sighed. "Where is she?"

It was Thursday, Mom's usual day off. "Probably at home. But it doesn't matter, I'll just call her cell."

He looked at her as if she had three heads. "Well, the jail is in the opposite direction."

"My mom's not in jail." Her temples throbbed. Massaging them, she said, "Look, I know you have to stay in character, and I will probably fail the class, but I really, really want to go home now."

"Then go!" Sam scowled. "I don't know if this is a joke, but I have things to do. I'm a very busy man!"

Kino groaned. "Well, can you at least point me in the direction of the palace?"

"Gladly."

He walked outside and pointed down the road. "Head that way. Look for a grove of palm trees. The palace is just beyond there."

Kino thanked him and left in the direction he'd indicated.

The hot sun cast little shadow on the ground. Her shoes offered some protection from the rocky terrain, yet she still stumbled on occasion due to their ill fit and high heels.

Several carriages and a few pedestrians passed Kino on the street. Everyone stared at her. It may have been because of the streaks of blue paint still in her hair. Or because she had pulled most of the long skirt up over the twine, so that now the hemline stopped at her knees. The clunky shoes looked ridiculous on her bare legs.

Sweat rolled down the sides of her face and saturated the high collar. Kino loosened her top buttons, and felt the immediate kiss of cool air on her neck. When she spotted the glistening ocean through a row of palm trees, the desire to stick her feet into the water overcame her. She hurried toward the beach, not taking her eyes off the shimmering blue.

As she reached the wet sand, Kino pulled off her shoes and ran into the surf. Gentle waves unfurled and dissipated into a white foam of bubbles that pushed past her ankles. Her headache receded with the water. Then she looked up from her feet at the horizon – and gasped.

What the...

In the distance was Diamond Head. It was on her left and not too far away, which meant that she was somewhere around Ala Moana. But where was the mall, the hotels, and the high-rise buildings? Not to mention the cars, busses, and people? Even if the immediate town were a movie set, that wouldn't explain the lack of any buildings or houses on the mountains.

Kino backed up out of the water, tripped on her shoes, and landed on her butt. She turned her head to the left and fixed her gaze on the unmistakable Oahu landmark.

How is this possible?

Her rapid heartbeat felt as if it was thumping in her ears. Her head started to hurt again. She brushed as much sand off her feet as she could and put her shoes back on. Taking a deep breath, she struggled to stand and trudged up the beach.

After she'd walked for several minutes on the road, a large cluster of palm trees loomed up ahead. Kino hoped that it meant she was getting close to her destination.

Rectangular and triangle-shaped hales dotted the landscape around the palms. Two men sat outside one of the grass huts, pounding poi on elongated boards. Kino recognized the round-bottomed, bell-shaped stone pestles that they used to mash the taro, even from a distance.

Anxious to get to the palace, she picked up her pace. A group of small, naked kids ran around near the road, laughing and playing. She guessed them to be around five or six and could hear them speaking in fluent Hawaiian. It was the first time she ever heard kids conversing in the language.

The children stopped and stared at her with wide, curious eyes. Kino dropped her gaze, pushed her hair behind her ears, and walked past as quickly as she could. They giggled and whispered to one another before running off.

A big dust cloud headed toward her. From it emerged two horses, side by side, pulling a black covered carriage. Before Kino had a chance to step away from the road, they galloped by. Dirt flew from the horses' hooves and the wagon wheels. It only took a matter of seconds to pass her, but it left her covered in a fine layer of red dust.

Frustrated and disgusted, Kino continued on. Her feet ached and burned. The ill-fitting shoes rubbed her toes raw. She stopped and pulled them off. The skin on her pinky toes and the backs of her heels had lifted into blisters.

A small pond in the distance caught her eye. She could at least wash her hands and face in it and find some relief for her inflamed feet. Dropping the heavy shoes, she hurried over to the water's edge and stepped down into the cool, wet mud. Water rose up over her knees, forcing her to pull her ballooned skirt up almost to her waist. Squishing the soft, wet soil between her toes, Kino sighed and closed her eyes, enjoying the moment.

"'Ae'a kapu!" a man's voice boomed from behind her.

Startled, Kino flinched then turned around. A hulking, muscled Hawaiian man in a red malo pointed a long wooden spear at her.

Too stunned to say anything, she dropped her dress and put her hands in the air. Her skirt slowly sank into the murky water.

"Hele mai!" He prodded the air between them.

Kino knew that meant he wanted her to go with him. She put her hands down and plodded out. He gestured with his chin the direction he wanted her to start walking.

"Please, sir," she implored, putting her hands back up. "I don't mean any harm – I was just trying to cool my feet."

He jabbed the spear at her, prompting her to move. She bit her bottom lip and did her best not to freak out.

Was this part of the re-enactment?

The man herded her toward a compound, which was surrounded by a twenty-foot fence made up of sharp-pointed wood posts. A pair of statuesque, dark skinned, well-toned men guarded the entrance. They each wore a waist-length ti-leaf cape, red malo, and stoic expression. Each man held a tall wooden spear like the one pointed at Kino.

The pair stared straight ahead, not making eye contact with anyone. They reminded her of the expressionless English guards at Buckingham Palace.

10

'Umi

Once through the gates, Kino found herself in an enclosure, twice the size of a city block. In the center of the spacious compound stood a two-story thatched building. Smaller grass huts of different styles and sizes were scattered throughout the area. Some of these were shaped like the more traditional house in the Bishop Museum, others like tall triangles. Pavilion-like structures and lean-tos held workers in the midst of their labors.

Men and women toiled in the yard, dressed in the old, traditional Hawaiian attire. The males wore dark-colored malos; the females were dressed in pa'u skirts in bright colors and patterns, with coordinating sleeveless cloaks worn off the shoulder. Kino surprised herself when the word "kihei" popped into her head. Her short-term memory had not been so reliable during the language part of her museum class.

In one area, four women with wooden clubs pummeled a long, white sheet of cloth. Kino recognized the fibrous material from the time her museum class made kapa using similar tools.

A pair of older men tended a mound of banana leaves with smoke piping out of it, scenting the air with the rich smell of roasted pork. Nearby, a small group of dark-haired women sat under a thatched lean-to, weaving baskets with dried lau hala leaves.

The guard guided her toward the main building. Two sentries, each holding a large, red-and-gold kahili, guarded the entrance.

The first time she'd ever seen a kahili, Kino thought they were feather-covered cylindrical lampshades on ten-foot poles. Years later, she found out they were standards to indicate Hawaiian royalty.

As she approached the open doorway, a boy dressed in a crisp, white, long-sleeved shirt, matching pants, and a gold-embroidered vest came out. The man turned the spear vertical and put it on the ground, then bent down on one knee in immediate submission. He bowed his head and didn't look at the boy.

Kino eyed the kid. Who the heck was he, and why was he dressed that way? He must be someone important, based on the reverence that the guard showed him.

The boy had big, brown eyes, full lips, dark-brown skin and short, wiry black hair; and he was several inches taller than Kino. His white shirt was trimmed at the cuffs and collar with ruffles, and buttoned all the way up to his chin. He stood with his shoulders back and his spine straight, giving him a dignified air. There was something oddly familiar about him that Kino couldn't quite identify.

The boy asked the guard a question in Hawaiian. The man didn't dare look up and spoke his answer to the ground.

The boy turned his focus to her. "'Ōlelo Hawai'i 'oe?"

Kino dropped her hands. "I'm sorry, I don't speak Hawaiian."

"Why were you standing in the ali'i taro pond? It is kapu. Forbidden."

"I'm sorry. I didn't know. I just wanted to cool off. I didn't see any taro shoots." Her clammy fingers fiddled with the tiny buttons on her bodice.

He surveyed her blue-streaked hair and filthy clothes. The muddy water had dried to a red, dusty layer on her legs and the bottom half of her dress. Sand still clung to parts of her skin and clothes.

With authority in his voice, the boy chastised the guard in Hawaiian. The man bowed his head, stood upright and left.

The boy studied her from head to toe.

"Who are you?"

"My name is Kino. Is this the palace?"

"Yes. Do you have business here?" He stepped closer to her.

She looked up at his eyes. "I'm lost and I'm trying to get home. I need to call my mom."

"Is she here?" He gestured toward the yard.

Kino shook her head. "No, she's either at work or at home."

He narrowed his eyes. "Why would you come here to call her? Would it not make more sense to go to where she is?"

"I came here because I was hoping to use your phone."

"What is a yourfone?"

Not this again.

Sighing, she said, "Look, I just want to get home. Can you please tell me who to speak to so I can make a call?"

"I do not understand what it is you need. You want to call your mother who is not here, and you would like to speak to someone who will give you permission to do so?"

She looked at him and nodded.

"Well, I give you permission." He planted his hands on his hips. "You may go to wherever your mother is, and call out to her."

She couldn't help but laugh. Was he serious?

"What is your name?" She hoped she would recall where she saw him before.

He puffed out his chest and said, "My name is Keaweawe'ula Kīwala'ō Kauikeaouli Kaleiopapa."

She blinked hard twice then stared at him, expressionless.

"You can just call me Kauikeaouli," he smiled.

"K-Kaui-ke-kuli?"

"Kaui-ke-a-o-u-l-i," he said, slowly.

"Kaui-ke-" she said, just as slowly.

"A..."

"A..."

"O..."

"O..."

"Uli," he said with a nod.

"Kaui-ke-a-o-u-li," she said, haltingly. He mouthed the last three syllables as she said them. "Kauikeaouli."

"Well done!" he grinned. "What is your name?"

"Kinohiloa Wahinenohopono Kahele." For some reason she felt compelled to curtsy but stuck her hand out instead. "But you can call me Kino."

"You are not from here, are you?" He looked at her dirty palm. His left brow arched as he eyed the dried red mud on her fingers and the back of her hand. He hesitated before extending his.

As soon as their fingers touched, she felt a strange and immediate connection, as if she had known him all of her life. Yet this was the first time she had ever met him. She was certain of that.

He must have felt something, too. The awkward meeting was neutralized in an instant. His formal demeanor became far more relaxed. He furrowed his brow and tilted his head. "Have we met before?"

"No, not that I know of. What school do you go to?"

"School? I have several tutors who teach me different subjects, but I do not go to an academy to learn. I am educated here." He pointed at the main structure.

Aah, homeschool.

Kino peered closer at his face. "Have you ever gone to the Bishop Museum? I have to go there every day." Maybe that's where she'd seen him before.

"I am not aware of this Bishop Museum," he said. She fell into stride with him. "However, my brother spoke of a magnificent museum in England that holds the world's treasures. He plans to visit it on his tour through Great Britain. He said he would bring me something from there. Maybe an artifact from history!"

Kino stopped walking.

"How old are you?" she asked, looking up at him.

"I am eleven years old. How old are you?"

"Twelve," she said, trying to stand taller. He had a good four inches on her.

It began to rain.

"Come with me." He ducked and ran toward the building. Just as they passed the two kahili bearers, the gentle sprinkle turned into a downpour.

The room they entered took up the entire space of the tall, thatched structure. Although it looked like a two-story building from the outside, inside there was no second floor. A grander version of the lau hala mat she sat on in class spanned the entire ground. Two beautiful and intricately carved chairs sat opposite a velvet chaise longue in the center. The ornate Western furniture stood in stark contrast to the simple thatched ceiling and walls.

A young Hawaiian girl posing with a three-foot long, brown feather-covered stick stood stiffly in one corner. A white flower lei crowned her black, wavy, shoulder-length hair and matched the one around her neck. Her elongated face held a slight, rigid smile. A cape made of red and yellow feathers, trimmed with opalescent black ones, draped across her shoulders and down to the floor.

In front of her, a gray-haired Haole man in a blue painter's smock sketched her image on a large canvas. The girl glanced at the pair as they entered the room.

"That is my sister Nahienaena," Kauikeaouli said.

"Yes, I recognize her from the painting hanging in the Honolulu Museum of Art. She looks just like her, I mean the real Princess. This whole re-enactment experience is really believable. I love the attention to detail."

"She *is* the real Princess. What is a "re-enactment experience"? What do you mean?"

Kino sighed. Explaining anything would be pointless. They would probably act as though they had no idea what she was talking about, in order to stay in character. But the girl standing in front of her looked *just* like the postcard of the portrait she had purchased from the museum gift store, to put in the scrapbook she'd made for Grandpa. She was well acquainted with the princess's image. The resemblance was uncanny.

Her eyes shifted to the boy. What were the odds? *Now* she realized why he had seemed so familiar. He looked identical to a painting that hung with Nahienaena's in the Museum of Art. Two actors chosen to play people they *actually* look like. She had to say something. It was pretty amazing.

"The two of you really look like the prince and princess in the paintings I saw."

His eyebrows knitted together.

"What paintings? This is the first time that anyone is capturing our image like this." He gestured toward his sister. "And I told you, she *is* the princess."

A strange sensation struck Kino that somehow he was telling the truth.

"Where are we?"

"In the palace of my brother," Kauikeaouli straightened with pride, "Kamehameha the second, King Liholiho."

Kino gawked at him, then at the girl in the cape, and then back at him. It was all coming together. Somehow, someway, she had ended up in the past – in a time before big buildings, cars and tourists. No wonder the landscape looked completely different.

The room started to spin. Glancing at the girl and boy again, Kino understood. She was in the company of young Kauikeaouli, the actual Kamehameha III, and his royal sister, Nahienaena.

She felt faint. Her knees buckled and she dropped to the ground. Alarmed, the prince called out, and two men in malos ran in. The last thing that Kino remembered was the feeling of floating.

When Kino opened her eyes, both Kauikeaouli and Nahienaena were kneeling in front of her. Their brows furrowed in concern. Princess Nahienaena still clutched the feathered scepter.

"How do you feel?" asked Kauikeaouli.

Kino pushed herself up on the chaise. "What year is this?"

The princess raised her brows and said, "It is eighteen hundred and twenty-five, of course."

If Kino weren't already sitting, she would have fallen again. Her legs were still weak from the first shock.

"How could this be?" Kino looked around as if searching for something. She swept her fingers through her hair and tugged at the ends.

"How could *what* be?" Kauikeaouli asked.

Kino stood up and started to pace. "How could I be here? In the nineteenth century?"

The siblings looked at each other then at the girl who was having a meltdown in front of them.

Kino grabbed her head, turned, and paced away from them. She paused, "I was in the museum…" She ambled back toward them.

"Hiding in the grass hut…" she marched away again. "Then I woke up and…" She turned, faced the pair and said, "You're not going to believe me. Heck, even *I* don't believe me!" She walked back toward them. They both stood in front of the couch. "You may want to sit down."

The royal pair sat at the same time.

Kino perched on the edge of the chair opposite them.

"What is this about?" Kauikeaouli frowned.

"I don't belong here," Kino shifted her gaze from one sibling to the other. "I'm from a different time."

"What time? Night time?" Nahienaena asked.

"No, I mean from the year 2016."

The pair stared at her with blank expressions.

"I'm not crazy," Kino gripped the cushion she sat on. "I don't know how it happened, but somehow I ended up here, in this time, and now I need to get back home – to the future."

Nahienaena narrowed her eyes. "You sound crazy. What sort of trickery is this?" She stood up. "What is it that you want? Money? Because we can have you arrested." She walked toward the door.

Kino felt lightheaded. Everything was happening so fast.

"Wait," Kauikeaouli said. "I believe her."

Nahienaena stopped, crossed her arms, and scowled. "Are you pupuple?"

Kino stifled a giggle. She knew that the word meant "insane," in Hawaiian.

"I don't know why, but I can feel she is telling the truth," said Kauikeaouli. "I believe her, so, we will help her."

They both stared at Kino. She wished she could turn invisible.

"Well, she looks crazy." The younger girl dropped her arms. Directing her next question at Kino, the princess asked, "Why are you so dirty?"

Kino glanced at Kauikeaouli.

He smiled. "It is a long story. However, now she is our guest and we must treat her as such. Extend your aloha, my sister, and welcome her."

Nahienaena glared at him for a moment, sighed, and said, "Ho'okipa i ka Kino."

11

ʻUmikūmākahi

Kino's stomach let out a loud groan. She doubled over and covered her belly in embarrassment. Her breakfast of fruit and eggs had been hours ago, and she was famished.

"Lunch will be ready soon. Would you like to join Nahi and me? Kauikeaouli asked.

Nahienaena eyed Kino from head to toe. "She cannot eat with us. Look at how lepo she is."

"Nahi is right," said the prince. His sister's mouth curled into a coy smirk. "We need to get you cleaned up before you eat with us."

His sister shot him a look.

The prince called out, "Mai!"

A slender, six-foot-tall woman with brown, wavy hair entered the room, followed by a shorter, full-figured woman with long, black hair. They both wore matching gray kīkepas, and purple crown flower wreaths around their heads. The heavier woman was closer in height to Kino than her much taller counterpart, with cocoa colored skin, a round face, and a smile that came easily, reminding Kino of Makani.

He instructed them in Hawaiian, giving direct orders to each woman, while gesturing and pointing at Kino.

"Go with them," Kauikeaouli said. "They will take care of you."

The women escorted Kino outside, and around a screen of tall bushes, to a thatched, covered pavilion. Under the inverted V-shaped roof stood a large, cast-iron, clawfoot tub. It looked out of place in such a minimal structure. Although there were no fixtures, and it lacked running water, it was a luxurious upgrade from the metal bucket she had last bathed in.

She walked over to the tub and waited for them to leave. Instead, the tall lady stepped up and started unfastening Kino's buttons.

Surprised and shocked, Kino recoiled.

"Uh, I can do it." She turned her back on them, undid the rest of her dress, and let it drop to the floor. It was such a relief to get out of the dirty, heavy clothes. She sighed and stood there for a moment, just enjoying the cool air, before stepping and sinking into the warm water.

The shorter lady walked over with a cloth, dipped it in the bath, rubbed it in coconut-scented soap and started scrubbing Kino's shoulders. Although it was odd to be bathed by an adult, let alone a stranger, she decided that it was a lot easier to let them do their job so that she could get to lunch. Her stomach rumbled in agreement. Next, the woman washed Kino's hair. Remnants of blue paint floated in the dirty water as she rinsed Kino's head.

The tall lady gathered the heap of filthy clothes and left the room. When she returned, she set some folded clothing on the table near the entrance before leaving again.

As Kino patted herself dry with a sheet of beige kapa, the shorter woman went to the table, retrieved its contents, and brought it back to the tub. She handed Kino the white garments on top.

They turned out to be long, old-fashioned cotton underwear that went down to her knees, and a matching undershirt. Next, the woman gave her a knee-length peach dress with short, puffy sleeves, and white-lace trim on the collar. The style was a lot more fitting for a girl her age than the gown she'd had on before. She guessed that it belonged to Nahienaena.

The stout woman buttoned the back of Kino's dress and tied the white sash into a big bow, just as the tall lady returned with a pair of black leather shoes. Rolled up in one of them was a set of white stockings.

Kino picked up a sock, leaned against the tub, and pushed her foot into it. The material stung her blisters. She winced and pulled the sock off.

The shorter woman bent down and examined the raw skin on Kino's feet. She said something in Hawaiian to the tall lady, who nodded and left for a moment, then came back in with a wooden bowl and a stool. She placed the bowl on the ground at Kino's feet and the stool beside her, then gestured Kino to take a seat.

The shorter woman kneeled, and then applied a dark-green poultice to Kino's blisters. Her sore feet stopped stinging in an instant.

The tall lady poured a few drops of liquid into her palm from a small gourd before rubbing her hands together. Kino caught the scent of kukui nut oil as the woman combed her fingers through Kino's hair and styled it into a single braid.

The other woman rinsed the paste off Kino's feet, then helped her put on the socks. The shoes were a little big, but they fit a lot better than Sophie's. The soft leather was also a lot more supple, and it felt good on her feet.

When the tall lady stood, she picked something up and put it into Kino's skirt pocket.

Kino reached in and felt the object. She immediately recognized the smooth, cool wood of her compass.

The women escorted her to a pavilion where Kauikeaouli and Nahienaena were seated on a woven mat on the ground. Between them, an amazing spread of Hawaiian food, and fruit enough for a small dinner party, sat on a two-foot-high table.

"You look different when you are clean." Kauikeaouli smiled as Kino sat down next to him.

"Thanks." Kino felt her cheeks get hot. She often felt like that lately when boys spoke to her. She had no idea why.

"I will attend to my lessons while you eat." Kauikeaouli stood up.

"Is there any way I can get to Kalihi? Maybe there will be a clue on how to get me back to my time. I need to get back as soon as possible."

"We can go there when I am finished."

"Awesome. Thanks!"

He raised an eyebrow, stared at her for a moment, then excused himself and headed toward the main building.

75

Nahienaena, now wearing a white dress similar in style to Kino's, gazed at her from across the table. Kino was too hungry to talk. She ate quickly, shoving the food into her mouth with her fingers. The princess just stared at her and chewed her own food slowly. They ate in awkward silence.

When the meal was over, the two female servants cleared the table. Kino could no longer stand the silence, or Nahienaena's staring. She crossed her eyes and stuck out her tongue on one side of her mouth.

Nahienaena giggled, then made a funny face of her own. They both burst out laughing.

"How old are you?" Kino asked.

"I am ten years old," said the princess.

Kino noticed that Nahienaena was a lot less bold without her brother around. She studied the girl for a minute. Although she was two years younger, she was already the same height as Kino.

"What's it like living here? Do people live in all these buildings?" Kino pointed at the differently shaped grass structures in the compound. She wondered what the difference was between them.

Nahienaena stood up and said, "Only some of the hales are used for sleeping. The other ones are work huts and storage. Would you like to see?"

"Yes!" Kino stood up. She hoped she wasn't coming across as over eager, but she knew that this was a unique opportunity to understand what life was like at this time in history. So far, it was nothing like she had imagined it would be.

They walked across the courtyard to a row of rectangular grass buildings and peeked into the first one.

Inside, three women sewed inch-long, bright-colored feathers onto a cape similar to the one Nahienaena wore in the painting.

"It takes hundreds, sometimes thousands of feathers to make one ahuʻula," Nahienaena said.

"Wow." Kino knew that the practice of capturing these native birds for their colorful feathers had contributed to the birds' extinction, yet she couldn't help but marvel at the painstaking work.

The princess leaned in and asked, "Do you want to see something?" She almost whispered that question.

Kino guessed that it must be something they shouldn't be doing.

"Umm, sure."

"Come with me."

The younger girl looked from side to side as she crossed the quad. Kino chuckled. The eight-year-old's attempt to be inconspicuous made her way more obvious.

Nahienaena stopped in front of one of the larger huts then glanced from left to right. The nearby workers were too busy to notice them. She shot Kino a knowing look and entered the building.

"This is Kauikeaouli's hale moe. He sleeps out here when it gets too hot in the main house." She made her way across the room and stopped in front of a table. On it was half of a coconut shell, filled with clear liquid and a single flame in the center, casting dim light throughout the room. The smell of roasted kukui nuts filled the air. Next to that was a large glass jar containing a stick with three green ovals hanging from it. A small fishing net secured with a cord served as a lid.

When Kino peered into the glass, she realized the ovals were butterfly chrysalises.

"Do not tell him I showed this to you. I am not supposed to be in here," Nahienaena said in a hushed tone.

They finished their walk around the grounds, and just as they reached the main building, Kauikeaouli came out.

"Your turn, Nahi."

The princess left without a word. She didn't look too eager for her lessons.

Turning his attention to Kino, he asked, "Do you want to see something?"

"Okay."

She wondered if he was going to show her the cocoons. Sure enough, he led her into his hut.

As the prince lit several more candles, Kino saw rich colors of red, gold and black appearing along the tops of the chrysalises that she had not noticed the first time.

"They are very rare monarch butterflies." He bent down and put his hands on his knees, smiling as he admired his prized collection.

"Wow, cool." Kino leaned closer to the glass.

"I think they just might be the last of their kind."

She wasn't sure whether to believe him or not. She moved around the table to see them at a different angle. "When will they hatch?"

"They were just formed yesterday. The monarch's chrysalis usually hatches in about seven to ten days." He straightened up. "I have arranged for a carriage. It should be here shortly."

"Where are your parents?"

"Both my father and my mother are no longer alive." He headed toward the door. "One of my father's wives, Ka'ahumanu, is my guardian now. She is kuhina nui, the co-ruler, and she helps my brother govern the kingdom. She is currently in Lahaina, on the island of Maui."

They walked out to the gate, and as they reached it, a black, closed-compartment buggy pulled up. Harnessed to it was a black horse with blinders on. A Hawaiian driver in a long-sleeved white shirt and black vest sat on his perch atop the cab with reins in hand.

One of the gate guards held the door open as Kino and Kauikeaouli climbed in. They sat, facing each other, in silence.

Several minutes into the ride, the prince asked, "What is it like in your time? Does the island look the same?"

Kino thought for a moment. She knew she needed to be careful about what she said, from watching her share of time-travel movies.

"There are a lot more people in my time, as well as way more houses and buildings."

Kauikeaouli's eyes shined as he sat forward in excitement.

"And what about the kingdom? Who is ruler now?"

"I don't think I should tell you too much. I don't want to say anything that could change history. That could end very badly for me." She let out a big yawn. "And I'm too tired to talk."

"Oh." The prince slouched and sat back. "Perhaps in time, you will tell me more."

The ride was a long and bumpy one. The scenery, although lush and beautiful, varied very little. There were big plots of bare red dirt, patches of wild grass, trees, and fields filled with sugar cane and sweet-potato plants. Kino recognized their triangular leaves and purple blossoms from the plants in Gramma's garden. On occasion, they passed small clusters of houses and taro ponds.

Kino glanced at Kauikeaouli who had his eyes closed. His head nodded gently with the motion of the cab. She too felt sleepy, but she managed to keep her eyes open. Or so she thought.

She awoke when the carriage came to a stop. When Kino opened her eyes, she saw only open land with random clusters of dense brush.

They both stepped down from the buggy and looked around. She stood there for a moment, then shook her head before putting her face in her hands.

"There's nothing here."

Kauikeaouli asked, "Is your home nearby?"

"No." She dropped her hands, shook her head and let out a big sigh. "I don't know what I expected to see. Let's just go."

Kino clambered up into the carriage. Kauikeaouli climbed in after her. "Is there anywhere else you want to go that might help?"

"No," she said. "I can't think of anywhere."

"Do you have a place to stay? You can be my guest at the hale ali'i."

Kino thought about Sophie and kind faced Makani.

"Thank you, I have a place."

They returned to the palace, and from there, Kino was able to navigate her way to Sam's general store and then up to Sophie's.

Makani waved from the yard as the carriage pulled up to the house. A broad, toothy grin appeared on her face when Kino stepped out.

"Aloha!" The woman bustled toward them.

When Kauikeaouli emerged, Makani stopped in her tracks, dropped to her knees and prostrated herself.

Sophie emerged from the house. Her face brightened when she saw Kino.

"You're back!" Sophie clapped her hands, then gathered up her long, blue skirt and hurried toward them. "And you brought a friend! Wonderful!"

Kino smiled and said, "This is Kaui-kea-o-uli." She said his name slowly. She had been practicing it in her head for a while.

Sophie said, "How do you do?" Her eyebrows lifted as she gazed at Makani, still kneeling, face-down, on the ground.

79

Kino blurted out, "Oh yeah, and he's the prince."

Sophie looked at the boy with surprise and said, "Oh, my! What an honor to meet you, your majesty."

She gathered her skirt up once more and curtsied.

"How do you do." He smiled, bowed slightly then gently said something to Makani in Hawaiian.

The woman stood up and brushed the grass off her dress. She kept her eyes averted.

"I am guessing that you were unable to find your mother?" Sophie asked.

"No, and you won't believe why!" Kino gushed.

Sophie's eyes widened. "I would love to hear everything. You can tell us all about it over supper. It would be an honor for us to have you join us, Kauikeka-ol-i..."

Kino shook her head. "Kauikea-o-uli."

"Kauikekouli."

Kino said his name again, this time slower, "Kaui-kea-o-uli."

"Kauikeaoli. Ka..." Exasperated, she put her palm against her forehead. "Oh dear. Can I just call you Kaui? I do not mean to insult you; I just know I will butcher your name each time I try to say it."

The young prince laughed and said, "It is not customary, but yes, you may do so."

Kino raised her eyebrows and asked, "Do you want to stay and eat?"

He nodded. "Yes, thank you."

12

ʻUmikūmālua

During the meal, Kino told the two women about her discovery that she was in the wrong century. She could tell that they were skeptical at first, based on Sophie's sympathetic expressions, her tone, and the looks she exchanged with Makani. But they saw that Kauikeaouli believed her, so they couldn't help but accept her story as possible truth. Or at least they acted as if they did.

"So, what are you going to do?" Sophie asked.

Kino looked down at her hands and said, "I don't know."

Makani said, "My hoahānau is da kahuna at heiau hoʻola Kamananui. You go see him for kōkua."

Kino was impressed with herself. She actually understood that they should go to a particular Hawaiian temple to seek help from Makani's cousin who was the priest there. Frowning, she said, "I don't know how to get there. And I can't speak Hawaiian. How will they understand me?"

"Do not worry, Kino. I will find out where it is and take you there in the morning," said Kauikeaouli.

Kino smiled at him. "Thanks. I'll be ready."

At the end of the meal, Kauikeaouli announced that he needed to leave. Makani walked him out.

Kino sensed that Sophie wanted to ask her more about him, so she let out a big yawn, making sure her eyes watered a bit, before she closed her mouth and met Sophie's gaze.

"Sorry. It's been a long day." Kino stretched her arms out and let out another yawn.

Sophie smiled. "I understand. I will mind my own business. She cupped Kino's chin with her hand. "Just know that we are here for you, no matter what." She released Kino's face. "I am going to Honolulu early tomorrow morning, and I may be gone when you wake up. I'll see you at supper."

*****

That night Kino dreamt she was holding a big, wooden bowl. In it were vines covered in round, black berries, several leaves, and three trumpet-shaped blue flowers.

A large brown-and-white owl flew toward her, gripping a long, golden feather in its talons. The owl let go, and the feather transformed into a fern as it spiraled into the bowl. When the leafy frond landed, it curled into a round fiddlehead, the most center part of the plant. The fiddlehead glowed and began to pulsate, slowly at first, and then in short, rapid beats. It exploded into a bright flash of light. As the light faded, only blood-red liquid remained in the bowl.

Kino awakened with a start and sat up. Her heart stampeded in her chest.

What the heck was that about?

She thought about turning on a light, and then realized that it would entail fumbling around in the dark to locate a match. Deciding it was too much trouble, she lay back down. Eventually, she drifted off to sleep.

In the morning, Kino dressed in a hurry and found Makani in the kitchen, preparing food, when she emerged from the bedroom.

"Aloha kakahiaka. Breakfast is ready." The woman placed a plate of cut fruit and a boiled egg on the table.

"Aloha kakahiaka." Kino smiled and sat down. "Thank you, I mean, mahalo."

Kauikeaouli showed up just as she was swallowing her last mouthful of food. This time he was alone and on horseback. Kino ran outside to greet him.

"Do you have something to climb on?" Kauikeaouli asked as he maneuvered the horse toward her.

Makani hurried out, carrying a stool. On her hip was a small ipu, a dried gourd container at the end of a twine strap.

She placed the stool between Kino and the horse. Unlooping the cord from over her shoulder, she placed it over Kino's head. The gourd hung like an oversized pendant.

"For water," Makani said. "E hoʻi āwīwī mai." She held Kino's face between her palms and touched their noses together. "Hurry back."

Kauikeaouli scooted forward in the saddle to make room as Kino stepped up on the stool.

As they headed down the road, Kino leaned forward and said, "About the heiau we're going to, is it one where they do human sacrifices? I don't want to see that."

Kauikeaouli laughed. "No, that is called a luakini heiau. Human sacrifice is kapu and no longer practiced."

Kino sat back and thought of her grandfather. Maybe the kahuna would know how to help him. She started missing Grandpa dearly, but she pushed the thoughts out of her head.

Kauikeaouli held the horse at a trot until they neared the palace, then he kicked his heels in and brought the animal to a gallop, hurrying past the royal household. He slowed down their pace once they were well past.

"You aren't supposed to be doing this, are you?" she asked.

He chuckled. "No. I am never allowed outside of the palace grounds without an attendant. But don't worry, I put a coconut and lauhala pillows in my bed, then covered it all with a kapa blanket. The servants will just think I am sleeping late. It will be a while before they miss me."

Kino giggled. That was not the behavior she expected from a future king.

After two hours on the main road, they arrived at a narrow trail running up the mountain through a canopy of lush shade trees. The ground became uneven and rocky the higher they ascended, and the air felt cool and moist. The greenery around them appeared denser than the shrubs and trees on the main road. Before long, they heard the sound of running water and followed the sound until they found its source – a rippling stream.

"Do you know how far we have to go?" Kino asked.

"The heiau is supposed to be just past the waterfall." He turned the horse and guided it uphill, alongside the running water.

When they reached the falls, the horse faltered and snorted, swinging its head from side to side. Kauikeaouli snapped the reins and kicked his feet into the horse's sides. "Imua," he ordered.

The animal hesitated, then grudgingly obeyed and moved forward. The trail wound around the pond and through a thicket of trees. Kino felt the hair on the back of her arms rise. There was a change in the air, as if sudden electricity had charged it. She rubbed the bumps of her "chicken-skin" limbs.

Kauikeaouli must have felt it too. He pressed his elbows into his sides and said, "Brrr…" shivering a little. "The air is different."

Kino murmured in agreement.

The wind swirled around them. The horse stomped its feet and neighed. Kino held tighter to Kauikeaouli.

"Do you hear that?" he asked.

All she could hear were the leaves whispering with the wind. Then she heard it, and understood what he meant. The rhythmic beat of pahu drums and the hollow sound of music ipus being pounded on, coupled with chanting drifted toward them. They were definitely near the temple.

The sounds of the rustling leaves, drumbeats and chants grew louder and more intense as they neared the top. When they reached it, everything went quiet and still.

A large, walled enclosure made of tight fitted dark brown stones, sat several hundred yards from the summit. They trotted toward the gate.

Two tall, muscular Hawaiian men in dark brown malos stood at the entrance. Just like the guards at the palace, they each held a nine-foot spear. They stared, as Kino and the prince dismounted. One of them addressed Kauikeaouli sternly in Hawaiian.

Kauikeaouli stood up straighter, pushed his shoulders back, stuck his chest out and answered him. The man eyes narrowed as he scrutinized their clothes. He looked skeptical.

The guard said, "Alia," then nodded at his counterpart before proceeding into the heiau.

Kauikeaouli said, "The man said to wait."

"How do you know they will help us?" asked Kino.

He put his hands on his hips and said, "He has to help us. And I am ali'i nui, and the son of Kamehameha the Great."

"Have you met this guy before?"

"No." Kauikeaouli dropped his hands.

"Then why would he believe that you are descended from King Kamehameha? Is it the clothes? I guess regular Hawaiians wouldn't be wearing what you're wearing."

"It is not my clothing," Kauikeaouli said. "It is the mana, the life-force of these islands, that flows through my blood and the blood of my ancestors."

Kino wondered if that's what made Kauikeaouli seem so different than any other kid she'd ever met.

"The kahuna will see and know," said the prince. "You must remain out here. It is kapu for females to enter."

That was fine with Kino. The whole place gave her the creeps.

The guard returned, followed by a thin old man with white, shoulder-length hair, wearing a white malo and kihei. He leaned on a dark walking stick with intricate carvings. Around his neck was a necklace that resembled one made from human hair, and a carved whalebone hook like one she had seen once in the museum.

The minute the old man saw Kauikeaouli, he dropped to his knees and prostrated himself. Both guards followed suit.

Even though Kino had seen this happen several times, it never got old. She wondered what it felt like to have adults kowtow the moment they met her. She bit her lips to stifle a giggle.

Kauikeaouli didn't even blink an eye. "E ala."

The guards stood up, but kept their eyes averted. The kahuna approached the prince and blessed him, then gave Kino a nod.

"I will return shortly," Kauikeaouli told her, as he handed her the reins.

She led the horse to a shady patch of grass then sat down on a flat rock that was large enough to stretch out on. She sat down and glanced at the gate. The guards were no longer paying attention to her.

Inside the enclosure, the drumbeats and chanting had resumed. She lay on her back and watched as the leaves above her fluttered to the rhythm of the song. She could feel the power of the chant, and the almost palpable energy emanating into the ground and vibrating up through the rock.

Kino closed both eyes as vivid images appeared in her mind. Birds of all types, sizes and colors flew over the land. The earth blossomed into rich greens and jeweled tone flowers, and big white waves crashed onto black, cragged rocks. Plumes of gray smoke billowed out of the water and blew over the black rocky shore. From the smoke, a beautiful young woman with long black hair wearing a red pa'u appeared.

The mysterious female approached and reached her hand out. Kino held her hand out as well, and just before their fingers touched, she heard, "What are you doing?"

Her eyes flew open. It was Kauikeaouli. He was standing over her, looking down at her outstretched body.

Kino realized that her arm was sticking straight up in the air. She dropped it and rubbed her bicep. "Uh, nothing. Just a cramp."

The boy pulled her to her feet. "Kahu Pauo'le said he was expecting us."

Kino wondered if Makani had somehow sent word to her cousin between last night and today.

Behind Kauikeaouli stood the old man with the white hair. This time a pair of male attendants flanked him. One man clutched a water gourd, decorated with an elaborate pāwehe pattern of black triangles burnt onto the sides. The other man held a wooden bowl with similar markings as the ipu.

Kauikeaouli continued. "Kahu said he dreamt of us coming. He also said our ancestors have chosen you to be the one."

"The one what?" she asked, uncertain if she should feel honored or concerned.

"The one chosen to save the land."

"How am I supposed to do that?" she directed her question at the kahuna.

The man answered in a gravelly voice. "Our ancestors did not say."

"You speak English?" Kino was surprised and relieved.

"Some," said the man.

"I don't understand," Kino frowned. "How can I be the chosen one? How can I save the land? I don't even know how I got here. I just want to go home."

"You will go home. But first you must complete a task." The old man leaned on his walking stick and hobbled toward her.

"What kind of task?" she asked.

He held up a scroll of beige kapa by one end then let the roll drop. Crude markings on the inside showed an outline of the island, as well as marks and symbols.

"In order to fulfill your destiny, you must first gather four sacred objects." The man leaned heavily on his staff as he bent down to place the map on the rock.

"You must collect a branch of the special pohuehue blossoms from the top of Mokoli'i Island in the east, in the morning, when the flower is still blue. It turns pink later in the day." He pointed at a small crooked circle off the eastern shore with the tip of his stick, and then followed a thin line up along the coast to the north, along jagged triangles Kino guessed were mountains, then down the center of the island.

"In Kipapa, you need to descend into the gulch to find a sacred black rock." He tapped at a wide dark line to the left of the mountains.

"Then you must go to the summit of Ka'ala." He drew an invisible line across the island to another set of jagged lines to the west.

"There you must get the fiddlehead of a rare hapu'u fern. It is the heart of the plant and glistens like gold in the sunlight."

That last item sounded oddly familiar, but she couldn't place where she had heard it.

"Last, you must go to the largest of the eight waterfalls of Ka'ala and gather sacred kane-pōpolo berries by moonlight." He continued the invisible line and stopped it at the base of the largest triangle. Three small symbols, which looked like shepherd's crooks, indicated the waterfalls.

"After you gather these items," the kahuna continued as he set his cane down, "you must bring them to the Kaniakapupu heiau." The kahuna pointed at three Hawaiian petroglyph symbols near the south of the island. "But once you gather the first item, you only have six days to get it all to the heiau."

"Then what?" asked Kino.

"If you are successful, you will return home upon the seventh day once the prophecy is complete."

Kino looked at Kauikeaouli.

"Can we go from here?" she asked.

Before he could answer, the kahuna interjected.

"It is not that simple."

Of course not.

"You must wait for the first two of the three signs before you can begin your journey. You can return home to your time, after you complete your task, and the third sign comes to pass."

Before Kino could ask the obvious, Kauikeaouli blurted out, "He said we must look for the following three signs." He stuck his thumb up. "The first is the death of a monarch."

Kino pictured the chrysalises in Kauikeaouli's hut, and wondered what their life expectancy was.

"Second, the return of a king." Kauikeaouli made the shape of an "L" with his fingers as he named them. Sticking his middle finger out he said, "The last is the new rain."

"What do we do until then?" Kino asked.

"You wait," said the priest. "The journey cannot start until the second sign has come to pass."

Exasperated, she threw her arms out to the side. "Why can't we just head out after the first sign?"

"Because you will not know where to go." He picked up the kapa by the same end he had held to unravel it. It curled back into a scroll, which he passed to Kauikeaouli.

"What do you mean? You just handed him the map."

Kahu Pauo'le said, "That is just a piece of kapa. It will be of no use to you until the time comes."

Kauikeaouli pulled the scroll open and gasped. He turned the paper toward her. It was blank. Before she could say anything, the kahuna gestured toward the attendants.

"You will take these items to help you on your journey."

The men stepped forward. One held a dark, dried gourd container similar to the one they drank from earlier. The priest picked it up by a cord that was wrapped around the neck of the vessel.

"The first very kahuna nui carried this ipu ʻawaʻawa from Tahiti centuries ago. It has been blessed by the god Lono." He handed it to Kauikeaouli, who hooked the container over his shoulder.

"We already have this one," Kino pointed at the one on her hip.

Kauikeaouli said, "This one is sacred." He held up the gourd. "It has been filled by the mana of my ancestors. It will always have water in it for me to drink. But it is kapu for you to drink from it."

She narrowed her eyes. "What about when *I'm* thirsty?"

"I can pour the water into your ipu for you to drink – you just cannot drink from this directly," Kauikeaouli answered.

Kino shrugged. "Fine. I'm not thirsty anyway."

The second attendant presented a reddish-brown wooden bowl, half the size of a bowling ball, to the priest. Kino guessed it was made from koa, the prized wood of the islands.

"Let me guess. That's a magic bowl to go with your magic gourd." Kino said flatly.

"Yes! How did you know?" Kauikeaouli clearly did not understand sarcasm.

She shook her head and sighed.

"This sacred calabash was brought to this land by our ancestors from Tahiti. Like the water ipu, it has been blessed by the god Lono – and it is kapu to eat from it unless you are a descendant of the highest rank of aliʻi."

Kino fought the urge to roll her eyes. While she understood the importance of tradition, these rules were pretty hardcore. The fact that they were forbidden made her want to use them even more.

"It will be getting dark soon. We need to head back." Kauikeaouli carried the bowl and ipu and loaded them into one of the horse's saddlebags before taking the reins and returning to the group.

"Is that it, then?" she asked the kahuna.

He nodded and told her he would see her again soon. Then, after bowing at Kauikeaouli, he walked back into the compound.

13

‘Umikūmākolu

"Let me get this straight." Sophie counted on her fingers. "You are waiting for the death of a monarch, the return of a king and the new rain?"

Kino nodded. "What do you think it all means?"

Sophie thought for a moment and said, "Well, the death of the monarch could be one of Kaui's butterflies, since maybe not all of them will hatch properly. Or perhaps one of them might get smashed accidentally or something."

Kino wondered if Sophie meant to imply that she should kill one to get the signs going. But this would never be an option for Kino. The only bugs she liked to smash were mosquitos, flies, and cockroaches.

"The return of the king must be Kaui's brother, King Liholiho," said Sophie. "He's in England, visiting their king. I do not know when he is supposed to come back, but I know he's been gone for some time now. I remember because I arrived to this island the same week that he left, in November of 1823. He had quite a big sendoff."

"That makes sense!" Kino fidgeted with excitement. "Kauikeaouli mentioned that his brother was in Great Britain. Maybe he expects him soon."

"I wonder what the 'new rain' means. It rains almost daily." Sophie glanced out the window.

Kino thought hard. Could it mean a storm? Perhaps a hurricane? Tornado? She pictured the hale pili spinning around in a twister and landing in the spot she'd woke up in when she arrived in this century.

"Don't worry, I'm sure you'll know it when the time comes." Sophie placed a reassuring hand on Kino's arm.

"Your 'amakua will help guide you," said Makani. "Do not be afraid to call on them when you need help."

That night, as Kino lay in bed, she pondered the three indications of her time to go home. She fell asleep wondering what "the new rain" meant.

After breakfast the next morning, she walked to the palace. The guard who had discovered her in the taro patch stood at the gate. This time, though, he paid no attention to her.

She made her way across the large yard to the main building, and met with a familiar sight when she entered. A feather-cloaked Nahienaena, kahili in hand, stood poised and perfectly still. The princess glanced at Kino before returning her eyes to the same spot she had been staring at while the artist worked.

"He will be with you shortly," Nahienaena said to the spot.

Kino didn't mind waiting. On her way to the palace, she realized that until she made it home, she needed to soak up as much of her experience here as she could. She had to admit, despite being in the wrong century, that her time here had been interesting so far. And now they had a quest. Kino had always wanted to go on a quest. The closest she had come to one before was a neighborhood-wide scavenger hunt at a birthday party last year.

Kauikeaouli burst into the room.

"I have something to show you!" He wore only a red malo. "Come with me!" He took her hand and pulled her out of the door. Once outside, he dropped her hand, then led her into his hut and over to his butterfly collection.

Kino's eyes widened in wonder as she bent closer to the jar and peered in. The green little ovals that she had seen two days ago had morphed enough for her to see the wing markings of the butterflies they held taking shape. They were still rimmed with gold, red and black, but the majority of the green had melted away into a rich, dark purple. The unmistakable striped and dotted pattern of a monarch was now clearly visible.

"They are transforming quickly. I have never seen such a speedy process, and I have hatched butterflies before." Kauikeaouli's eyes shined with excitement.

"Why do you think that is?" Kino tried to remember how long it had taken for the caterpillar in her fourth grade class to turn.

"These are a very rare type of the monarchs." Kauikeaouli put his face an inch from the glass. "Perhaps their biology is different."

Someone yelled Kauikeaouli's name from outside.

"Someone's calling you," Kino said, uncertain if he had heard it or not.

"Yes, I know. Quick..." he darted across the room, then pressed himself against the wall right next to the door. Slowly he stuck his head out and looked both ways.

"Shouldn't you go see what they want?" Kino asked.

He pulled his head back in and motioned for her to stand next to him. "I know what they want. It is time for more lessons. I do not want to study right now."

She hurried over and pressed herself against the same wall. He stuck his head back out, looked both ways, and then said, "Follow me."

They left the hut and made their way between a few other buildings, before ducking behind a row of orange hibiscus bushes along the fence line.

"There." He pointed at a back gate. It was wide open. "We just have to get past them."

Three men were unloading a horse-drawn cart as two guards watched over the open gate. Searching the ground for something, Kauikeaouli stooped to pick it up. He opened his palm and showed her a rock just smaller than a golf ball. He stood up and chucked it at the horse. It hit the animal on the rump, and as the horse reared up in alarm, it lifted the cart. The cargo crashed to the ground and scattered.

Two of the men rushed to settle the horse while the third man and the guards hurried to pick up the items that had spilled. Kauikeaouli grabbed Kino's hand, and, still crouched, they scurried between the fence and the bushes until they reached the gate, before breaking into a run. They continued sprinting until they arrived at a cluster of trees and hid behind the thick trunk of a large rainbow eucalyptus.

They waited another minute, each panting and peering out from their own side. Once they were certain no one had followed them, they both relaxed.

"I take it this isn't your first time doing this." Kino leaned on the multicolored bark to rest.

Kauikeaouli grinned at her. "What gave you that idea?"

Kino laughed and shook her head slowly.

"What?" he asked.

"Nothing." She giggled, "You're just not what I expected a king would be like."

"That's because I'm not a king. That's my brother's job." Kauikeaouli darted off.

Kino chased after him. "Where are we going?" she called, and ran as fast as she could to catch up to him.

He stopped several yards away and waited. When she reached him, she struggled to catch her breath.

"Can you puh-leez," she huffed and puffed, "stop running and tell me where we are going?"

Kauikeaouli said, "You'll see." He wagged his eyebrows. "But we have to hurry." Pointing at the trail heading up the mountain, he said, "This way."

Kino looked at what seemed like a steep climb, and she hurried to keep up. Her leg muscles burned as she trudged up the hill. The higher they hiked, the more she found herself gasping for air.

When they reached level ground, she saw a group of older, bigger Hawaiian boys, dressed in malos. Each held skinny, pointy ladders at least six feet tall, made of bound dark wood that was only five inches wide. One of them had two stacked and slung over his shoulder. Kino wondered what they were.

As if reading her mind, Kauikeaouli pointed and said, "Those are papa hōlua sleds."

She had heard of those, but had never seen one in person.

"You are fortunate – usually commoners are not allowed to watch the aliʻi play," he said.

Kino turned and looked at him. She was about to say she wasn't a commoner, but then she realized that at this time, in this company, she actually was.

Walking close behind him, she followed Kauikeaouli in the opposite direction of the boys. He led her through some bushes to a plateau.

"You can watch from here." He gestured toward a big rock with a flat top. "Just meet me at the bottom."

"Okay. Wait. What? What do you mean at the bottom?" she yelled.

He was already gone.

She took a seat on the rock. From that vantage point, Kino could see Kauikeaouli catch up with the other five boys. They climbed a little higher up the mountain onto a wide landing. In the center of it was a broad track of slick dirt and stones that sloped all the way down the steep hill.

The shortest of the boys was stocky and wore a dark-green malo. He walked over to the top of the track, looked down then walked back a few feet before placing down his sled. Another boy in a brown malo came up alongside him and put his board down. They each kneeled, straddling their sleds. The tallest boy, who seemed like the one in charge, gave the ready, set, go signal.

The two boys lay on top of their hōluas and propelled them onto the track. They zoomed down and were just about neck and neck, until the short kid leaned in too early on the turn and the other boy crashed into him. They tumbled off the track in a tangle. Kino held her breath. The boys lay motionless, covered in grass and black gravel. Then one of them stirred. They both stood and brushed themselves off. She exhaled in relief. The shorter boy held his forehead, but he seemed okay for the most part. He raised a hand and waved to the boys at the top of the track.

A dark, stout boy in a purple malo approached the slide, and a boy with big, bushy hair came up beside him. They waited for the signal then pushed off on their sleds.

The pair managed to race all the way to the bottom with ease, although Kino still held her breath as they made the turns. The first two boys walked down to the bottom of the hill and joined the second pair.

It was now Kauikeaouli and the tallest boy's turn. He and his running mate put their sleds on the ground before lying over them. They looked at each other and simultaneously bobbed their heads as they counted down from three together.

They zipped down the track and made it halfway down the slide when the tall boy's hōlua drifted sideways, hit a rock, and threw him off his sled and into Kauikeaouli. The collision knocked the prince off his sled, over a rock and into a tree.

Kino sprang to her feet and ran down the hill. The four boys at the bottom dropped their sleds and ran uphill. Kino reached the prince first. He lay in a crumpled heap at the base of the tree. His nose was bleeding and his right arm was bent at an awkward angle underneath him.

"Are you all right?" she asked, rushing toward him. She knelt and helped him prop himself up against the tree. A bump the size of a quarter loomed over his right eye. Dark flecks of dirt clung to his scraped road rash. Blood oozed from raw, dirty wounds. Kauikeaouli pulled himself together and sat upright, but didn't say anything.

"Can you stand up?" she asked, trying her best to keep her eyes on his face and not on his abrasions. They were too painful to look at.

"Auwe! Kauikeaouli is hurt!" the shortest boy in the group yelled, as he reached them and knelt down next to Kino.

"I'm fine, Manu. Stop fussing." Kauikeaouli said impatiently. He lurched forward to a squat, and leaned on his palms to push him upward. He let out an agonized yelp, fell backwards, and banged his head on the tree.

Kauikeaouli's right forearm dangled loosely at the elbow. Kino and Manu helped him to his feet, and the prince's face contorted in pain as he stood up.

"Where is my hōlua?" he asked.

"A part of it is over there…" said Manu, pointing to half of the sled lying on the other side of the tree, "… and the rest of it is down there."

He pointed further down the slope. One of the boys held the second half and walked toward them with the others.

Kino untied the sash around her waist and ripped it off her dress. After days of wearing the same clothing without a chance to wash it, the sash was not the cleanest it could have been. She took both ends of the fabric belt and tied them into a knot, then put the sash around Kauikeaouli's neck.

He arched his brows and looked at her with wide eyes. "Why are you giving me a dirty lei?"

Kino realized that her actions resembled a traditional lei greeting. Giggling, she said, "This isn't a lei." She moved it to his left shoulder and looped the other end of it under his right elbow. "It's a sling."

Kauikeaouli smiled gratefully. "Mahalo."

Kino noticed that his eyes were red and watery.

When the rest of the boys had joined them, Kauikeaouli introduced her to his friends. Pono, the tallest kid in the group, was the son of a chief of a nearby district. The boy in the purple malo was named Palani, the boy with the big bushy hair was Kaleo, and the boy in the blue malo was Inoa. The shortest boy, Manu, was Inoa's brother.

"You remind me of someone back home." Kino said, looking at Kaleo's shiny eyes and bright smile. She thought of Kawika. Boy, would he be surprised to hear about her visit.

Kaleo smiled uncomfortably and looked away.

"He does not yet speak English." Pono said, "His father is chief of a region on the other side of the Ko'olau Mountains. People on that side of the island have not yet embraced the new language. Many have not even heard it spoken."

Kino noticed that the boys who could speak English spoke it properly. There was no hint of pidgin. Back then there was no need for it. That blew her mind. She actually missed hearing the local slang.

"You are not from around here, are you?" Pono asked.

Kino's multicultural mix of nationalities made her features and build smaller than these pure Hawaiians. Her tanned complexion was light in comparison to their rich, brown skin tones. Her hair was finer, straighter, and lighter, and her eyes were more almond-shaped.

"No. I'm… uh, visiting. My father has business in Honolulu," she fibbed, glancing at Kauikeaouli.

"We must get the kahuna lapa'au to heal him," Manu urged the group.

"I will be fine," Kauikeaouli insisted. "I just want to go home." He winced and limped forward.

"Hold on," Kino said. She hurried back up the hill to some aloe plants she had noticed earlier, and broke a few inches off the tip of a leaf. The thick sap clung to the piece she held, and stretched out a line of clear goo like melted cheese from a hot slice of pizza. She ran back to the boys and spread it on Kauikeaouli's cuts and abrasions. He grimaced and bit his lip as she did so. She could tell it stung.

"What should we do with your hōlua?" Kino asked as she applied the aloe to the last cut.

"Leave it. I will send someone for it later."

The group took their time climbing to the bottom. When they arrived at the base of the hill, the boys picked up their sleds. Kino and Kauikeaouli parted ways with everyone except Pono and Manu.

They stopped several times so that Kauikeaouli could rest. Occasionally, Kino caught a glimpse of tears, but for the most part he remained stoic. Kauikeaouli either had nerves of steel or he was putting on a brave façade. She would probably still be bawling her eyes out if she were that badly hurt.

When they neared the palace, Manu left the group and ran to get help. Within minutes, several men came running, holding a wooden stretcher. They put it on the ground and helped Kauikeaouli recline, being very careful not to move his arm too much. He grimaced as the men lifted the board up. They took off without a word. Kino hurried after them, but they were too fast. She fell back to a regular pace and walked with Pono and Manu to the palace gate.

The guards seemed to recognize the two boys, and they bowed their heads as the kids walked past them. Inside the compound there was a lot of commotion. Several women workers knelt together in a group outside the main house, crying and wailing. The kahili bearers wore troubled expressions.

Kino wondered if all this activity had something to do with Kauikeaouli getting hurt. She hoped there was nothing seriously wrong with him.

As they walked through the entrance of the building, Kino spotted Nahienaena sobbing in the corner. The three kids rushed to her side. The princess held her face in her hands, and her shoulders trembled.

"What troubles you, Nahi?" Pono brows knitted in concern.

Nahienaena glanced up at Kino then directed her answer at Pono.

"A telegram just arrived from the house of Kalanimoku. My beloved brother, our King Liholiho, is dead!" She put her face back into her hands and wept.

Pono put his arms around her and she sank into him, burying her face in his chest. He hugged her tight. Nahienaena's shoulders shuddered each time she inhaled deeply. Manu shifted from one foot to the other, and stared at the ground.

Kino was uncertain of what to say. Then she thought of how it felt when she lost her dad. He had died when she was just four, so she didn't remember any details aside from crying a lot and being carried often. She recalled feeling really sad and confused, and kept expecting him to walk through the door, but he never came. Before she realized it, she too joined the pair and put her arms around both of them in a group hug.

Nahienaena lifted her face and met Kino's gaze. They looked at each other for a moment. There was a softness in the younger girl's eyes, Kino hadn't seen before.

She wanted to ask the princess where her brother was, but she didn't know how to inquire without sounding inconsiderate. She decided to wait for the right time. Clearly, this wasn't it.

Pono gave Nahienaena a squeeze, then let go. Kino let her arms drop as well.

"My dear cousin, where is Kauikeaouli? He was with us earlier, but was injured on his hōlua," he said.

Nahienaena dabbed at her eyes with a white handkerchief. "He is in his hale..." Frowning, she blurted out, "And who is to look after us? My father is gone. My mother is gone. And now my dear, beloved brother is gone. It is just Kauikeaouli and I left." She ran, sobbing, out of the room. Manu ran after her.

Kino and Pono exchanged looks then headed outside towards Kauikeaouli's grass hut. More people had gathered to mourn. Some of them held each other and wept quietly. The group of women who were wailing "Auwe" in unison outside the main building had grown, and the sound of their cries made Kino's heart feel heavy.

The pair reached the door of Kauikeaouli's hut. It was dark inside, but as Kino's eyes grew accustomed to the low light, she could see an oblong, light-beige horizontal form on a sleeping mat.

"Kauikeaouli?" Pono asked.

"Leave me alone," said the beige figure. It looked like a long kapa wrapped cocoon.

Kino and Pono stood there for a moment. Then Pono said, "I'm sorry about Liholiho…"

The form on the ground did not respond or stir.

"I will remember him fondly." Pono took a step closer. "I loved him as a brother as well."

The form on the ground sat up. The light-beige material fell to the sides, and she could make out the profile of the boy who had been swaddled in the cloth.

"He is not your brother! He's mine!" Kauikeaouli blurted out. "Get out, Pono! I do not want to speak to you!"

"There is no need to get upset. I was just trying to tell you…"

"I said, go away!"

Pono paused for a moment, then he shook his head and walked out.

Kino glanced at the door. She wasn't sure if she was supposed to leave with Pono.

"Kino?" asked Kauikeaouli.

"Yes? I'm here." She moved closer to him. "Your arm…" Kino said as she watched him light a candle with a match. The flame illuminated his tear-stained face.

"Oh, my elbow. It hurt a lot, but it is fixed now."

Kino sat on the ground next to him.

"Have you ever felt alone?" Kauikeaouli asked.

Being an only child of a single mom, she didn't have to think about her answer.

"Most of the time. Probably because I'm always by myself." She shrugged.

"I mean really alone. Like there is no one out there who is looking out for you, alone."

Kino thought about it for a minute. Being solo never bothered her. Frankly, she never gave it any thought. It was just something she was used to.

"You're not alone – you have Nahi, your uh, servant people, and your aliʻi friends." She put on her best smile in hopes of cheering her up.

He remained despondent. "It's not the same. They do not understand me. My brother understood me... and now, he is... gone."

Kauikeaouli lay back down on the mat and said to the air above him, "I would like to be alone now. Tell the guards at the main house that you are ready, and they will see that you get home to Sophie's." He rolled over and turned his back to her.

Kino stood up, brushed herself off, and said, "I'll check on you tomorrow."

14

ʻUmikūmāhā

Makani stepped out onto the porch when the carriage pulled up to the yard. A broad smile appeared on her face as she saw Kino climb out of the cab. "Aloha!" she waved.

Both Kino and the driver waved back at the woman and returned her greeting. Kino loved that the word meant goodbye to him, and simultaneously hello to her.

Makani greeted her at the front door. Out of habit, Kino kissed her on the cheek as she did with all her relatives. The woman beamed.

"You're back!" Sophie said, entering the kitchen. "I have something for you! Come in! Come in!"

Kino wondered what it was as she sat down at the table.

"Close your eyes and I'll be right back," said Sophie.

Kino obeyed and shut her eyes. A flashback of her grandmother's similar instructions on her birthday came to mind. She hoped it wasn't another rock.

Sounds of movement and whispers followed by a soft thud on the table made Kino scoot forward in anticipation.

"Surprise!" Sophie gushed.

Kino opened her eyes. A pastel-pink box with a white bow lay in front of her. She wondered what it could be as she untied the ribbon and lifted the lid. A navy-blue dress lay inside. Kino held it against her body. "Thank you so much, Sophie! I really needed something else to wear."

Sophie nodded at the box. "There's more in there."

Kino put the dress aside and pulled out a beige cotton frock that looked like a combination sleeveless dress and apron. Sophie explained that it should be worn over the navy dress to help keep it clean. Under the cotton coverlet were more items: a white camisole on top of matching bloomers. Beneath those were two pairs of beige stockings.

Grinning, Kino put the clothes down and hugged Sophie.

"Thank you again. You didn't have to spend so much money on me."

Sophie gave her a squeeze and said, "I wanted to. You needed something else to wear, aside from the dress you have on. Besides, since I can't have any children of my own, it's nice to be able to indulge in someone else's." She winked at Kino.

"Da tub is filled. Go 'au 'au," Makani said, "Leave your dirty clothes outside. I wash dem laytah."

After washing up and changing into her new clothes, Kino felt refreshed. She had almost forgotten the day's events – that is, until they all sat down to dinner and Sophie asked how her day had gone.

First, she told them about how one of Kauikeaouli's monarch butterflies had hatched. Then how she had snuck out of the royal compound and ended up watching the young ali'i boys race their hōlua sleds. She thought it was funny how Sophie's eyes looked as big as a lemur's as Kino described each race and their various results.

When they heard about how Kauikeaouli had wiped out and dislocated his elbow, concern washed over both their faces. She finished by telling them of the news that the king had died. The women sat there, dumbfounded. It wasn't something that either of them expected to hear. Tears came to Makani's eyes, and she excused herself.

After a few minutes of silence, Sophie said, "Kino, I think you just received your first sign."

Puzzled, Kino frowned. "I don't think so. The monarch looked like it was alive, just still really wet, it probably needs time to dry out its wings. The other two chrysalises hadn't hatched yet, but they still looked okay."

Sophie shook her head. "That isn't what I meant. Do you know other words to describe royal rulers?"

Kino answered, "You mean like kings, queens, dukes and earls?"

Sophie nodded.

"I don't know," Kino said, "Don't you call them his or her highness?"

Sophie asked, "I meant what do you call the group of royals?"

Kino thought for a moment. Then it dawned on her. "Monarchs?"

"Yes!" Sophie clasped her hands together. "What is the second sign again?"

"The return of a king," said Kino. "Do you think that means he comes back from the dead?"

Sophie laughed. "I hardly think so. Perhaps it's when they bring his remains back from Europe."

"Aaaaaah," Kino nodded. "That makes a lot more sense."

"What was it you were supposed to do after you start seeing the signs?" Sophie dabbed her mouth with her napkin.

Kino did the same with her own napkin and said, "We are supposed to go to different places on the island to collect items to bring back to the kahuna."

Makani returned to her seat at the table. Her eyes were still red and swollen from crying, but she put on a cheerful front.

Kino told them of the objects they needed to get, and where they should find them. Makani mentioned that they could walk out to Mokoli'i Island during low tide, but warned that they needed to leave before the tide gets high because people have drowned trying to cross at that time. Kino asked as many questions as she could about the potential journey and Makani indulged her in tales and legends of the past.

That night Kino had another dream. She was standing on a hill, overlooking a lush, green valley. At the far end of the valley was a small dirt field. The sun shone brightly, and she could see different-colored songbirds chirping and flitting about. Next to her was a young Hawaiian man in a white malo. Tribal-patterned tattoos covered one shoulder and part of his chest. Around his head was a wreath of green ferns that matched the lei on his collarbone. He wore similar bands of ferns around each wrist and ankle. He reminded her of the male hula dancers she'd seen at the Polynesian Cultural Center, a place her museum class had visited.

Although he spoke only Hawaiian, she understood what he was telling her in his native tongue. He expressed the importance of keeping the land sacred. That Madam Pele's blood and fire had helped forge it, and that nothing should be done to upset the balance of nature. And that to preserve the sanctity of the land is to preserve the health of the people.

As she stood watching, a dust funnel started forming on the field. It picked up speed, turning into a small cyclone. Red dirt and debris filled the air as the twister ripped up trees and bushes, leaving nothing living in its wake. Any plants that the dust storm didn't destroy died when the red dirt landed on them, as if the soil were poisoned. Slowly, like a scourge, the field of dirt grew and grew until it had overtaken almost all of the greenery in the valley. The exotic songbirds that filled the air with their chirps were now silent, and their colorful little bodies lay dead on the ground.

Kino looked at the lifeless birds and her heart ached. She wanted to cry. She gazed at the young man. There was something familiar about him. She looked at his arms. His smooth, unblemished skin was now marred with sores similar to her grandfather's. She stared at him and only saw confusion in his eyes.

The approaching dirt funnel was now just yards away from them. The man looked down at his sores, then up at her again, pleading with his eyes to help him. Before she could say or do anything, the whirlwind scooped him up and he disappeared into the cyclone.

Kino screamed and bolted upright. Her heart was pounding hard and fast. She looked around and saw that she was safe in bed in Sophie's house.

It was just a dream.

Dressing as quickly as she could when she awoke the next morning, she ate a banana, then left a note and quietly snuck out of the house before Sophie and Makani awoke. Kino was determined to get Kauikeaouli to help her.

Gray clouds hung in the sky, casting a gloom on the hour-long walk to the palace. When she arrived, everything looked different. The guards at the outside gate wore black capes over their red malos. Their usually stoic expressions had given way to long, sad faces. Inside the compound, the sorrow was almost palpable. The crowd of wailing women had grown, and their lamenting had become even more anguished. All the palace workers wore troubled expressions, and hardly anyone spoke to one another.

Kino headed toward the main building but stopped just outside the door. Inside were Haole men in formal suits, speaking in hushed tones. It didn't look as if the prince was in there, so she made her way to his hut.

She found him inside, still curled up in same position as she had left him the day before. He had his back turned toward her.

"Kauikeaouli, are you awake?" She knelt down next to him.

"What do you want?" he asked, not making any effort to face her, let alone move.

"I wanted to know when you will be ready to get started on our journey so I can get back home?" she asked gently.

"I don't want to go anywhere or do anything."

"But you said you'd help. I think the news of your brother was the first sign that we were supposed to look for. The 'death of a monarch,'" she said.

"Is that all you care about?" Kauikeaouli sounded annoyed.

Kino sat back. He was right. She *was* coming across as self-absorbed, considering the circumstances.

"I'm sorry," she said. "I didn't mean to sound like I was happy about the first sign being about your brother."

They sat in awkward silence for a few minutes.

"Is there anything I can do? Maybe get you..." She tried to sound helpful.

"No," he answered. "I just want to be alone."

Kino looked at his back for a minute, then stood up and said, "I'll come and check on you tomorrow."

They repeated that scene over the next three days. Kauikeaouli, still overcome with grief, refused to budge from his hut; so every day Kino made the long walk to the palace and the long walk back, then spent the rest of the day helping Makani and Sophie around the house and yard.

On the fourth day, Sophie woke up the earliest and had breakfast on the table by the time Kino had washed up.

Sophie said, "I thought you'd enjoy coming with us to Honolulu today. I need to pick up a few things. Makani has packed up some food that we can take into town and have a picnic down by the water later."

"Yes! I'll go with you." Kino looked forward to seeing how the city looked back then.

Sophie said, "Let me finish getting ready, then we will head into town. From there we can take a cab to Honolulu."

Makani entered the kitchen and set a bag down on the table before pulling on a wide-brimmed straw hat.

Sophie returned, wearing a purple-and-lavender bonnet that matched her long dress. After putting on gray, elbow-length gloves, she picked up her small beaded purse and said, "Are you ready?"

Kino nodded. She followed Sophie out and Makani closed the door behind her. They hurried to Sam's general store, where two hansom cabs waited. They climbed into the closest one and Sophie instructed the driver to take them to the city.

Minutes down the road, they saw a large crowd of people near the harbor. Most of them were Hawaiian in traditional attire. Intermixed were Haoles in suits and dresses. The water was filled with many canoes and big woods ships with sails. The largest of the vessels was docked on the shore.

Sophie stuck her head out the small side window and asked the coachman, "Driver, what is going on there?" He had slowed the horse down to a walk. Other cabs and carriages inched along, and the crowd continued to grow.

"It is the return of the H.M.S. Blonde, madam. The ship is carrying the bodies of the royal party, including King Liholiho's," the man answered, steering his horse away from the crowd. "I cannot get you any closer to town. I will drop you off here."

Sophie paid the driver and they hurried toward the center of the activity. They didn't get very far, since there were too many people crowding to see the royal procession.

"Let's go this way," Sophie said, moving away from the growing congregation. "I have a feeling they will end up at the mission church."

Kino and Makani followed her to a simple, wooden, thatched-roof chapel. Kino wondered if this was the predecessor to the landmark Kawaiaha'o Church in modern Honolulu.

A small cluster of mourners gathered on the lawn in front of the building. Their numbers grew by the minute as people clung to each other and wept.

They found a spot under some trees and sat down to eat the food that Makani had packed earlier. Just as they finished eating, Kino heard a small marching band playing a funeral dirge. They stood and hurried to the road.

Kino watched as twenty solemn kahili bearers dressed in black, some with handsome feather cloaks on their shoulders, led the way. Behind them were sailors from the ship, then the band, all followed by a group of uptight-looking Haoles in heavy clothing. Kino guessed they were missionaries, walking alongside a man with a priest's collar and long black coat.

Then came a large group of men, all of them well over six feet tall and wearing red and gold, the colors of the ali'i. Kino counted forty pairs of men, pulling the two royal coffins on black, canopy-covered carts.

"Do you really think that this is the second sign?" Kino asked, never taking her eyes off the crimson velvet-covered caskets.

"It's the only thing I can think of that would make sense," said Sophie.

The prince appeared next, dressed in a midnight blue, formal, royal-military-type suit with brass buttons joined with gold braids. He sat atop a platform carried by four servants. His expression looked pained and he stared straight ahead. Walking alongside him was a wiry man in a green top hat. Kino had seen him at the palace. She remembered hearing him speak with a British accent to another man who spoke the same way.

That second man wore spectacles and walked with a slight limp. He accompanied the platform carrying Nahienaena. The young girl wore a somber black lace dress with long sleeves and a collar that came up to her chin. She seemed dazed and unfocused. Her eyes, puffy and red, stared off into the sky above the crowd.

A whole slew of men walked behind the royal pair. Kino guessed they were chiefs by their red-and-gold feather capes, followed by sea captains and other well-dressed Haole people in fancy hats. It took a while, but the cavalcade finally filed past them.

They waited a bit for the crowd to dwindle before heading back into the town. Sophie pointed out the shop where she had bought the new dress that Kino was wearing. After purchasing some smoked meats and cheeses, they headed back home. This time they took a cab directly from the town to the house.

At dinner, Kino informed them that she was going to go to the palace in the morning to speak to Kauikeaouli. If he wasn't going to help her, then he could at least tell her what to do – she hoped.

The next morning, she put on Nahienaena's old dress that Makani had washed. Kino had figured out that she could go three days in the same clothes, if she was careful and didn't sweat too much. The coverlet that went over her navy dress bought her an extra day, but after learning how tedious it was to wash clothes by hand, she really didn't want to create extra work for herself or Makani, so she tried her best to stay clean.

She missed her own clothes. They might have been cheap and some of them used, but at least she had more options than the same two dresses that she had been alternating between. She couldn't wait until she was back at home.

*****

At the royal compound, everyone still wore mourning colors. The throng of grieving people no longer gathered in the yard, but sorrow still lingered like a low-hanging rain cloud over the space.

Kino stopped first at the main building and found Nahienaena and her tutor engrossed in a lesson. Not wanting to interrupt, she backed out of the building and made her way to Kauikeaouli's hale.

He wasn't in the hut, so she decided to take a walk around the grounds. In a far-off corner, past the cooking hale, stood a set of palm trees. Kauikeaouli sat on a bench under one of them with his back facing her.

Kino's first instinct was to sneak up and scare him, but as she neared, she could see his trembling shoulders. Wanting to give him ample time to collect himself, she yelled, "Hey! There you are!"

Kauikeaouli quickly wiped his eyes. By the time Kino reached him, he had regained his composure and stood up to greet her.

"Aloha, Kino." the prince said softly. "I apologize for my behavior the other day."

"That's okay," she replied, "I understand." She paused then said, "I'm really sorry about your brother."

The man that had walked with Kauikeaouli in the funeral procession approached and addressed the boy. He gave a nod to Kino, and in a British accent said to the prince, "Come along now, your highness. We will start your lessons early today."

Kauikeaouli protested. "But I told my friend I would help her with something. I want to do my lessons later."

The man eyed Kino then turned his attention back to the young prince. "There is no time for that," said the man. "You will go to Chief Kalanimoku's house after your studies."

Kauikeaouli frowned at Kino. "I promise I will help you later."

"No problema," she said, not wanting to sound disappointed. He looked at her and was about to ask her something, probably what a problema was, when the man cleared his throat.

Kauikeaouli smiled helplessly as he walked away.

She watched them head back toward the main building. *Great.* She'd walked all this way for nothing. Kino dawdled on the way back, and by the time she reached the front gate, a horse and carriage were already waiting to take her home. Disappointed, she climbed in and headed back to Sophie's.

She didn't say or eat much at dinner. Sophie and Makani didn't pry, but they did give her sympathetic looks when she looked at either one of them. At the end of the meal she excused herself and went to her room. After blowing out the candle on her nightstand, she turned and half fell, half flopped onto the bed. She lay there, staring at the ceiling, listening to the crickets and trying her best not to cry. Now, more than ever, she wished she were at home.

111

The drone of the insects soon lulled her into a light sleep, and she felt as if she were floating.

A tapping on the window above her head snapped her awake. A dark head peered at her from the other side of the glass. She was about to scream when a familiar voice said,

"Kino, it's me, Kauikeaouli!" He spoke in a hushed voice.

"What are you doing here?" she whispered, as she pushed opened the window.

"I ran away," Kauikeaouli answered softly.

"YOU WHAT?"

"Shhhhhhh. Come outside." He gestured with his thumb over his shoulder.

Kino found the matchbox next to her bed and lit the kukui nut candle that she'd used earlier. She cupped the flame with her hand as she hurried outside.

"What do you mean you ran away?" Kino asked. "And why?"

"Well, I promised to help you," Kauikeaouli answered, "and my brother's spirit sent me a sign that it's time."

Kino's brows rose. "What do you mean? What kind of sign?"

"He appeared to me as a gold-and-black pulelehua."

From what she remembered, the word meant moth or butterfly in Hawaiian. Kino had heard stories about deceased people visiting their loved ones in this form.

"It landed on the scroll and I knew it was time. When I unrolled it, the map was on it already." Kauikeaouli looked around. "Is there anywhere I can sleep?"

"Why don't you come into the house? Sophie has a couch." Kino gestured toward the door.

Kauikeaouli shook his head. "No, it is best that they do not know I was here."

"Why?" She knew Sophie wouldn't mind if he slept in the living room.

"Because if the guards come looking for me, I do not want your friends to get into trouble or have to lie for me."

That made perfect sense to Kino. He was really smart for his age.

"There is a small shed where Sophie keeps the empty crates from the furniture that her husband brought on his last trip. No one goes in there. You can tie the horse up behind it." Kino pointed at a small building, several hundred yards from the house.

Kauikeaouli said, "Aloha ahiahi," and turned the horse in the direction she had pointed. Kino spotted a rolled woven mat, and guessed that was what he would be sleeping on that night.

"Goodnight..." She turned back toward the house. "Does that mean we can start on our quest tomorrow?"

"Yes," Kauikeaouli answered over his shoulder.

Kino went back into the house with a big smile on her face.

Finally! Progress!

The next morning, Kino packed her shorts and t-shirt into a fabric bag Sophie had given her the day they went into Honolulu. It was large enough to hold her clothes and still had room for the items they needed to collect. She also made sure to pack her compass. Even if it didn't work right, maybe it could at least lead her back to the hut with her rock in it.

"You look a lot happier than you did last night," Sophie commented, as she entered the kitchen the next morning. Kino had not realized she was humming.

"I think today is the day that Kauikeaouli will agree to help me," Kino announced confidently.

"Wonderful!" Sophie said with a smile. For second, Kino thought she saw sadness flash in the woman's eyes. "Does that mean you will be home for dinner?"

"Probably not," Kino answered, "If it's late, I'll eat something at the palace." She hated lying to them, but it was important that the women didn't know.

She stood up and headed toward the door. She was about to step outside, but then she paused and turned. "Um, I don't know how long everything will take. It might be easier for me to stay there so we can start early every day. But don't worry; I'll be okay. I'll make sure to come back as soon as we get everything."

Makani handed her the same dried-gourd container on a cord that Kino used on her excursion to the heiau.

"Well, you know where to find us." Sophie smiled.

Kino put the cord around her neck and shoulder, looked at the two women then rushed back in to hug them both. She was grateful that they had been so kind to her. Even though she was eager to get back home, she wasn't quite ready yet to say goodbye to them for good.

Kauikeaouli was already up when she made her way to where she had last left him. Kino had taken two boiled eggs from the bowl that Sophie kept on the counter and offered them to him.

"No, thank you, I already ate."

Kino shrugged and said, "Okay, so where do we go first?"

Kauikeaouli reached into the saddlebag and pulled out the kapa scroll that the kahuna had given him, and opened it for her to see.

Kino looked over his shoulder at the map.

"I wrote down the destinations on a separate piece of paper. The kahuna said we needed to go to Mokoli'i Island, Kipapa Gulch, the top of Mount Ka'ala, and the largest waterfall at the bottom. Here, hold the corner." She did as he instructed.

"We are here," he said, pointing at a space on the south side of the island. "Mokoli'i Island is here." He tapped a small circle off to the east coast of the island.

"Here are Ka'ala and the falls." He touched the other two landmarks. "We should start at Mokoli'i Island." Kauikeaouli folded the map and stuck it back into his pocket. "If we leave now, we should get there by tomorrow night."

"What? I thought the whole thing was only going to take a day or two! Not just getting to the first place!" Kino lamented.

Kauikeaouli asked, "How long does it take to get there in your time?"

Kino thought for a moment. It looked as though the area they were supposed to go to was in the Kualoa region of the island.

"I just went there with a class I'm in, and it took us about an hour from the museum. But we took the highway."

"You mean the mountains?" Kauikeaouli asked.

"Never mind," Kino shook her head. "I'll explain it later. Let's just get on the road."

15

‘Umikūmālima

“Do you know where we’re going?” Kino glanced at the trees and bushes around her. She had no idea where they were, other than that they had just passed Diamond Head, and were following a trail uphill.

“There is a main road that goes around the outer edges of the island,” Kauikeaouli answered. “We can get to Mokoli‘i if we follow it north. We just have to get to that road first.”

As they headed toward the coast, Kino gauged her surroundings. The area they had traveled from was a lot more populated than the area they were traveling toward. Aside from open fields and small plots of land used for farming, most of the landscape consisted of broad, grassy meadows, thick shade trees and dense bushes. On occasion they came across a grass hut or two. Sometimes the inhabitants were working nearby in the yard or in front of the house. Other times they were nowhere to be seen. Now and then, Kino and Kauikeaouli crossed paths with other travelers walking or riding in the opposite direction.

The narrow trail eventually connected to a much wider one that ran along the coast. They decided to stop and take their first break shortly after reaching that main road.

Kauikeaouli pointed at a grove of trees. “We will rest there.”

Kino was happy to hear that. Her butt hurt and her thigh muscles ached from straddling the horse.

When they reached the trees, Kauikeaouli jumped out of the saddle then helped her down. It felt good to straighten her legs. She bent her right leg and grabbed her foot at the ankle, then pushed her heel into the back of her thigh.

Kauikeaouli mimicked her actions, watching carefully for any movement changes, and moved with her when she switched sides.

Kino did her best not to fall over as she stood on each foot.

"That felt good. Where did you learn that?" Kauikeaouli asked.

"PE class at school." Kino replied, amused that he copied her motions. Taking a wide step sideways, she bent at the waist and touched the ground. He did the same, but he looked up a couple of times to make sure she was still in the same position.

"What is a PE?" Kauikeaouli asked from between his ankles. She straightened up and put her hands on her hips. He did so as well.

"Physical Education. It's a class where you have to exercise and play stupid games like volleyball and basketball." She bent over again.

"Ball? That sounds like fun," he said, bending as well. "I envy you. I would love a class where I could just play. You are lucky. Is that your favorite subject?"

She straightened up for a moment then bent back down. "No, actually I hate it."

Kauikeaouli straightened up, then bent over again and asked, "Can I ask why?"

"Because I am not good at any sports..." she straightened up. Kauikeaouli did the same. "And I always get hit in the face with the ball."

Kauikeaouli stared at her for a second, then sucked in his bottom lip, bit back a smile and did his best to stifle a giggle. He looked so funny that Kino started to smile. Their eyes met, and they both burst out laughing.

As their laughter subsided, Kino said, "I'm so thirsty."

"I am too." Kauikeaouli replied. He walked over to the horse that was nibbling on grass a few feet away. He unbuckled one of the saddlebags and pulled out the water gourd that the kahuna had given him.

Stepping away from the horse, he held the gourd in his left palm with his right hand on the neck of it. He closed his eyes and murmured something Kino couldn't quite make out, but from the sounds she heard, she knew it was in Hawaiian.

He let out a small gasp as his hands dipped down, as if the gourd had unexpectedly become heavy.

"Do you have your ipu?" he asked, walking slowly toward her.

She nodded and pulled the cord over her head to free her gourd from around her. "Here you go."

"Hold it out." The prince poured water from his ipu into hers. Then he lifted his gourd up to his lips.

Kino followed suit and drank the sweetest, cleanest water she had ever tasted in her life. She immediately felt reenergized and refreshed.

"How did you do that?" Kino asked then swallowed the last sip. She wasn't sure what she had seen, but it looked as though the gourd had been empty to start with by the way he had lifted it with ease from the saddlebag, sideways. Then, suddenly, he could barely walk with it – either because it was too heavy or too full.

Kauikeaouli made loud noises as he gulped down his water and finished with a satisfied *aaaaah* sound after the last sip. Then he burped. Loudly.

Kino found it amusing and gross at the same time.

He held up his water container. "Astonishing, is it not? Mana from my ancestors did it all."

"Oh yeah, that's right, the kapu ipu." she uttered. She didn't mean to sound so sarcastic as it actually came out.

He either was unaware of her tone or didn't care. "Yes, it is quite remarkable. We are fortunate to have it."

He was right; she didn't know why she had such a resentful tone when it came to the special gourd. It was silly, and she felt ashamed for a moment.

"It's really cool," Kino admitted. She took another big sip.

"Yes, the water is quite cold, but the container itself is actually rather warm. The leather of the bag acts like an oven and traps warm air inside of it, so the ipu was almost too hot to touch. It has cooled down a bit, but I think it is still warm."

"I mean the trick it does with instant water was really cool, not that the ipu itself was."

Kauikeaouli matter-of-factly stated, "I told you, it is the blessings of my ancestors that makes it possible. It has nothing to do with temperature."

She suddenly realized that cool meant something different in modern day slang than it did in 1825. She face-palmed herself. He smiled. She wasn't sure if he was joking or not.

"Would you like a mountain apple or guava? I picked a few yesterday." Kauikeaouli headed back to the horse and opened one of the bags.

"Mountain apple, please," she answered.

He pulled three out and handed one to her. He bit into one of his as he picked up the reins and started once more down the road.

"Since you will not tell me what life is like in your time, you can at least tell me about yourself," Kauikeaouli said without looking at her.

Kino shrugged and asked, "What do you want to know?"

He turned to face her and continued walking backwards. "How old are you? Do you have any brothers or sisters? What is school like? What is your hale, I mean house like? Who…"

"Whoa! Slow down with the questions!" Kino interjected. She couldn't help but chuckle. He must have been dying to ask them for a long time.

Kauikeaouli smiled and looked at the ground in embarrassment, then turned back to face the direction they headed.

"Let's see. I just turned twelve and I'm an only child. Uh, I like school for the most part. Except for these mean girls. And I live with my mom and grandparents right now. They have a small house that my mom grew up in. But I think we have to move soon."

He rattled off another set of back-to-back questions. "Who are the mean girls? Why are they mean? And why do you have to move?"

Kino thought of her bullies and rolled her eyes before she realized she had done so. Must be a reflex. She answered, "There are four of them: Chanel, Tiffany, Cyan, and their ringleader, Maylani. She's the worst of them all. We used to be best friends a long time ago. I think they are mean to me because my family doesn't have money, the way theirs do."

"Are they children of the ali'i? Is that why they have so much money?" Kauikeaouli asked.

"No," Kino murmured, "Tiffany and Cyan have dads who are surgeons, Chanel's dad is a lawyer and Maylani's step-dad is the president of GRANDAGRA."

Kauikeaouli tipped his head. "GRANDAGRA?"

"It's some big company that is buying up land and forcing families like mine to move because we don't own the land our house is on."

"Of course not. The 'aina belongs to the kingdom."

"Actually, Kamehameha the Third made it possible for people to… buy… land…" She caught herself only after she had spilled the beans.

"I did?"

Kino put her hands on her head and made a frustrated sound. "Auuugh!"

Kauikeaouli and the horse stopped.

"Are you all right?" His concerned expression returned. Kino dropped her hands and looked at him.

"I can't tell you any more. I don't want to do anything that can affect…"

"History," he cut her off. "I know."

By now they had traveled several miles on uneven terrain, mostly uphill, and Kino's legs felt tired and weak. She slowed her pace and asked, "Can we stop soon? I'm hungry, and it's hot."

"Yes, I am as well. Let us look for a suitable place to rest."

She smiled to herself when he said the word "suitable." It was easy to think of him as just another eleven-year-old boy like the ones she'd gone to school with last year. But when he said things like "suitable," she was reminded that he came from a time when people spoke English differently, and kids were more mature for their age.

Ahead of them, the tree-lined road curved left and upward at an angle. The dusty ground gave way to more compact dirt and rock as they climbed further up the hill. After a while they arrived at the summit.

Sunlight danced off the teal-blue water, making the ocean shimmer and sparkle. The sky was clear with no clouds in sight. She watched the lush, green leaves and grasses flutter in the breeze. In the distance she saw the islet called Manana Island. She pointed at it and told him that most people knew it as Rabbit Island in her time.

He didn't take his eyes off of it as he walked, but tilted his head as he looked at it.

"Is that because it looks like a rabbit's head?"

"I thought that too," Kino answered, "but then I learned that it was also used for many years as a rabbit habitat."

He continued to glance at it as they continued down the hill towards the island.

"That's pretty cold."

Kino asked, "What did you say?"

"That the island shaped like a rabbit had rabbits on it was, how did you say it, really cold?"

Kino giggled. At least he was trying. "The word is cool. When something is great or you really like something, you say it's cool."

"Cool? Cool, I will remember that." He looked at her with confidence. "This seems like a good spot to stop." He pulled the horse to a patch of shade trees, several yards off the road.

"Great, I'm starving." Kino joined him on the grass. She lifted the strap of her bag over her head and placed it on the ground. Kauikeaouli pointed to a small grove of green ti leaf plants and instructed her to pick five leaves.

Removing the wooden bowl that the kahuna had given him from the saddlebag, along with his special ipu, he walked to her bag and sat down in the grass.

Kino returned and handed him the leaves, then sat down and faced him.

Kauikeaouli laid one in front of her, one in front of him, and used the last three leaves to cover the empty bowl. He began softly chanting a prayer. A gust of warm wind blew by that gave her "chicken skin."

When his praying was over, Kauikeaouli lifted the ti leaves off the bowl. Fragrant steam rose from a leaf-wrapped bundle that filled the container. He gingerly picked it up by the top stems glistening with moisture, and carefully placed it on the leaf in front of him.

Could it be?

Kino watched fascinated and hopeful as Kauikeaouli untied the knotted bundle.

"Oh wow – lau lau!" Kino couldn't help herself. It was the largest one she had ever seen.

To her surprise, her favorite Hawaiian dish – made up of steamed fish and pork, wrapped in luau leaves similar to mild tasting spinach – filled the bowl.

"Hand me your ti leaf," he instructed, ripping a section off the one in front of him. He served her half the contents of the bundle, then wiped his hands on his pants.

Kino's stomach growled in anticipation. He replaced the three leaves over the bowl, and then he reached for his water gourd.

"Hand me your ipu."

She did as he instructed. He poured water into it from his then handed her gourd back to her.

"Pour it on my hands." Kauikeaouli said as he put his own gourd down and held his palms up.

Confused, she asked, "Uh, can I have some of it to drink?"

"Yes, I will pour you some water. I just need help washing my hands."

"Okay." She slowly poured as he washed up.

"Now, give me back your ipu." He picked up his. She handed her gourd back to him and he refilled it.

"Thank... uh, I mean mahalo." Kino said, marveling at this magical meal.

"One more thing." Kauikeaouli lifted the leaves off the bowl. Inside of it was a generous helping of poi.

He pushed the bowl closer to her leaf dish, scooped his fingers into the poi, twirled up a gob and then placed it on her leaf. He was about to serve a second when she stopped him.

"Whoa, that's okay – that's more than enough," she said gratefully. He shrugged and ate the poi off his fingertips. She noticed that he had served her, instead of sharing the bowl "family style" as she had done at Sophie's.

It didn't matter. She was famished. She didn't even bother to wash her hands before eating. The food practically melted in her mouth. She ate quickly and loudly. She'd had a bunch of questions about the bowl when she first saw the huge lau lau, but forgot them quickly once she'd had her first bite.

If the bowl made food this good, she didn't care how it worked – she was really grateful they didn't have to rely on non-perishable rations like dried fish and meats. And no matter how much she loved it, she couldn't imagine living on island fruit for every meal of every day, for however long it took for them to finish their journey.

By the time they set up camp and started a fire, it was dark. She reclined on her mat and looked up at the stars. The sound of waves crashing on the shore was loud and almost distracting. As her thoughts drifted to her mom and grandparents, the sound seemed to fade. She missed them so much and wished she could be home right now, sitting at the table with Mom and Gramma. And she wished that Grandpa would finally be out of the hospital, so that he could be there with them.

16

ʻUmikūmāono

Kino dreamt she was standing outside as it started to rain. She was getting wet, but couldn't seem to move. Water hit her head.

"Aloha kakahiaka."

She opened her eyes. Kauikeaouli, in a dripping wet malo, stood over her, grinning. She sat up and wiped the water off her forehead. "Good morning. Thanks for the shower. How long have you been awake?"

Kauikeaouli held out his hand and pulled her up.

"I awoke at sunrise," he said, covering the special bowl with ti leaves. Holding his hands over the bowl, he shut his eyes and whispered a prayer in Hawaiian. Kino watched, fascinated.

At the end of the prayer, he lifted the broad leaves off of the bowl. Perfectly ripe island fruit filled it with color. Generous chunks of pink papaya, bright-orange mango, and golden pineapple glistened with juicy freshness. He poured water on his fingertips to rinse them and divided the fruit.

"It was early, the tide was still high, and I did not want to disturb your sleep," said Kauikeaouli. "So I decided to take a walk along the beach. I came upon two great honus – turtles – and followed them into the water, where I explored the reef a bit. There are many fish with beautiful colors living among the rocks." He ate a piece of mango.

"I love sea turtles. I hope to see some too."

Kauikeaouli continued. "I also saw sharks."

Kino's hair on the back of her neck rose when he mentioned those lethal predators. She wouldn't know what to do, aside from panic, if she came face to face with one. She had heard that people sometimes pee when they get really scared. That would probably happen to her too.

"If I saw a shark in the water, I'd freak out."

Kauikeaouli knitted his brows. "Freak out?"

"Yes! You know, freak out!" She raised her hands and shook them in the air.

He laughed and asked, "Would you really do that?"

"Maybe," she said. There was no need to share her theory of possible incontinence. "Or I'd scream and pass out."

"I do not suggest you do either," Kauikeaouli chuckled. "Besides, I have nothing to fear. Sharks are one of my family's 'amakua."

Kino thought back to the helpful owl at the beginning of her strange journey. "I think the pueo is our family's guardian. But can you have more than one type?"

Kauikeaouli nodded. "Yes. Some families have more than one, but usually one animal is more prominent."

"That would be cool if I had more than one type of 'amakua," said Kino. "I could use all the help I can get."

*****

Pink hues tinted the clouds, indicating the sun's gradual descent. The journey north had taken many hours up and down the rocky trail, even with only two bathroom breaks and a short lunch.

"I'm tired. How much farther do we have to go?" Kino asked. Her body had wanted to stop hours ago, but her spirit wanted to forge ahead.

"We should be seeing our first destination when we reach the top of the hill."

"Good. Finally!" Kino walked faster.

Kauikeaouli sped past her, yelling, "Race you!"

Kino sprinted after him and met him on the summit.

"There it is," Kauikeaouli pointed at an inverted cone-shaped island across the water. "Mokoli'i."

Kino had been wondering where this island was, since it didn't sound familiar. She only knew the island by the name "Chinaman's Hat," as most folks called it in her time.

"Have you been there before?" Kauikeaouli asked, laying out their sleeping mats.

"No," replied Kino. "I'm not that great a swimmer. But I've always wondered what was on it.

Kauikeaouli walked over to the horse and returned with two stones that he used as flints. "We should wait until low tide, then we will be able to walk to the island."

She sat down on her mat. "Do you know when that is?"

"I think it is around sunrise. And the flower that you need has to be gathered in the morning."

Kino was about to ask why; then she remembered that the flower changes from blue to pink later in the day. She needed the flower to be blue when she picked it.

Settling in, Kauikeaouli started a fire just as the daylight disappeared. They stayed up later than they had the night before, laughing, comparing scars and talking about nothing in particular. And she taught him how to play the alphabet game.

She soon regretted doing so. He loved it so much that he insisted they play it over and over, with the rule that a word can only be used once and not repeated in the next game. After the seventh round she said, "T for time – time to go to bed now, because we have to wake up early."

Kauikeaouli said, "But I'm not even tired."

Kino watched his eyes slowly start to water and his jaw drop, making his closed lips open into a small "o." He could no longer hold it and let out a big yawn.

She laughed and said, "Nighty-night, don't let the bedbugs bite."

"Bedbugs?"

"Never mind; it's not something you have to worry about." She let out a similar yawn and lay down. Closing her eyes, she said, "If you wake up before I do, wake me up, okay? I want to get an early start."

Kauikeaouli also lay down, curling on his side to face her. "I will. And you do the same as well."

125

She opened her eyes, said "Okay," and closed them again.

That night she dreamt she stood on the peak of Mokoli'i, staring down at shark-infested water. Dark shapes with dorsal fins circled the island. Terrified, she refused to get into the ocean. No matter what Kauikeaouli said or did, nothing could budge her. She would not go further than a rock about six feet above the surface.

A ten-foot shark loomed up in front of her, standing upright on its tail on the surface of the water. It turned into a man, who climbed up to the rock where she was and faced her. His dark skin glistened as beads of water rolled off his muscular physique. He crouched down and stared at her. There were no whites in his eyes, just the blackest of black pupils.

He smiled at her with razor-sharp pointed teeth, then picked her up, put her on his back and dove into the ocean. It happened so quickly that she didn't have time to gulp in any air before they plunged underwater.

Panicking, she kept thinking, *I need air. I need to breathe.* She tapped him on the shoulder. He offered no reaction. She grabbed his hair, which withdrew from her hands and sank into his skin. His head turned back into a shark's head, but his body remained human, allowing him to keep a firm grip on Kino as he dove deeper into the dark-blue ocean.

Her lungs felt as though they wanted to burst. She gave up and let out a big exhale. Surprisingly, there were no bubbles. Before she could figure out why, her feet touched the ocean floor. Other than sand and coral, it looked nothing like the pictures in science books. She was in an aquatic paradise. She could breathe, but her inhale felt muffled, as if she were breathing under a blanket.

Brilliant colors surrounded her. Little fishes swam in small schools that flashed silver whenever they changed directions. Various sizes and types of bright blue, yellow, and red fishes darted in and out of openings in the coral reef.

She found that she could walk very slowly on the sandy bottom, like an astronaut on the surface of the moon. The shark man held her hand and led her through a curtain of seaweed. As they came out on the other side she saw people, or rather saw through them, to the fishes and reef on the other side of the curtain. A transparent man turned, smiled, and came towards her. When she looked, the shark man was gone. In the distance, she saw a dark-gray form swimming away.

She looked back at the transparent person. He looked familiar, though she knew she had never seen him before. He reached out to her and beckoned her to follow him. She did so, and he led her past bright, shimmering fishes into an area that looked like a garden. In it, more people turned and greeted her with warm smiles. Somehow, she knew that they were her ancestors.

She felt safe and very loved in their presence. She wanted to stay there forever. But they encircled her, lifted her up, and pushed her to the surface. She tried her best to protest, but it didn't matter; they just kept pushing her upward.

Suddenly she heard, "Wake up – the tide is low!"

Kino opened her eyes, sat up and looked out at the rippling, steel-blue ocean. The sun had just risen above the peak of the little island across the water, casting bright sunbeams that pierced through the few dark clouds above it, painting a column of gold in the water that ran from the island to the shore.

"I need to change," Kino said, and reached for her bag. She pulled out her t-shirt and shorts then stared at him. "Ahem."

Kauikeaouli stared back at her. "Oh. Right." He blushed and turned his back to her.

She pulled off her pantaloons and pulled on her shorts. Next, she put her head into the t-shirt and left it hanging like a necklace as she unbuttoned the top of her dress. As she pulled her arm out, she stuck it through the t-shirt sleeve, then did the same for her other arm. Then she stood up and pulled her shirt down properly. Her dress fell around her ankles.

"Okay, I'm ready."

Kauikeaouli turned to face her. "What are you wearing? Is that your underwear?"

Kino laughed and answered, "No, this is the kind of clothes that kids our age wear every day."

"Who are those boys on your shirt?" he asked, not taking his eyes off her as he stood up.

Kino glanced down. "Oh, that's One Direction."

"Which direction?"

"No – One Direction. They used to be a 'boy band.'" She didn't want to get into what that was. "Do you have anything we can put the flower in after we pick it?" she asked, changing the subject.

"I have something we can put everything that we gather in." He walked over to the saddlebag and returned with a round gourd with a flat cover, wrapped in tightly woven makaloa grass, a method ancient Hawaiians used to make containers waterproof. A loop of cord was threaded to its side that he slung over his head and across his body.

They waded out to the island in water at waist-high level, slowing down only to maneuver over rocks and reef. Once on the island, they spotted a trail. Kauikeaouli took off running as soon as he saw it. Kino ran after him.

"Slow down!" she yelled. He stopped and waited for her to catch up.

Kino followed his footprints as they climbed up the steep incline. When they reached the top, she turned around to face the shore.

"Wow!" she said in awe. The breathtaking view of the majestic Koʻolau Mountains sat before her. Sunlight bathed the sharp ridges that ran down the mountainsides like solid, emerald green waterfalls. Below her, teal water encircled the little island, blending into darker turquoise that covered mottled spots of dark reef under the surface.

A few yards below her on the hill were the blue, trumpet-shaped flowers of a pohuehue plant.

"I see them," she replied. "Here, help me." She held out an open hand.

He grabbed her outstretched arm at the wrist, and she turned her palm to grab his. Squeezing slightly, she took a step toward the flowers and stretched her other hand down. Her fingertips grazed a leaf, which she used to pull the vine up off the ground a few inches. Slowly she shifted her weight to her back foot, let go of Kauikeaouli's wrist, and brought her hand down to meet the one holding the plant. Gently breaking off a branch that had two flowers and three leaves, she passed it up to Kauikeaouli. He put it in the gourd container, then offered his arm for her to grab on to.

"Woohoo! We got it!" Kino hooted. "High five!" She swung her open palm upward toward him.

He stood there with a big grin on his face.

"Don't leave me hanging – hit me," she said.

"I beg your pardon?"

"Hit me!" she waved her open palm in the air.

He squinted at her. She waved her hand again.

Shrugging, he waved at her with his left hand then hit her in the shoulder with his right.

"Ow! What did you do that for?" She rubbed her shoulder with her opposite hand.

"You told me to hit you."

Kino slapped her forehead. "I meant hit my hand with your hand." She held her open palm up again. He held his hand up, hesitated then slowly clapped her open hand with his.

"Good! Now do it again," she encouraged. She held her palm up again and prompted, "High five..."

He swung and missed her hand, clipping her fingers with his palm.

"We'll work on that. Let's get going," she said.

Kauikeaouli looked disappointed.

"I promise, we'll practice later, but we have to go before the tide comes in."

On their way to the island the water had been calm, and its level had reached only to her midsection at its deepest point. Now, just several yards from the island, the water was almost to her chin. The winds picked up, making it harder for her to touch the bottom while keeping her head above water.

"We need to hurry," Kino said, treading water to pass him. She figured it would be easier to dog paddle at this point, instead of trying to tiptoe her way back to the main beach. She turned to face Kauikeaouli. Her blood ran cold.

A large, dark-gray, pointed dorsal fin was heading right at them.

Before she could say or do anything, another dorsal fin emerged, slicing through the water on her left. Frozen with fear, Kino stopped paddling. Kauikeaouli's face was the last thing she saw before being pulled underwater.

The first thing she thought of was that the sharks had gotten her. She fought her way to the surface, waiting for the water around her to turn bloody. But the only things surrounding her were white, foamy bubbles. Then she realized she was caught in the undercurrent.

Kino swam harder, trying not to flail her limbs in panic. Her lungs burned.

She broke through the surface to gasp a mouthful of air before being pulled under again. The water twisted and turned, pulling her deeper. She couldn't hold her breath any longer and exhaled into the stream of bubbles around her head before everything went black.

Her mind flashed to the dream she'd had earlier. Was she still dreaming? Would she open her eyes and be surrounded by loving, ghostly ancestors, giving her a boost?

Finally, her face broke through the surface and she gasped for air. She could feel something smooth under her, propelling her forward. Salt water burned her nose, throat, and sinuses as she sucked a big gulp of air and choked down a mouthful of briny water.

When she opened her eyes, she saw she was moving toward the beach. Suddenly her feet touched the sandy bottom, and whatever had been under her pulled away. She crawled the rest of the way onto the shore, coughing the water out of her lungs.

Where was Kauikeaouli?

She looked back at the water. Did the sharks get him? She didn't see blood. What if something happened to him? It would be her fault that history had changed.

She heard her name being called in the distance. Looking up the beach she saw the young prince running toward her. She let out a sigh of relief. He didn't get eaten, thank goodness. History remained intact.

He rushed to her side. "Kino, are you all right?"

She went to say something and coughed again. Her throat hurt from hacking up water. Instead, she nodded. He helped her sit up.

He frowned. "You were caught in the undertow. I could not reach you."

She looked across the water. Mokoli'i Island seemed to be a lot farther away now. Kino cleared her throat and asked, "How did I get back to shore?"

Kauikeaouli looked at her with surprise. "You do not know?"

She looked at him blankly. "No, what?"

"Before I could reach you, you disappeared from the surface. Then I saw na mano. The sharks. They left me then started swimming quickly down this way, toward you. I made it to the sand, and by the time I ran down here, all I saw was you lying here and two grey fins swimming away. I think they helped you. Sharks must be one of your family's 'amakua, as well."

Kino couldn't believe her ears. If it hadn't happened to her, she would not have accepted any of it. She hugged her knees and shivered.

Kauikeaouli said, "You stay here; I will get the horse." He jogged away.

Kino gazed out at the breaking waves, still shaken from the event. Her nose hurt when she inhaled and her eyes burned. She kept her eyes open to let her natural tears build up then blinked to rinse the ocean salt out. As the tears rolled down her cheeks, her eyes felt a little better – which was more than she could say about herself.

She stared out at the water again. She just wanted to be home with her mom and grandparents. She even missed her small bedroom with its thirty-year-old décor. At least there were no sharks or chance of drowning there.

Kauikeaouli returned with some water in her ipu. She nodded with as much grateful sincerity as she could, and drank it all without pausing. The cool liquid immediately soothed her sore throat. He helped her to her feet and they made their way to the mats he had laid out. Kino sat and drank more water while he prepared their food. She ate in silence, and tried not to think about anything – especially what had just happened.

17

'Umikūmāhiku

After the meal, Kauikeaouli pulled out the map, unrolled it, and laid it out on the ground between them.

"Our next destination is here," he said, placing his fingertip to the left of the jagged lines. "And we are here," pointing at a spot on edge of the island to the east. "The road will take us along the coast for most of the way," as his finger followed the shoreline north and west. "Then we go here." He drew an invisible line south, from the top of the island to just about the center of it.

Kino stared at the map. "That looks like it will take forever."

Kauikeaouli said, "I believe it is more than a two-day journey. Or, we can go this way." He pointed at their starting point and dragged his finger west, across the jagged mountain symbol to the next destination area.

"I don't know," she said with uncertainty. "How will we know which trail to take?"

"There are many trails on this island," he said. "We take the first one we find, until it connects to one that takes us uphill. Then we keep climbing, and heading west, until we reach the top."

"Isn't a lot more dangerous to go that way than to take the main road?"

"Perhaps a little," he grinned, "but it is not any more dangerous than drowning."

Kino shot him a look. "That's not funny."

"Sorry." His grin said otherwise. He stood up, offered her his hand, and pulled her to her feet. "So, are we in agreement?"

Kino hoped that her summers of hiking with Kawika and his older sisters would make this trek less difficult for her. Just last August they had completed Oahu's Olomana Trail, a difficult hike even by experienced adult hikers' standards.

"Yup. Let's take any shortcut we can, even if it's over the Ko'olaus." She picked up her mat and began rolling it. "I want to hurry and get this whole thing over with."

"Splendid. We have only a few hours before nightfall. Let us head north and take the first westward trail we find."

An hour later, the pair arrived at a path heading toward the steep hill. The terrain went from brown, dried sea grasses, light-green plants, sand and rock, to lush, deep-green grass, trees and bushes, the higher they climbed.

When they arrived at a broad landing at the base of the larger mountain, Kauikeaouli stopped the horse and climbed off.

"Why are we stopping?" Kino asked. "We should try and get up there," she pointed up. "We can camp on that ledge."

"It will be dark very soon." The young prince unloaded the sleeping mats.

"That's even more reason for us to hurry!" Kino insisted.

"No. We must stay here and rest for the night. We can start early in the morning."

Kino jumped off the horse. "By morning, we could be on the opposite side of the mountain, instead of just starting out from where we are."

Kauikeaouli shook his head. "I am hungry and tired." He pulled out the bowl and the ipu calabash from the saddlebag.

"Fine. If you change your mind, you know where I'll be," she announced as she walked away, certain he'd follow her. Without bothering to look back, she hurried up the trail. Soon, the path curved past a cluster of tall bushes, blocking her view of Kauikeaouli and the horse.

As Kino climbed higher, darkness continued to descend, shrouding her vision in dusky gray. She shut her eyes for a moment and opened them again, trying to adjust to the lack of light. It was of no use. The only thing she could make out was the contrast between the light, sandy trail and the dark patches of rocks and colorless grass.

She glanced around. No sign of Kauikeaouli. It was too dark to continue at a normal pace, so she decided to find a place to sit and wait, confident that he was on his way. Further up the trail, she spotted a cluster of light-colored boulders. Kino made her way to them and climbed up on top of one. The sound of the ocean whispered in the distance. She pulled her knees to her chest and hugged them. Maybe he was just taking his time; trying to psych her out into thinking he wasn't coming. She expected him to jump out from behind a bush to try to scare her.

After several minutes, Kino gave up on waiting. The trail ran between two coconut trees. She scrambled up the steep incline, and found that it crossed a path leading up the mountain.

Although the sky was layered with thousands of stars, the moonless night seemed to envelop her. A sudden draft of cold air pushed past her. In the distance, she could hear chanting, and thought of the lovely singing she had heard at the pond when she first arrived in 1825.

Could it be? Menehunes?

Kino cupped her hands behind her ears and turned toward the noise. It sounded more intense now, and less melodic. And there was another sound. Something she could not quite place, but she knew she had heard it before.

As the combined noises drew closer, she could see, in the distance, two distinct rows of torches heading toward her. The chanting was drowned out now by something that sounded like it was screaming across and up the mountain. Wind.

The plants and bushes shook and bent as the wind howled. A thick cloud of fog descended in front of her, making it difficult to see the glow of the torches through it. She squinted and hunched over, made her way to the nearest tree, and hugged it. The angry breeze felt as if it were about to blow her off the slope. Yet, it didn't affect the dense cloud that floated a foot off the ground.

In an instant, the space between Kino and the mist became still and silent. The wind sounded muffled, as if someone had covered her and the thick haze with an invisible dome. She watched a wide circle of plants around her frantically shake in silence. The scent of flowers and kukui nut oil filled the air, along with another, more acrid smell that Kino couldn't identify. It put a bad taste in her mouth and she grimaced. The chanting resumed. It came from the approaching fog.

Kino stood there, transfixed. The mist began to swirl toward her like smoke in a jar. Seven-foot-tall, dark-skinned, shirtless men emerged from the cloud. Their tattooed, well-defined muscles glistened with oil that reflected the light from the torches. They wore red loincloths and some donned fierce gourd helmets that partially covered their faces. Two men wearing pointed dog-tooth necklaces blew on large conch shells as they emerged. The other two carried torches. She could see more torches burning in the mist behind them.

Then she noticed something horrifying. These men had no feet. She could see them clear as day, but they had nothing else from the shins down. A cold shiver shot down her spine and her mouth went dry.

Night Marchers!

Her heart leapt into her throat. She stood there, mouth agape, frozen in fear, with her heart beating into her ears. More men emerged from the mist. One of them stopped. She squeezed her eyes shut and prayed that he hadn't seen her.

In an instant, someone tackled her.

That's it. I'm dead now.

Her body hit the ground.

"Curl into a ball and do not look up!" Kauikeaouli commanded. He lifted himself several inches off her. Kino tucked her knees under her body, held her breath and pressed her knuckles against her mouth. It was the only thing she could do to stifle a scream. He covered her once more with his body.

She could feel the intense warmth from the torches on the back of her neck. The heat wavered in the gap between the passing torchbearers. The skin on her neck prickled. Although her eyes were squeezed shut, she could tell that fire was being held just above her.

...And over Kauikeaouli. God, please don't let anything happen to him!

Kino could feel him across her back, weighing her down. It was the only thing that kept her from shaking uncontrollably. She wanted to puke.

It felt like forever before the light moved away. The night air felt cool again. Relieved, she exhaled. Her head felt as though she was spinning.

Kauikeaouli rolled off Kino's back and sat down next to her. She remained in a ball, her nose pressed against the hard earth. Dirt and sand clung to the snot and tears on her face.

"They are gone now. You are safe. You can sit up," he said softly.

She didn't budge. Her heart felt as if it was about to explode out of her chest. She was pretty sure she'd peed a little.

Kauikeaouli put his hand on her shoulder and gently pulled her up, until she was sitting on her knees. Kino wiped her face with the back of her hands, folded her arms across her chest, and shivered. She still felt a little shaky.

"They are gone now. And they will not come back." He patted her shoulder.

"Weren't you scared?" she asked, surprised at his calm demeanor.

"A little, at first." Kauikeaouli said. "But once an ancestor in the procession claimed me, I knew I would go unharmed. So there was nothing to fear. I believe they did not see you."

"Thank GOD!" Kino declared. She sat back, crossed her legs at the ankles, hugged her knees and rocked back and forth.

"Will you be all right?" he asked.

Kino nodded. She just needed a minute to regroup. He waited patiently without a word. She took a deep breath and held it before exhaling slowly several times, in an attempt to resume her heart's normal rhythm.

"Yeah. Thanks," she said at the ground. Then she thought about it for a moment, blinked, and looked up at him. "And thank you, for covering me."

He smiled and said, "No problem-a."

Although she was still shaken, she couldn't help but giggle as she wiped her face on her sleeves.

Kauikeaouli scanned their surroundings. "We will need to stay up here tonight. I cannot see a thing."

Kino replied, "That's what I'd planned to do. I thought you'd eventually follow me up here."

"That's funny – I thought you would eventually come back."

They both laughed for a moment. Then Kauikeaouli said, "No, seriously, I thought you would come back. I set up camp down the hill."

"Why didn't you just bring everything when you came up?" she asked, annoyed.

"I had already finished unpacking everything, thinking you would return. Something spooked the horse and it ran off. Then I saw the torches coming down the mountain. I had a feeling it was the Huakai'po, the procession of spirits of the dead, and I wanted to warn you."

Kino couldn't see his face well, but she could tell by his apologetic tone that he felt bad. In a way, she was glad that he did. He wasn't the one who almost drowned, and he also hadn't faced possible harm by the night marchers. A lump formed in her throat.

He hung his head and said, "I should not have let you go on by yourself. If you had been harmed, that would have been my fault."

Kino's self-pity party was over. She stood up and swallowed the lump.

"No. It's my fault that we're even up here. It was stupid of me to continue. I shouldn't have left you." She offered him her hand. "So, let's figure out where we are going to spend the night." She pulled him to his feet. "We're way too close to the edge here."

They both glanced around. The light sand made the trail fairly easy to see in the starlight, even though they couldn't see much else. Several yards up, the path widened on one side.

They made their way over and found a small turnout that was wide enough for them to lie side by side between the mountain and the trail. Exhausted, Kino unhooked her bag from around her shoulders and let it drop to the ground. Kauikeaouli sat down next to the satchel. She flopped down next to him.

Pulling her dress from the bag, Kino folded it lengthwise and rolled it up, before doing the same to the fabric bag and handing it to him. She picked up her rolled dress, put it on the back of her neck and lied down. He watched her for a moment before tucking the rolled bag under his neck.

The sky was amazing to look at. Thousands of stars covered the moonless sky. Big stars, little stars, ones that twinkled, and others that just shone bright and steady. Kino wished she knew the names of the constellations above her.

"Kino?" Kauikeaouli asked softly.

"Yes?"

"What do you think would have happened to us if the night marchers hadn't recognized either of us?"

Great. She was purposely focusing on the stars so she wouldn't have to think about what had happened earlier. Just a glimmer of the thought itself made her squeamish.

"Shh! I don't want to think about it," Kino said. "Don't ever bring it up again." She hoped he couldn't hear the fear in her voice. "Nothing happened, and we are both fine. Now let's get some sleep, so we can cover as much ground as possible tomorrow." She lay back down and exhaled. Her heart was just starting to slow down to normal.

Kauikeaouli said nothing for a long time. Just when she thought he'd fallen asleep, he said, "I was told I will have to accept the throne – and I don't want to." His voice sounded thick, as if he had something caught in his throat.

Even though she couldn't see him well, she could tell he was frowning. She didn't know what to say; she just wanted to make him feel better. She said brightly, "Well, isn't it a good thing? I mean, I think it would be awesome to be king, or in my case, queen of my own kingdom. My family wouldn't have to struggle to pay bills or worry about having a place to live. And I'd get to do whatever I wanted, whenever I wanted." She reveled in the idea of not having to go to school or do any chores. "And," she continued, "I'd have ice cream for breakfast, lunch and dinner."

He turned his face toward her and asked, "What is ice cream?"

"You don't know what ice cream is?" Kino was shocked. She reminded herself that she was in 1825, and probably no one had introduced this amazing treat to the islands yet.

She faced the stars, closed her eyes, and imagined eating an ice cream cone. "It's sweet, frozen milk made into a creamy texture."

"Frozen milk?"

Kino wanted to smack herself. She had been doing her best to keep their conversations simple, so she wouldn't have to tell him things he would have no idea about.

"Let's just say it's something that's sweet, tastes really good and is super cold." She faked a yawn, "And I'm super tired. Let's try and get some sleep."

Just as she felt herself floating off to dreamland, she heard Kauikeaouli softly say, "Kino?"

She opened her eyes once more and looked at him.

"Yes?" Her voice carried a sharp edge.

"You may call me Kalani," he said quietly.

"What?"

He looked at the sky. "My family calls me Kalani. You may call me that too."

Kino's annoyance dissipated. His cherub-like profile reminded her that despite being the future king, he was still a young boy.

She smiled at him, "Okay, Kalani. Sweet dreams. I'll see you in the morning." Rolling away from him, she closed her eyes and tried to fall asleep. But every time she did, she swore she could hear drum beats. As far as she knew, the marchers only walked in one direction per night. She scooted backwards until her back met his. She felt him lean against her too. Grateful for the comforting support, she finally drifted off.

18

ʻUmikūmāwalu

Kino woke up feeling refreshed and full of hope. Sunlight winked through the treetops above her. The air, alive with the sounds of many kinds of birds singing their melodic songs, felt cool and crisp.

Yawning, she glanced over at Kauikeaouli's empty mat. Next to it lay two ti leaves. A mélange of tropical fruit was piled in the center of one of the leaves. Several bits of pineapple and papaya lay in an arbitrary pattern on a shiny layer of fruit juice on the other. She sat up and ate her breakfast before drinking some of the water that he had left in her ipu.

She stood up, stretched and looked around. Where could he be? He didn't answer, no matter how loud she yelled his name. Kino's contentment was quickly dissolving into anxious frustration. She wanted to get a strong start, first thing in the morning, so that they could get to the next target. With Kauikeaouli gone, they were wasting precious time.

She figured correctly that he would be down by the water she could hear, and made her way toward him.

"Kalani-i-i-i!" she yelled.

The young prince turned toward her and frowned. Placing his hand over his brow, he shielded his eyes from the sun.

At first, Kino thought he'd forgotten that he'd told her to call him that. Then she realized he wasn't looking at her, but at something behind her. She turned, and fear gripped her, freezing her in place. A gnarled old woman dressed all in white stood less than a foot away. Long, stringy gray hair covered her face. The woman stretched out a bony hand and almost touched Kino, who screamed, stumbled backwards, and fell into a bush.

Kauikeaouli rushed over and helped her up.

Kino glanced around her. The woman was gone.

"Where did she go? The old woman?"

"What? Who?" Kauikeaouli asked, looking around as well.

"Didn't you see her? She was right here." Kino pointed at a spot on the ground in front of her.

Kauikeaouli shrugged his shoulders. "No – I just saw you and a strange light that was right behind you. Then you screamed and fell."

Kino scanned her surroundings again. She was certain that an old woman had just tried to touch her. But there was no one else in sight other than Kauikeaouli. Her skin prickled as a chill ran down her spine.

"Did you eat?" Kauikeaouli asked, leading the way up the path to their camp.

"Yup. It was good. Oh, and I packed everything up already. I figured we could just follow the stream, and hopefully make it to the next place before it gets dark."

"Brilliant! Well done," he said over his shoulder.

Kino smiled at the ground as she followed his exact footprints.

They loaded up as before, and headed back to the trail.

*****

Much of the day was spent in concentrated silence. The narrow, uneven trail was not well maintained, forcing them to spend much of the climb on their hands and knees, crawling either under or over fallen trees and branches. Kino had never thought she would wish she had a machete, but she did now.

The overgrown path ran through a wall of red hibiscus trees covered with flowers in full bloom. Most of the foliage started at chest level to Kino, so ducking under the leaves between branches wasn't an issue for her.

Kauikeaouli, too tall to do the same with ease, had no choice but to push through. The trees showed no mercy. Just as he pushed one branch aside, another one followed right behind it, ready to smack him in the face.

At first Kino thought it was funny. All she heard was "shuffle-shuffle-shuffle-OW," every few minutes, but after the fourth thicket she felt bad for him.

"Why don't we stop for a bit and take a break?" she suggested, as they came out of the last row of bushes.

Once they were in the clear, he turned and faced her. She couldn't help but burst out laughing. Yellow, fuzzy dust covered him, from his head down to his hips. It looked as if he had been squinting his eyes and pursing his lips as he went through the ferns, so that when he relaxed his face, his eyes and lips were clean, like a weird, canary-colored ski mask.

He scratched his head. "What is it? Why are you laughing?"

She pointed at one of his arms, covering her giggle with the other hand. Kauikeaouli looked down and saw the layer of pollen covering him. He looked like one of those street performers who spray-paint themselves bronze or silver and act like statues, while tourists take pictures with them for money.

"Augh!" he said, attempting to dust the spores off himself.

She took out a handkerchief from her bag and swatted at the pollen she had on her own clothes. It was barely anything compared to him.

"Here," she handed him the cloth.

He mumbled, "Mahalo," and grumbled under his breath as he wiped at his face and hands.

Kino looked around and spotted a pair of guava trees not far off the trail. The one furthest away had the most, and the ripest fruit.

"Ooh, guava!" she pointed. "Want one?"

"Yes, thank you." He didn't bother looking up. He was too busy trying to shake the pollen from his bare belly.

She walked past the first tree and stopped under the one with the yellowest fruit. There were many golden guavas, but most of them out were of reach. Kino looked up and slowly walked around the tree, looking for the lowest-hanging fruit. She was in luck. A cluster of four yellow orbs dangled just a tiptoe reach away.

She stood under them, took a deep breath and jumped, simultaneously reaching for the fruit. She was able to grab one of them and pulled the branch down enough to where she could stand normally. Clutching the branch, she pulled off one guava, bent her knees and gently dropped it on the ground. She did the same with the next two. Their plump, firm bodies were ripe and ready for the picking. The last one gave Kino trouble. She twisted and turned it, but the stem refused to give. She gave up and let the branch go. It sprang back up and shook the rest of the tree, pelting her with fruit. She stood there for a moment feeling like an idiot. Hopefully, Kauikeaouli wasn't watching.

She glanced back at him. Thankfully, he was still working on dusting off all the pollen. Then, something caught her eye behind him that alarmed her.

Several yards from Kauikeaouli, between a set of paperbark trees, stood the old lady with white hair in a long, white dress. Although her eyes were hidden, Kino swore she felt the woman's stare. A blast of cold shot through Kino's body.

Kino screamed and glanced at Kauikeaouli, who had been dancing around, trying to fend off a bee. He stopped in his tracks and ran over to her. The bee hovered close behind.

"What's wrong?"

Kino's eyes grew larger. "The lady!" She pointed and looked in the direction where she had seen the woman. There was no one there. Kino rubbed her eyes then blinked hard twice. When she looked again, there was nothing but trees.

"I do not see a lady. Maybe you need to rest. And drink some water. Here, sit down."

"I swear," Kino insisted. "There was an old lady dressed all in white. I think it's the same woman I saw earlier."

She plopped her bag and herself down. Was she losing her mind?

Kauikeaouli placed everything down and asked for her ipu. He handed it back to her once he had filled it and she took a sip. Almost immediately, she felt a little more energized. She gulped down the rest of the water greedily. It tasted so good.

They took a short break to eat the guavas and rest their feet, but it wasn't long before Kino insisted they push forward. If the forest was creepy like this during the day, she didn't want to be in it at night.

It was nearly dark before they reached the top of the gorge in the center of the island. The Kipapa Gulch, their next destination, was the scene of one of the bloodiest battles in old Hawaii. Kipapa meant "the paved way," as in the bodies of the dead paved the area after the battle.

Although Kino had never been there, she had heard stories and legends about the spirits that still lingered in the area. She didn't remember any story specifically, just that the area was one of the most haunted places on Oahu, according to the TV news. That's why she had insisted that they camp out before heading into the gulch.

They ate in silence, both exhausted from the day's hike. Kino found herself zoning out, staring at the dancing flames.

Kauikeaouli lay on his back, looking up at the stars. "Do you really have to go back?"

Kino's mind snapped back to the present. "What?"

Kauikeaouli said, "Do you really have to go back? You can stay and live at the palace."

Kino reclined on her mat and looked at the night sky too.

"I have to go back," she said. She felt hollow. "I really miss my family."

"You do not like it here?" he asked, turning on his side to face her.

"It's amazing to see Hawaii during this time." She rolled and faced him. "But I don't belong here. I need to get back before my family finds a new place to live without me."

Kauikeaouli propped himself up on one elbow. "If you stay, you never ever have to worry about having a place to live, or money... or seeing those mean girls again." He put his finger in the air. "And," he added, "You can help me rule the kingdom. I cannot do it alone."

She propped herself up on her elbow too and looked at him.

"Yes, you can. You become one of Hawaii's most influential kings ever."

"Ever?"

"Ever," she nodded.

His eyes sparkled in the firelight as he stared off for a moment, then he returned his gaze toward her. "I still wish you could stay." He rolled onto his back and let out a big yawn, while stretching his arms over his head and pointing his toes.

Kino lay back down as well. Her eyelids felt heavy and her mind started to drift.

She listened to his deep, slow breath, and she soon found herself breathing in rhythm. Then she rolled onto her stomach, and soon drifted off to dreamland.

Suddenly she couldn't breathe. Or move. Or open her eyes. Someone or something was pressing on her back. Then the pressure worsened, as if someone had sat on her.

Was Kauikeaouli lying on her? Her heart started racing. Was she dreaming?

She struggled to move her arms and open her eyes. On instinct, she immediately started reciting the Lord's Prayer in her mind. The pressure subsided a bit and she opened her eyes. Kauikeaouli lay just a few feet away from her, sleeping soundly.

Terrified, she tried to scream, but nothing would come out. Her rapid heartbeat banged in her ears. Still praying, she clenched her hands into tight fists, squeezed her eyes shut and flipped herself over just as cold, unseen hands wrapped around her throat.

She gasped for air, but she felt what little breath she had in her lungs escape instead. She didn't dare open her eyes, as she knew that the image would give her nightmares. Something breathed its hot, fetid breath on her face. The stench made her want to throw up.

The icy grip around Kino's throat tightened, as images of her past flashed before her still-closed eyes. Brief snapshots of her mom making dinner, her first visit to Hawaii, playing with a little girl from across the street. Then saying goodbye to her friends in California, moving into a run-down house, and that little neighbor, now several years older, surrounded by her friends Cyan, Tiffany, and Chanel.

Finally, an image of her grandfather in the hospital flashed into her mind, and she realized that she couldn't let anything stop her from completing her quest. She felt herself get hot and angry.

ENOUGH!

She wasn't sure if she said it aloud, or just in her head. A loud piercing screech filled her ears.

She opened her eyes just as something gray and misty drew back and disappeared into the night, chased by a large owl.

Kino bolted upright. Her heart was beating so hard that she could see her shirt palpitating. She looked over at Kauikeaouli, who was still fast asleep.

"Kalani!" She shook his shoulder. "Wake up!"

"Huh?" he sat up. "What is going on? Is it morning already?"

"No. But we need to stay awake."

"What? What are you talking about? It is still nighttime," he rolled onto his back. "Time to sleep." He closed his eyes and smiled contentedly.

"No," Kino insisted, shaking him again.

"I couldn't remember what Makani had said about this place exactly – until now. She said if we saw the lady in white, we shouldn't fall asl…"

"I do not recall anything like that. And I did not see the lady; you did. Or at least you say you did." He kept his eyes shut as he spoke. "You just had a bad dream."

"It wasn't a dream," she insisted. "I remember now – she told Sophie and me. But it doesn't matter; we just shouldn't go to sleep until we are far from here," Kino pleaded.

Kauikeaouli rolled his head toward her and opened one eye.

"I am tired. I am going to sleep. Wake me if anything exciting happens."

Kino insisted, "You don't understand. I was just choked! I fell asleep and felt like someone was sitting on me. Next thing you know, I felt something squeezing my throat. I couldn't breathe!"

Kauikeaouli yawned, "It was all just a bad dream." He reached over and patted her foot. "Goodnight. Go to sleep."

He rolled onto his side and faced his back to her.

It was no use. She was exhausted and didn't want to spend any of her remaining strength arguing. It didn't matter too much; she would just have to guard him.

Kino sat for a few minutes, just staring at the ground. She felt heavy, and she really wanted to lie down and close her eyes. But she didn't dare. She didn't want to risk another encounter with whatever had choked her. Just thinking about it made the hair on the back of her neck prickle.

She then spent the next several hours fighting sleep. She started to lean over to one side, without noticing at first. Gravity was beckoning her to give in. When she realized what was happening, she immediately sat upright and slapped her cheeks.

Soon she found herself leaning over once more. This time she stood up and shook her entire body, as if she were doing the hokey pokey. Her body felt weak. She did some leg lifts and stretches, trying to get some circulation into her muscles.

The fire had died to down to smoldering embers, so she added more wood and poked at it until flames appeared, then she stood there staring blankly at the flames. Her eyes felt dry and stung a little.

Kauikeaouli stirred in his sleep. Kino looked down at his sleeping form. He was curled on his side and had his hands in prayer position under his head. His round, boyish features appeared almost angelic. It was hard to believe that in just a few days he would become King Kamehameha III.

Tired of standing, she headed over to a nearby tree and sat at the base of it. Kauikeaouli snorted, turned on his back, chuckled then rolled onto his side, facing Kino. At first she thought he was waking up, and waited for him to say something. But instead he exhaled and snorted once more. Then he farted.

Kino giggled. He may be the next king of Hawaii, but he really was just a kid – a kid who didn't want to be king. She knew *that* feeling. Not the king part, but what it felt like to be thrust into a situation without any say in the matter.

Hues of light blue, pale yellow and gold started pushing away the gray at the horizon and pierced through the clouds as the sun slowly emerged. She looked at the changing colored sky.

Maybe this thing only attacks at night. Hopefully.

Either way, the approaching dawn gave her great relief. She settled back against the tree. Her eyelids felt so heavy that she had to lift her eyebrows every time she blinked. She slapped her cheeks again.

Focus on something else.

She looked at Kauikeaouli. Kino didn't know a lot about him in history, other than that he was the second son of Kamehameha the Great and that he was proclaimed king at age eleven. And she knew that he had brought back old customs, like dancing the hula, after they were banned shortly after Christian missionaries had arrived in the islands.

King Kamehameha III was the monarch who had allowed land to be purchased by foreigners, which helped transition Hawaii into a more attractive place for industries, such as ranching and agricultural farms, which still exist. He also penned the state motto: Ua Mau ke Ea o ka 'Āina i ka Pono. Kino couldn't remember its exact translation, just something about the life of the land being preserved in righteousness.

Beyond that, she didn't know much else about him or the Hawaiian monarchy. Her class was just starting to study Hawaiian history, but they were still covering ancient times.

Her eyes glazed over as she imagined the king on a fancy, jewel-encrusted throne in a big, stone castle. Then she remembered that it was Hawaii, so it would be more like a woven chair in a grass hut. Kino wasn't sure. She liked her own version better: Kauikeaouli in medieval royal clothing and a gold-and-red velvet crown on his head, like the old kings of England.

Her blinking gradually slowed down as her lids started to spend more than a couple of seconds shut at a time. This added to the temptation to doze off, so she tried squinting each eye separately instead. From far away, Kino looked as if she was winking at the ground. Soon that slowed too.

I'm not going to fall asleep. I'm just going to rest my eyes.

She let her eyes relax and remain closed. Instantly, she felt relief. Her body felt lighter, as though she were floating on the breeze. She continued to drift, then felt as if she'd started to fall. A hand grabbed her shoulder.

Kino screamed and opened her eyes.

Kauikeaouli withdrew his hand with a look of shock and surprise on his face.

"What is wrong?"

Kino stood up quickly. She felt embarrassed, but tried to play it cool. "What? Oh that. I-I was having a bad dream. I'm fine." She pushed past him and started rolling up her sleeping mat. "Let's get going. I want to find the next thing and get as far away from this place as possible."

19

ʻUmikūmāiwa

Low clouds skimmed the top of the gulch, casting a dank gloom over the mountain and shrouding their descent into the canyon the next morning. The plan was for Kino and Kauikeaouli to get down into the gulley and locate the next object, then make their way out before sunset. But the narrow trail was wet and slippery, causing them to go slower than they had planned.

Halfway down, Kino asked, "What is it that we're supposed to find again?"

Kauikeaouli pulled out the piece of paper from his bag, and read it without bothering to stop.

"It says we have to find a special black pōhaku," he called over his shoulder.

Kino scanned the rock-lined trail. Further ahead lay the river, which meant even more rocks. "How are we supposed to do that?"

"I don't know." Kauikeaouli jerked back, then leaned forward, as he almost lost his footing. "Whoa!" He grabbed an overhanging tree branch to catch himself. "Be careful right here – it's really slippery." Stepping off the path, he carefully made his way around an elongated slick of mud by walking through the bushes.

"What did you say?" Kino asked, rushing to catch up.

"I said watch out for the…"

Her foot hit the wet stretch of dirt. She yelped, slid forward, lost her balance, tumbled once, and skidded the rest of the way down.

"Kino!" Kauikeaouli hurried onto the dry trail.

Wincing, Kino pushed herself up from the ground to a sitting position. Dirty scratches and abrasions made the skin on her palms sting. Her body ached and her head throbbed. Blood, mixed with the mud and dirt, oozed from the patch of missing skin on her right elbow, matching the long strip of bloodied, exposed flesh that ran from the side of her right knee and up her thigh.

Exhausted from not having slept the night before, and now hurt and filthy, she bit her bottom lip to avoid crying. Unable to control her emotions, she wept hot, salty tears that ran down her face and splashed small, clean circles on her mud-covered lap.

The journey had been a lot harder on her than she had expected. So far, all she had found was the first element of her search, and they still had much farther to go. She was tired and didn't want to continue. So what if she's stuck here. Staying in 1825 was a far easier option than trying to get back to modern time.

Then Kino thought of her mom, and Gramma and Grandpa. She missed them so much that her heart ached. She sobbed even harder.

Kauikeaouli ran and knelt beside her, his brows knitted with concern. "Are you all right?"

She nodded and shuddered as she inhaled.

"You are hurt. Here," he pulled his special ipu, whispered a prayer, then poured water on her legs.

Kino grimaced as the ice-cold liquid touched her scraped skin. At first it felt really good. Then it started to sting. "Ow, it's burning! Stop!" She rolled her knees away.

"Shhhh. Hold still and close your eyes," Kauikeaouli insisted, as he pushed her legs back up. The water gushed down from his ipu as if it were flowing from a bottomless container. Kino swore she heard a sizzling sound, like steak frying in a pan. Steam rose from her wounds. The boy continued to pour until the noise and smoky tendrils subsided then withdrew his ipu.

Kino's knees felt cool and tingly. Her eyes grew bigger when she looked down. Her limbs were wet, but aside from that, they were completely intact. No sign of broken skin, not even a scar lingered.

"How the heck…" She stopped herself. She already knew that the answer had something to do with his sacred mana.

Kauikeaouli held up his ipu. "Now hold still so I can wash the rest of your wounds."

She gazed at him in wonder as he tended to her elbow and palms. When he sat back, she looked down.

"Wow, thanks!" She admired the front and back of her hands. "That was amazing."

Kauikeaouli poured water into Kino's ipu before handing it to her. She drank greedily. The refreshing liquid did more than quench her parched throat – it completely restored her energy. When she had finished, she wiped her mouth with the back of her hand and asked, "So what now? How do we find a rock among rocks?"

"I am unsure." Kauikeaouli stood up and waded into the shallow stream. Standing in knee-high water, he scanned the banks on each side. "Maybe we should head downstream?"

She joined him in the water. "How do you know it's downstream and not upstream?"

They both looked up and down the narrow waterway.

"Well, we could either split up and meet back here in a bit, or we can head in one direction, and if we are unable to find it in a few hours, we can return here," he suggested.

Kino didn't like the idea of separating, and the second option seemed like it would take a lot of precious time. "Too bad we can't flip for it," she said.

"Flip for it?"

"Yes, you know, with a coin?" She pantomimed a coin toss with her thumb.

"Do you have one?" he asked.

"No. Maybe we should do rock, paper, scissors."

Before he could ask what that was, a butterfly – with the same vibrant red, green and gold colors and markings as Kauikeaouli's monarchs – flew between them, and hovered at eye level, before fluttering to the opposite bank.

They both stared at it, transfixed. The butterfly flew back between them, paused then returned to the other side once more.

"I think it wants us to follow it," Kauikeaouli said, without taking his eyes off the insect.

Kino admired the rich, velvet colors of the butterfly then remembered the pueo, the owl that had guided her. "I think you're right."

"It may be a ho'ailona, a spirit that helps people of great mana with signs from nature." He crossed to the other bank. "We must go." He picked up a smooth, gray rock on the water's edge, paused, bowed his head, then continued the slow pursuit, through the trees and off the beaten trail. Several minutes later they arrived at a clearing.

A stout tree stump of a beautiful rainbow eucalyptus sat in the center. In the middle of the tree's multicolored rings sat a rich, black rock, just a bit larger than Kino's palm. It had the same concave design as the rock her grandmother had given her, as well as the ribbon of gold that ran throughout the stone.

The butterfly fluttered over the rock and then touched down on it, keeping its wings up. Kino noticed that the design of the white-and-black markings made it look as if it had an eye on the underside of each wing.

She had walked up to the stump and started to reach for the rock, when Kauikeaouli stopped her hand with his.

"We cannot just take this sacred pōhaku. We must leave something in its place as a ho'okupu... an offering." He held up the smooth rock that he had picked from the water's edge. "We must also offer our promise to cherish and care for the item we are removing." He handed her the stone. "Fill your heart with aloha as you offer this pōhaku."

She held it in her hands, and silently promised and offered it her aloha. While exchanging the rocks, she wordlessly thanked the spirits of the land.

Kauikeaouli opened the container that held the blue flower from Mokoli'i Island. Kino placed the black rock in it and let out a sigh of relief. Kauikeaouli closed the container, secured the lid then grinned.

"Two down, two to go."

20

Iwakālua

"We need to be careful." Kauikeaouli wiped his mouth with the back of his hand and stood up. "Surely, by now, people are looking for me. The last thing we need is to get caught."

Kino nodded in agreement. She finished her mouthful of mountain apple and pushed herself up. "Where are we heading to next?" she asked, scanning the terrain.

Kauikeaouli pointed west at the mountain range in the distance. "Do you see that point?"

She shaded her eyes with her hands. "You mean there? The highest peak on that mountain?"

"Yes."

Kino groaned and smacked herself in the forehead. "Of *course* it's the at the top of the tallest mountain." Her tone dripped with sarcasm.

Kauikeaouli looked amused.

"WHY," she threw her arms outward dramatically, "is it always at the top or bottom of hard places to reach?" Unhooking her ipu, she held out it out as Kauikeaouli poured water into it from his own.

"Thanks!" She gave him a nod and drank from her gourd. The ice-cold liquid calmed and refreshed her. It was as if the wondrous water had washed away her frustration.

She exhaled deeply then looked at the mountain peak once more. It was still a formidable undertaking that she wasn't looking forward to, but at least it no longer annoyed her to look at it.

They followed the dirt road past cultivated fields of sugarcane, pineapple, and dry-land taro. Interspersed between the fields were random clusters of shade trees and other natural brush. The road curved around a tight cluster of banana trees.

As they approached the turn, Kauikeaouli paused. "Do you hear that?"

Kino tuned in to the sound of horses trotting toward them. The trees blocked the view of the road on the other end of the curve.

Kauikeaouli grabbed her hand and pulled her into the dark grove. The canopy of low-reaching leaves provided good cover for them to spy from. They knelt at the base of a broad tree in the center, and watched as a trio on horseback came into view.

"Maleko!" Kauikeaouli whispered the name like it was a curse.

The leader of the group had a square jaw, thick neck, and broad shoulders. He rode in front, followed by two men with tattoos on their muscular arms and legs, wearing matching dark-brown loincloths.

"What did you say?" Kino whispered back. She glanced at him, uncertain if he had sneezed or actually said something.

His eyes never left the three men. He knitted his brows and said, in a low voice, "Maleko is the head of the royal guard, and those are his men. I had a feeling we would run into them sooner or later. He always returns me to the palace when he catches me."

The pair watched as the lead man signaled the other two to slow down. He then nodded at the smaller cluster of trees on the other side of the road. Each guard rode to the grove they were nearest to. The one that approached wore an elaborate tribal tattoo across his right bicep. Kino and Kauikeaouli ducked down lower as Maleko slowed the horse and peeked through the trees at the edge of the grove.

Both men returned to their leader. Maleko guided his horse in front, and they resumed walking.

Kino felt something land on her back and crawl down her shirt. She almost let out a scream. Kauikeaouli quickly put his hand over her mouth, stifling her to a short yelp.

Maleko held his hand up. The guards stopped. Kino could feel her heartbeat in her ears as she and Kauikeaouli froze. It was dark enough in the center where they crouched not to be seen at first glance. But any sudden movement would easily give away their position.

Whatever had fallen down the back of her shirt now crawled around to her belly. It felt like it had a bunch of legs. She bit her

KINO and the KING

bottom lip and clenched both hands into fists. It took everything she had not to jump up, scream and tear her shirt off. She let out a slight squeak. Kauikeaouli shot her a look and increased his pressure over her mouth. She held her breath and didn't move a muscle.

The guard peeked around the trees one more time, shook his head then joined the other men. Maleko kicked his horse into a trot and the guards followed.

Kauikeaouli released his hold on her. She exhaled. A long, bright-red centipede fell from the bottom hem of Kino's t-shirt and landed on her feet.

Gross!

Kino glanced at the road. The men were now a safe distance away and out of earshot. She recoiled and ran screaming out of the grove. Once away from the trees, she shook herself and her shirt out while jumping and wriggling, all the while yelping, "Ew, ew, ew, ew, ew."

Kauikeaouli giggled, watching her freak out.

Bending at the waist, Kino tossed her hair forward so that it hung over the top of her head, and shook her fingers through her tresses while swinging her body from side to side. She didn't care if she looked insane. Finally, she flipped her head back and stood upright.

Kauikeaouli hunched over, clutched his stomach and howled with laughter.

Kino planted her fists on her hips. "Done yet?"

He covered his mouth with his hand as he struggled to catch his breath. Wiping tears from his eyes, he excused himself and walked toward the bushes, saying something about "making mimi." Kauikeaouli returned a minute later, still chuckling and shaking his head.

He looked at her and pursed his lips. His eyes grew larger as the corners of his mouth turned upward. "Umm, your ah," he motioned at her head.

"What?" She raised an eyebrow at him.

"Ah," he again indicated at her head. "Here, hold still."

He put an arm on her shoulder, and with his free hand, pulled something out of her hair and tossed it in the grass. As soon as it left his hand she let out a shriek, jumped backward, and broke into another crazy bug dance.

"Ew, ew, ew, ew, ew!" She flicked her hair with her fingers.

"Do not be alarmed – that spider was harmless." Kauikeaouli walked over to the grass where the spider had landed. As he neared it, the brown arachnid ran away and up a tree.

Kino's eyes bugged out. She swore it was the size of a tuna can. "Spiders give me the heebie-jeebies." She folded her arms and rubbed her shoulders.

"Heebie-jeebies?"

"Yes, you know, like when something makes your skin crawl." She felt itchy just saying that. She scratched at her arms without thinking. Before he could say anything she said, "Imagine lying in a tub full of centipedes. Picture how it would feel with all those creepy legs climbing all over your body."

He paused, looked off for a second then shuddered.

"THAT," she said, "is the heebie-jeebies."

He gave her a knowing nod.

As they made their way across the valley, Kino asked the prince questions about his life and family. He told her about his early childhood in a place called Oʻoma, Kekaha on the island of Hawaii. Kauikeaouli explained that he had lived with another chief's family until he was five, and then went to live in Kailua, Kona after his brother Liholiho became king.

"What was it like being the son of King Kamehameha? It must have been pretty awesome!"

He looked at her for a second then chuckled as if he had just caught the punch line to a joke.

"I am still getting accustomed to the colorful way you speak." Kauikeaouli scratched the back of his head. "I guess you could say it was awe-some." He broke the word up into two distinct syllables. "I did not have much time to get to know him, as he died when I was just three years old. But it is an honor to have his bloodline, and his mana."

Kino could tell by his tone that her companion held his father in great reverence despite hardly knowing him. The boy continued to walk with a far-off look in his eye, as if visiting memories. Then he stopped and asked, "Do people in your time know of Kamehameha the Great?"

"Pffftt – who DOESN'T know about Kamehameha the Great." Kino said, "He is so famous, he has his own holiday!"

"Really? Like St. Patrick's Day?"

Kino thought that was a funny holiday to pick – she would have opted for Christmas or Easter, or at least Halloween.

"Sort of. It's a day where the people of Hawaii honor and celebrate the man who united all the islands. There are parades, festivities, hula performances, and different cultural events. There's even a big festival, a ho'olaule'a. And people make really long strands of leis and drape it on his statue. By the end of the lei ceremony, you can barely see his face. Just his helmet."

Kauikeaouli said in wonder, "A statue?"

Kino nodded. "A tall monument. I've seen the one in Honolulu. It is supposed to be a replica of the one on the Big Island."

A broad smile swept across Kauikeaouli's face. "Really? What does it look like?"

Kino stopped walking. "He stands like this, holding a spear with his hand held out." She stretched her right arm out with her fingers together and turned her hand upward. Then she made a fist with her left hand, and put it next to her left shoulder as if holding an umbrella.

"He's dressed in a gold malo, with matching cape and helmet. I think the whole thing is bronze. And it's tall. Like super, super tall." She broke her pose, stretched her arms up and swiped the air above him sideways.

His eye grew wider and wider every time she said "super." He grinned from ear to ear. Kino resumed her pose.

"So the statue is like this, on this tall pedestal stand, taller than you. On Kamehameha Day, people hang beautiful leis all over his neck and shoulders," she gestured, slowly sweeping her left hand down the front of her body, "and all down his arm to his wrist," as she waved her hand under the length of her extended right arm as if revealing a game show prize. "And that's just on Oahu. I think all of the other islands have similar celebrations too." She dropped her arms and resumed walking.

"That is really," he hesitated for a second, "cool."

It was Kino's turn for a broad smile.

"What is the date of his day?" he asked.

The deadline for the writing contest was the day before Kamehameha Day. Kino had noticed that when she wrote it on the calendar in her room.

"Wait. You have to promise me that if I tell you, you cannot do anything with this information." She held her gaze steady.

"Why not?"

"Because I don't think you were the one who created this holiday."

He held up his hand. "I swear I will not do anything with the information you are about to tell me."

Kino raised an eyebrow and asked, "And what happens if you break your promise?"

Kauikeaouli answered solemnly, "May my teeth be gnashed on a rock and my eyes gouged out with pointed sticks."

Kino hesitated then said, "June eleventh."

He smiled, "It will be June soon."

For the first time since she arrived, Kino thought about the date. Until now, it had never occurred to her to ask what day it was; she was too focused on getting home.

"What is today's date?"

Kauikeaouli mumbled to himself softly, as if he was thinking aloud. Then he announced, "Today is the twenty-ninth of May."

"I really need to get back. If it's the same date where I came from, my family has to move in two days. I don't know if we even have a new place to live yet." She walked faster. "Besides, my mom and grandma are probably worried crazy, and wondering what happened to me."

Kauikeaouli caught up to her. "I wish I could do something about that. Maybe I should not allow foreigners to buy land, and just keep it all in the kingdom."

"No!" Kino shook her head. "This is the reason why I didn't want to tell you anything. You cannot do anything different than what your gut, or heart, or whatever helps you make decisions, tells you to do.

"If you don't divide the land, progress won't happen, and all of the people I know wouldn't exist. Neither would I. Everyone I know in

Hawaii is a mix of different races and nationalities who all came to the..." Kino almost mentioned the plantations, but caught herself just in time. "The islands. They mixed, mingled, and married other races. Just like my grandma's family. Her mom was Hawaiian, Portuguese, and Chinese."

"Portugal and China. Those are countries a great distance away. People from there come here?"

"Yes," she nodded. "And many other cultures do also. Hawaii is called the 'melting pot of the Pacific' because there are so many different blends of people."

"I understand now," Kauikeaouli said. "It is one thing that I would affect Hawaii's future by knowing too much, but it did not occur to me that anything I did could drastically affect you, even your very existence."

She nodded. "Exactly."

21

Iwakāluakūmākahi

The pair took shortcuts through several fields before getting back on the main road. Up ahead, two boys stood over a man, cowering on his knees. While the taller kid laughed, the shorter one kicked dirt in the man's face.

Kino pointed. "Is that Manu and Pono?"

"AY!" Kauikeaouli yelled, stuck thumb and pinky in his mouth and made a loud whistle. The two boys stopped. "What is going on here?" The young prince motioned at the man covered from head to toe in a layer of red dust.

Kino felt bad for the man and went to help him. Manu stopped her.

"'Ho'opau!" he held his palm up. "Do not come any closer. This man is kauwa. He is unclean."

"Of course he's unclean! You guys have been kicking dust on him!" She rushed toward the man. She reached for his arm then hesitated. His right hand was missing; his arm ended at the wrist.

"What are you doing?" Pono pushed Kino.

"Ay! Don't touch her!" Kauikeaouli stepped between her and Pono, who was almost a head taller than him. It didn't stop Kauikeaouli from puffing up his chest and standing more erect. The taller boy looked down his nose at him.

"Why are you defending her? She is a commoner who touched a slave after I told her not to. They should both be punished." He advanced toward Kino again.

Kauikeaouli barked, "Lawa! Enough." He held his arm against the taller boy's chest. Pono didn't dare go further. The man remained crouched on the ground.

The young prince demanded, "Why are you mocking this kāne?"

Pono said, "We caught him stealing aliʻi guava."

Kauikeaouli looked at the trembling man and asked him something in Hawaiian.

The man shook his head desperately and spoke fast. Based on his actions and gestures, it looked as though he had simply been walking along when a guava fell and hit him on the head. He had picked it up just as the boys found him.

Kauikeaouli said to him, "E ae mai iaʻu eʻike. Let me see it."

The man held the yellow guava up. Kino took it from him since she was the closest. Her fingertips sank into the overripe flesh as she handed it to Kauikeaouli.

He examined it, picked up a similarly aged guava from the road and compared the two. He smelled both fruits and declared, "This man is telling the truth."

Kino asked, "How do you know?"

Kauikeaouli said, "The ground has not been disturbed around any of these trees." He pointed at the moist earth a few feet away. There were footprints on the ground but none that led off the road. "And the branches that hang over the trail are too high, even for you, Pono."

The taller boy stretched his arm up and stood on his toes. His fingertips barely brushed the lowest-hanging leaves.

"This fruit was not plucked fresh from the tree," Kauikeaouli lifted the guava. "It is clearly old and not fit for aliʻi. And based on the condition of the other ones on the ground, this one has fallen recently. Look."

He turned the yellow orb over. "The guava this man had only has a slight mark where it hit the ground." He presented the wide, mushy spot on the one he had picked up. "This other one has been there for more than a day. I believe him when he said he did not pick it from the tree." He handed it back to the man, who dropped to both knees and cupped it to his chest.

Kino could see that the poor man was shaking. "Why can't he have a better-looking fruit? One that isn't so rotten?" She stepped off the road and headed toward the nearest tree. Manu stopped her.

"What are you doing? You are not ali'i! You are not allowed to…"

Kino withdrew her hand. He was right. She wasn't royalty, and it wasn't her fruit to give away. Returning to the group, she pulled open the bag on Kauikeaouli's shoulder.

"He can have one of mine. I picked them yesterday." She fished around and pulled out two guavas. They looked a lot healthier and way more edible than the one the man held.

"Here," she held them out. The man looked up at her then at Manu and Pono, who stood motionless. He glanced at Kauikeaouli, then back at Kino, and reached a tentative hand halfway.

She looked at the boys. "Can you tell him it's okay?"

Pono said, "E ala."

The man slowly stood up, but kept his head lowered.

She stepped closer and offered him the guavas. He took them and put the fruit in the crook of his arm without a hand, and held it against his body.

"Mahalo, mahalo, mahalo." The man bowed toward her every time he said the word.

"Hele aku," Pono said with a nod. The man genuflected once more then ran away.

Pono turned to Kino and demanded, "How dare you do that? You are fortunate that these are not the old days – I could have had you put to death for defying me!"

She held her ground. "Sorry, but no one deserves to be bullied like that. You wouldn't like it if it someone did that to you."

Kauikeaouli stepped between the bickering pair. "Enough," he said firmly. "This is not the old days, so calm down. And Kino, Pono is right. You should not speak to an ali'i like that."

"But," she protested, "that guava was gross. And it's not like anybody would miss one."

She held an upturned hand toward the grove. All of the trees were full, and by the looks of the rotting fruit on the ground around the trunks, no one had bothered to harvest the trees. "Besides, would you eat the piece of fruit he found?"

Manu said, "That is not the point. That man does not deserve to eat the food of the aliʻi, or even the makaʻāinana. He is fortunate to get any scraps."

The makaʻāinana must be the regular people. So the kauwa must be the slave class.

Kino rubbed her temples. This debate was giving her a headache and costing precious time. She decided to concede.

"Look, I'm sorry if I did anything to offend anyone. I won't do it again." She glanced at Kauikeaouli, "We really need to go."

"Where are you going?" Pono asked.

"We need to get to the top of Mount Kaʻala to get a special fern," Kauikeaouli said.

Kino wished it were as easy as it sounded.

Pono said, "We are going swimming. Want to join us?"

"No, thanks, we really need to go," Kino said. Kauikeaouli nodded.

They said their goodbyes and went their separate ways. A few yards out, Pono turned and said, "Oh, when you get to Kaʻala, beware of Kamapuaʻa. I hear he likes the taste of children."

Kino frowned at Kauikeaouli. The young prince shook his head and said "Don't listen to him, Kamapuaʻa is a legend."

Kino said, "So are Night Marchers, and I saw those!"

*****

It was dusk when they reached the base of Mt. Kaʻala. The dense forest canopy kept most of the sunlight out, making the soil damp and muddy in places. Kino didn't mind. The humidity was a nice relief from the dry, dusty road they had been on. Her sinuses had been hurting from sneezing all day.

They located a narrow stream running down the mountain that someone had dammed up with rocks, creating a makeshift tub wide enough for two people. The design allowed the water to splash down from the hill above, into the pool, then over the rocks again to continue on. Not far from the rock tub was a tiered landing, flat enough for them to set up camp.

"Shall I put the mats here?" Kauikeaouli asked, pointing at the ground in front of him.

"No," she shook her head. "We should get further away from the water. There are some puddles near the water that look like they've been there awhile. I don't want to get eaten by mosquitos."

Kauikeaouli lifted an inquisitive eyebrow. "Mosquitos? Who or what is that?"

Kino was about to unfurl her mat when she paused. Come to think about it, she had not seen or been pestered by any the entire trip. She knew there had been something missing every night: the annoying, incessant, high-pitched buzz of the blood-sucking insects. For that she was grateful. They must have been brought to Hawaii at a later time.

"Mosquitoes are tiny, horrible, flying bugs that live on blood. Their bite leaves a super itchy welt on your skin."

Kauikeaouli made a face. "That sounds terrible. I am glad we have no such things." He unfurled his mat and sat down. "Is their bite painful?"

Kino unrolled her mat and sat down across from him. "You usually don't feel it until it's too late. But sometimes you can feel a tiny pinch. That's when you go BAM!" She slapped herself on the thigh.

Kauikeaouli flinched when she did that then chuckled. "What happens when there are a lot of mosquitoes?"

She looked at him for a second then slapped her body all over with both hands. He howled with glee and did the same to himself. She laughed, smacking herself faster. A wide grin wiped across his face. He sped up his patting. Soon they were going crazy hitting themselves silly. They both rolled backwards and laughed hysterically.

After dinner they lounged around the fire. Kino felt full and content. They had covered a lot of ground during the day, and their progress pleased her. She looked across the flames at Kauikeaouli, who seemed to be zoning out. He appeared different somehow.

Her mind flashed back to the memory of him taking control of the day's situations. She had to admit, it was impressive. She wished she had been as confident when she was eleven. Maybe then, Maylani wouldn't have intimidated her as much as she did.

Once again, she fought the reflex to roll her eyes at the sound of that name. She couldn't help herself. The image of her nemesis popped into her brain. Maylani Cho, in all her stuck-up glory, wearing her trademark scowl with her Louis Vuitton backpack on her shoulders.

But Kino had known her as an entirely different person.

Her mental image of Maylani now morphed into a much younger and shorter version, back when Maylani Cho was still Nalani May Rodrigues, a girl with glasses and a gap-toothed smile.

They played constantly for the first few summers that Kino visited. From the end of June until the second week of August, they made mud pies, rode their bikes and ran in the sprinklers. But as they grew older, their interests changed.

Nalani became interested only in playing dress-up; coming with up grand scenarios of a lavish lifestyle and fancy things she clearly didn't have but wanted. Kino would always suggest that they play outside, but she would end up giving in to Nalani's insistence. Then they'd spend the next hour or two playing with Nalani's Hello Kitty makeup set, while Nalani complained about her glasses and the gap in her teeth.

Kino recalled that every time she played over at Nalani's house, her parents were usually fighting. It wasn't bad at first, when she was younger. The arguments worsened over the years, though, and so did Nalani's bossiness. Then one summer Kino found out that Nalani's parents had divorced, and a new family had moved into the house across the street. That's when she met Kawika.

She didn't see Nalani again until last summer when she was at Ala Moana, the open-air shopping mall. Kino outwardly cringed at the thought of that moment.

Her mom needed to return something at a store, so Kino asked if she could get an ice cream cone and just sit outside to wait. It was a hot summer day, and although she sat in the shade, the cold treat melted quickly, trickling little rivulets of runny chocolate in several places. Kino twisted the cone, lapping at the flows. A familiar shrill laugh made her look up from her battle with the liquefying chocolate.

Coming toward her, in the midst of similarly styled girls, was her old friend Nalani.

Even without the glasses, Kino recognized her former playmate. She stood up in excitement and the top scoop of ice cream tumbled off her cone. Instinctively, she leaned forward at the hips and caught it between her hand and shirt. The cone in her opposite hand dribbled a river of chocolate down her wrist. Without thinking, she returned the scoop to the cone and slurped the dripping ice cream off her hand, unknowingly smearing the chocolate all over her mouth.

Nalani's face brightened as she saw her, until one of the girls scrunched up her face like she tasted something gross said, "Umm, do you know that girl, Maylani?"

Cyan!

Nalani hesitated and shook her head. By now the group stood only a few feet away from Kino.

"Nalani! It's me!" Kino gushed, looking into her old friend's eyes.

For a moment, she swore she had seen a glimmer of a connection, when Tiffany interrupted,

"She's probably mental. Just ignore her, Maylani."

Kino tried one more time. "Nalani! Don't you remember me? Kino? You used to live in Kalihi…"

"I'm not Nalani. My name is MAY-lani. And I live in Kahala, not Kalihi. You have the wrong person." She folded her arms and looked hard at Kino, then walked away. The rest of the crew scoffed then followed Maylani into the store.

Kino's mom later told her that Nalani/Maylani's mom had remarried, and that her new husband made a lot of money. It was during that time that Nalani had reinvented herself and transformed from nerdy, with gapped teeth, to stylish, with straight teeth. She had also traded her heavy, dark-framed glasses for contact lenses. Kino wished she could just revamp herself like that.

Enough. Stop thinking about Maylani. She shook her fingers through her hair, rolled onto her back and gazed up at the stars. All around her, crickets droned their incessant chirp. She could hear Kauikeaouli's even breathing. The rhythmic sounds soothed her and quieted her thoughts, so that she closed her eyes and soon fell asleep.

*****

"Are we almost there yet?" Kino huffed, as she continued the climb to the summit.

"Yes, it is not much further." Kauikeaouli called over his shoulder. Moments later they arrived at the top.

"There!" Kauikeaouli pointed at a patch of ferns with shiny gold fronds that sparkled in the sunlight. Kino hurried over to the tallest plant.

"I don't see the fiddlehead," she frowned.

Kauikeaouli walked toward her. "That is because you are looking at mature plants. The fiddlehead is a brand new fern all curled up. Look lower."

It took a moment but Kino finally found younger sprouts. Grabbing the stem of a round, curly center branch, she yanked and pulled. The rigid stem barely moved. She tried it again. It remained in place like stone. She tried one more time, this time twisting it and tugging it at different angles. It was no use. Her hands hurt. "You're stronger – you try."

Kauikeaouli stepped forward and grasped the base of the fiddlehead. Planting his feet firmly on either side of the fern, he bent at the knees and tugged.

"Oomph!" Only the outer leaves rustled. He tried once more. "It is impossible to remove."

Kino gazed at the plant. "Wait, how about an offering?"

"Yes," Kauikeaouli nodded. "That is a good idea." He removed his ipu from the bag, held the container with reverence, and murmured under his breath as he poured water on the center of the plant.

Kino whispered, "Mahalo and aloha," simultaneously pulling the stem upward. The plant released its grip. She pulled the fiddlehead vertically and held it in the air. The sun glinted off its golden surface. Kauikeaouli opened the container.

Kino gently bent the stem and placed the heart of the fern inside. She dusted her hands and asked, "Where to next?"

He pulled out the map, glanced at the sky, squinted and surveyed the land. A few seconds later he pointed over his shoulder and said, "The trail that will take us to the water."

22

Iwakāluakūmālua

Kino followed as Kauikeaouli led the way down the steep mountainside. The overgrown path narrowed in many areas and was often times barely visible. It took them over big rocks and through dense patches of woods. The trail leveled out slightly before continuing its steep downward slope. They agreed to take a short break, and found a fallen tree that made the perfect bench.

"Here." He pulled something the size of a protein bar wrapped in a ti leaf out of the wooden bowl and handed it to her. "Kulolo."

"Yummy!" She peeled back the wrapper, revealing the dense, reddish-brown dessert, and took a bite. The smoky, coconut-flavored taro practically melted in her mouth. As she took a swig of water, the bushes to her left rustled and two little, striped piglets the size of cats scampered out.

"Awwww, baby pigs! Look how cute they are!" She shouldered her ipu and put her hands on her knees, crouching down. "Here, piggy piggy," she called, holding her hand out.

They froze and stared at her.

She broke off two small pieces of her food and tossed them between herself and the baby boars, which they promptly gobbled up. One of them took a few cautious steps closer, sniffing the air with interest as it approached.

Kauikeaouli cautioned, "Their mother is nearby. We should keep going."

Kino dropped her hand. He was right; they had no time to stop. She stood up just as a little piglet reached her. Before she could react, the bushes shook as someone or something came crashing through the brush toward them.

"What the…" Before Kino could say anything else, a large black boar charged out from behind the leafy plants. She finished the sentence with a shriek. The animal's piercing, incessant squeals made her ears hurt.

Kauikeaouli rushed toward her and grabbed her by the hand.

"Quick! Up there!" He pulled Kino to a nearby tree and boosted her up. She clambered to the next branch. He went to pull himself up to her, but the branch she was on bent too far down. It wasn't strong enough to hold both of them.

She tried to scramble up the trunk to the next branch, but could not find a good place to grip. He jumped down and ran to the nearest climbable tree.

The wild pig rushed past Kino and followed its moving target. It reached the tree and leapt up on its hind legs. Kauikeaouli barely had time to shinny up the trunk. Just as he pulled himself up, a sharp-pointed tusk grazed the bottom of his foot.

"Augh!" He winced and tried to reach the next branch above him. It was too high. The tree shook as the tenacious pig head-butted the base of the branch he was on. He had no choice but to step further out on the bough.

Kino saw the tree limb arc under his weight, bringing him closer to the angry animal. The branch creaked and split partway at the trunk. He froze.

She had to do something. Spotting another tree just a bit down the trail, she hatched a plan to get Kauikeaouli to a safer spot. Cupping a hand around her mouth she yelled, "Kaui- Kalani! Run to this tree!" She pointed to where she was standing, then jumped to the ground and sprinted toward the one down the trail, yelling, "Hee-errrre, piggy, piggy, piggy!" at the top of her lungs.

"Stop, Kino! What are you doing?" The branch under him splintered with a loud crack and fell out from under his feet. He landed on the boar, which bolted forward into the bushes, launching Kauikeaouli off its back and into the ravine.

Kino screamed and ran toward the spot where he went over. As she reached the edge, her foot hit a slick of mud. She slipped and landed hard on her back. The steeply angled hill, mostly composed of dirt and rocks, left her nothing to grab on to.

She hit a patch of grass, which propelled her sideways, causing her to roll down the hill that sloped upward toward the bottom. For a moment she went airborne. She landed hard on her belly, knocking the wind out of herself.

*****

Kino opened her eyes and found herself stretched out on a lauhala mat in a small hut. Hearing voices, she sat up and looked around. The left side of her head throbbed in pain. She reached up and touched the area above her ear.

"Ow!" She winced and looked at her fingertips covered in thick, clear gel. She sniffed it.

Aloe. Yuck.

"I thought I heard you." Kauikeaouli appeared in the entrance, leaning on a shoulder-high walking stick. His ankle was wrapped in dingy gray kapa.

Relief washed over her. "Thank God!" She stood up and met him at the door. Glancing at his wrapped foot, she asked, "Are you okay? What happened?"

"I am fine," he chuckled. "This happened after we carried you back here. I stepped on a rock. I think it is just twisted."

"Who's 'we'? Where's 'here'?"

"Remember the man we met with Pono and Manu?" He shifted his weight and limped out in front of her.

"The one that they were bullying over a stupid, rotten guava? Yes, of course." She followed him to the side of the house.

The one-handed man and a scruffy young boy were working in tandem, pounding poi. The man held the board with the wrist of his missing hand, and smashed the elastic taro paste with a heavy stone pestle with his good hand, as the boy folded the mixture into a workable sphere between blows. They both looked up as Kino and Kauikeaouli approached.

Kauikeaouli gestured with his free arm. "This is Haoa and his son Lokela. They do not speak English."

Those names sounded vaguely familiar, but she couldn't figure out why at the moment. Kino smiled at them and waved, "Aloha."

Haoa lowered his gaze and said, "Aloha." His son smiled in silence.

Turning to Kauikeaouli she asked, "Are you okay? Last time I saw you, you were unconscious."

"Yes, I am fine. A bit bruised, but overall I am fine."

"Good. I'm glad you're okay, but it's going to be dark soon. We should eat then continue on. I'm starving." Her stomach grumbled in agreement. "What will the magic bowl make us?"

"Well," he grimaced. "I no longer have it."

"What? What do you mean you don't have it? Where did you leave it?"

"I lost it. The pua'a... the pig..." He rubbed the back of his neck.

"Dang it!" She knew the rest of the story. "Maybe these people have food?" She looked at the pair on the ground, still pounding and folding away. They were both very thin compared to average Hawaiians.

"Yes, they are preparing our food right now, and it looks like they are about finished."

Haoa scooped the poi into a wooden bowl, washed his hand then stood up. He carefully picked up the bowl and steadied it with his stump as he moved his good hand to its side. He walked up, bowed, and offered it to Kauikeaouli.

Lokela returned, holding a wooden platter. On it sat several sad-looking sweet potatoes, three small bananas, and two banged-up-looking guavas. Kino wondered if one of them was the infamous guava from the ali'i grove. Haoa said something in Hawaiian to the boy, who approached the pair.

Bowing, Lokela carried the plate and led them to a woven mat under a tree. He placed the plate down, bowed, and walked away, joining his father on a smaller mat next to the house.

"Aren't they going to eat with us?" Kino asked.

"No, they are not allowed to eat with anyone except their own," said Kauikeaouli.

"Why not?"

"Because they are kauwa," he explained. "Descendants of slaves and prisoners of war. They are not even allowed to eat with the commoners, the maka'āinana."

"What's the difference between them and us? Are they built differently? Do they have different color blood?"

"Of course not," he said.

"So what you're saying is, besides the class they're from, they are normal people. Human beings, just like you and me?" She tilted her head.

Kauikeaouli said, "Well, if you put it like that, the answer is yes."

"Then why can't you eat with fellow human beings and forget all this class stuff?" Kino held her palms up then dropped her hands.

Kauikeaouli shook his head. "It does not work that way. It has been like this for centuries."

Kino folded her arms. "Well, I think it's a silly custom. I'm going to invite them to eat with us. It's just the two of them and they look lonely. I don't think they get much visitors."

She stood up and walked over to them. When Haoa leaned back from the basket to face her, she saw a sleeping baby. It took her a second to get over her surprise, and she wondered where the mom was.

"Do you want to come eat with us? I mean, uh..."

Haoa raised his brows and looked at her with wide eyes.

"I'm sorry, I don't really know Hawaiian. I understand more than I speak... which isn't a lot." She scratched the back of her head. "What am I doing? They don't even speak English..."

Now both father and son stared at her, their brows lifted.

"Uh, do you..." she pointed at them, "want to uh, kau kau," she gestured eating with a spoon then she caught herself and instead motioned like she was eating invisible food with her fingers, "with us?" She pointed at herself and Kauikeaouli.

Haoa looked at the young prince for a moment, then at her, digesting the situation. She wondered if he understood. Not leaving anything up to chance, she repeated the last question and her gestures.

A look of comprehension washed over the man's face. He shook his head profusely, said something in Hawaiian then partially bowed as he nodded at Kauikeaouli.

Kino shrugged and said, "Fine then." She returned to her spot under the tree.

"I should have warned you," the prince said as she sat down. "The class structure goes both ways. They know their place, and they would not break kapu, even if I asked them myself."

"Wow. That's crazy, and really sad."

"Do the slaves in your time eat with the common people?" he asked. "I once heard an American man speaking of servants. I guess that is what you call your slaves?"

"We don't have slaves. Slavery was outlawed a long time ago." She tried to remember when Lincoln had given the Gettysburg Address, then remembered that the Civil War didn't start until 1861. So much for that reference.

"Why?"

"Because some people realized that human beings weren't supposed to be treated like property. Some of those freed slaves went on and invented very important, life-saving things that we use even in modern times. They couldn't have done that if they had just remained slaves."

"Interesting..." Kauikeaouli's expression looked thoughtful and distant.

Haoa walked up, stopped several yards away, and looked at the ground. The prince said something to him in Hawaiian, so he looked up and moved closer to them, stopping several feet from the mat.

Bowing slightly, he asked a question in Hawaiian. Kino looked at Kauikeaouli.

"He wants to know if we need anything, and if we will stay the night," the prince explained.

"We can't – we need to find the last item," she frowned. "What was it again? Some black berries we have to find at night?"

"Kane-pōpolo berries," he answered, "to be gathered by the light of the moon."

"Exactly," she said, standing up. "Can you ask them how to get to the waterfall?" She held out her hand.

Kauikeaouli reached up and pulled himself to his feet. Lokela hurried over, picked up the walking stick and readied it for the young prince, who nodded at the boy as he took it then asked the man the question.

The older man answered with enthusiasm, gesturing with both his hand and wrist appendage. He pointed at the sky, slid both arms down like there was an unseen pillar between them, then crossed and uncrossed his arms as if calling "safe" at home plate.

It looked to her like he was explaining the layout around the waterfall and the position of the moon. When he was done, he walked over to the ipu that he and his son had on their mat, picked it up, and slung the woven cord over his arm. Then he walked over to the ipu that Kino and Kauikeaouli were sharing and did the same. He returned to the group and held out the two gourds. Lokela took them and swung them over his shoulder.

Kauikeaouli explained everything to Kino in the meantime. "Haoa said the waterfall is not far from here. They get their water from it. Lokela will take us there."

The man walked back to the mat. The brown little baby sat up and smiled a wide, toothless grin. Haoa murmured something as he lifted a beige kapa cloth from the basket and placed the rest of the food from the platter onto it. He tied the corners together. Then he scooped up the baby and handed the bundle of food to Lokela, who presented it to Kauikeaouli.

"Are they giving us everything they have to eat? They don't have to do that. I'm sure we'll be able to find some fruit trees." Kino said.

Kauikeaouli said something to Haoa, who shook his head. Even though she didn't recognize any of the words, she could tell he insisted they take it.

"He says there are no fruit trees nearby," Kauikeaouli said. "This area is barren. That is how they can live here undisturbed. No one bothers to come here."

"Well, I guess we don't want to be rude. But we really need to get going. It's almost nightfall. Can you walk?"

"I will manage."

"Where's the container?" Kino asked. Kauikeaouli said something to the younger boy who disappeared into the hut momentarily, before returning with her grass-covered gourd.

"Thank God, I don't know what we would have done if this was missing." Carefully, she undid the clasp and sighed with relief. The precious contents were still there.

"Mahalo, Lokela. Can you take us to the waterfall now?" She knew he didn't understand English, she just felt weird not saying anything to him directly.

The boy smiled nervously at her, then looked at Kauikeaouli who translated. He grinned and nodded when he understood, then turned and disappeared once more into the hale. He reemerged with a rolled mat on his back. She recognized it as the small sleeping mat that she had woken up on.

Kino watched him say goodbye to his father and baby brother by pressing his nose against theirs and inhaling deeply. The tender way Haoa looked at his sons showed his devotion.

She felt a pang of envy. Her heart ached for home.

23

Iwakāluakūmākolu

Nearly two hours later, they spotted the waterfall through the treetops. The frothing water rushed down the sheer face of the mountain, cutting a swath of bubbling white as it cascaded between the greenery and the volcanic rock.

As they neared it they heard faint laughter. Lokela stopped, looked at them both then ran into the forest.

"Hey! Where are you going?" Kino called. She glanced at Kauikeaouli and asked, "Where do you think he went?"

"He has either left us or has chosen to hide."

"Why would he do that? We weren't even playing hide and seek." She scanned the area to see if she could spot him. Kauikeaouli shrugged and continued limping forward.

Following the trail around a dense cluster of broad-leafed 'ape plants, they arrived at a clearing where the falls emptied into a large pond. Long, thick, gray scarves of Spanish moss hung from branches all around them. Native islanders called this type of plant Madam Pele's Hair since it resembled the tresses of an old woman, which the volcano goddess often appeared as. In, and around the water were two familiar faces, and one she didn't recognize.

"Aloha!" Pono called from the center of the pond. Manu floated on his back a few feet away. A slender teenage girl stood naked on a rock next to the falls and waved at them before diving into the water. The three of them joined Kino and Kauikeaouli on the bank.

"Did you find what you needed at the summit?" Pono asked, wiping excess water off his chest, stomach, and arms with his hands.

"Yup." Kino patted the container on her hip.

"Aloha, Kauikeaouli," said the girl. She gathered her long, black hair and squeezed the water out as she walked toward them. Her whalebone hook necklace was the only thing she wore.

"Aloha, Nohea. This is Kino. I am helping her collect items the kahuna needs to get her back to…"

Kino coughed and shot him a look. Kauikeaouli held her gaze for a moment. He raised his eyebrows and cleared his throat.

"To… to help heal her kupuna kāne. He is very ill."

Kino recognized that the Hawaiian words meant grandfather.

The girl nodded and said, "Aloha, Kino."

"Uh, hi," she answered, glancing at the ground before resting her eyes on the water. It felt odd talking to a naked person and she didn't know where to look.

"What is wrong with your kupuna kāne?" Nohea asked as she picked up a long panel of brown kapa, wrapped it around her and tied it into a halter dress.

Kino felt a lot better once the girl was clothed. "My grandpa's skin is covered in painful sores, but his doctors don't know what's causing it. He just keeps getting weaker."

"That is unfortunate," the older girl said, slowly shaking her head. "You have my sympathy."

"Nohea is Pono's sister," Kauikeaouli said.

Kino saw the resemblance. Like her brother, Nohea was tall and slender, with dark-brown skin and thick, wavy, black hair. Hers came down to her waist.

The girl stared at her. Kino stared back. Nohea raised her right eyebrow.

Kino wasn't sure if she was supposed to bow, curtsy or shake her hand, or if a wave would suffice. The way Nohea eyed Kino's dirty clothing and messy appearance made Kino think she wouldn't be happy being touched. She hesitated, leaned over, and stuck her right foot behind her left one in an awkward ballet bow. She felt like an idiot.

The taller girl gave her a nod.

Kino straightened up. Inwardly she thought, *This is stupid.* Outwardly she said, "Uh, hi. It's nice to meet you." *It's not nice to meet her.* "I like your necklace." *I really do like her necklace.*

Nohea ignored the compliment and asked, "What are you wearing and why are you so dirty?"

Kino glanced down at her clothes. Between the falling and the sliding and the climbing and the crawling, her shirt was a dirty mess. The print on her t-shirt was smudged with dirt, so only parts of the boy band were visible, along with the partial word, "rection." Her shorts were equally filthy.

Think fast, Kino. "Uh, this is the latest rage, I mean style, where I come from in, uh…" she wasn't sure if California was a state in 1825 so she went with the city she knew from Sophie's package. "New England. All the uh, proper and elite kids wear stuff like this during the summer."

Nohea looked at her. "Stuff? Your manner of speech is strange."

Kauikeaouli laughed, "She speaks in a dialect of her region." He glanced at Kino.

Nohea turned her attention to the prince. "There are guards looking for you. They have come to our house two times already. What have you done?" She eyed Kino for a moment before focusing back on Kauikeaouli.

"I ran away. I promised Kino I would help her find the items to help cure her grandfather. I know what it is like to suffer loss. I do not wish that on anyone." Their eyes met.

Kino could have sworn that she saw the instant Nohea felt his words.

The girl looked at Kino and asked, "What is it that you need?"

Kino glanced at Kauikeaouli, uncertain if she should trust telling her. He gave her a slight nod so she told Nohea the final item they needed to find, and where they needed to take everything.

Pono said, "Kaniakapupu heiau is a long distance from here. A full day's journey on foot; much longer in your condition." He looked down at Kauikeaouli's wrapped ankle. "Your coronation ceremony is in two days, and half the island is looking for you. What are you going to do?"

Kino looked at Kauikeaouli. "Perhaps no one will notice?

"Impossible," said Nohea. "You both look too obvious."

The pair looked at each other. Their contrasting clothes made them stand out. On the trip, Kauikeaouli alternated between pants he wore rolled up to the knees and a malo, which he currently had on. Kino's choice of wardrobe was her t-shirt and shorts, outlandish at the time, and the ripped and stained dress.

Kino's heart sank. Nohea was right. The chance of getting caught before they could get to the heiau was higher the closer they were to the coronation date.

"Unless," Nohea said thoughtfully, "I may have an idea. But it is getting dark and we must head home before someone comes looking for us, too. I will help you. Tomorrow." She stared at Kino.

Kino returned her gaze then suddenly remembered to curtsy. Nohea nodded and walked away. The other boys followed suit.

Kino joined Kauikeaouli at the water's edge. "Am I supposed to do that to you every time I see you?"

"If you were from this time you would, but since you are not, I do not expect you to." He dipped a pensive toe into the pond. "Unless you want to."

"Why start now?"

Kauikeaouli laughed and hobbled into calf-deep water. He made a hissing sound as he sucked in air between clenched teeth. "Co-l-l-l-d!" He shivered. Favoring his injured ankle, he limped and waded to a row of larger rocks sticking out a few inches above the waterline. He followed them and stopped halfway between the shallow end and the falls.

"Haoa said that when the moon is high, we should be able to see them from somewhere right here."

"Do you see anything now?" Kino dipped her toes into the cold mountain water, shivered, and decided against joining him.

"No, the water is too dark," he said, craning his neck, toward the center of the pond.

Kino put her fists on her hips. "Well, how are we going to find small, black berries in dark water? That's impossible."

Kauikeaouli made his way back. "Well, I think we will find out soon."

She followed him out of the water and onto dry ground. Darkness grew by the minute, making it hard to see. She put a hand on his shoulder and let it drop when he stopped. He faced her and sat down.

"Now, we sit."

"Then what?" She splayed her hands out. "We don't have anything for a fire."

"We do not need anything." Yawning, Kauikeaouli laced his fingers behind his head and laid back. "It is best we let our eyes adjust to the moonlight."

"That makes sense," she said, sitting down. They sat in silence, just listening to the endless gushing water.

When the moon came into view, it was only half full.

"How are we supposed to find anything with that?" She gestured at it with her upturned palm.

Kauikeaouli said nothing. Kino glanced down at him and immediately became annoyed. People who could fall asleep anywhere irked her. Deep down she envied them.

The moon continued its excruciating slow crawl up the sky. Kino tapped her thigh in a repetitive, impatient rhythm for a minute, then threw her head back and moaned, "This is taking for-r-rever-r-r."

"Huh?" Kauikeaouli snorted and sat up straight.

"The moon. It's taking forever to…"

They both looked up. The lunar semicircle was now directly overhead, casting a reflection in the pond. Kino stood up and pulled the young prince to his feet.

"Do you want your walking stick?" she asked.

"No, leave it." He limped forward.

She followed him into the freezing water until it reached her knees. He stopped.

"I think you should stay here," he said. "The rocks are slippery and the pond is deeper than it looks. I am a stronger swimmer than you. There is no use in both of us falling in."

She offered no resistance. "Okay," she said. "But be careful."

He took his time navigating back to the halfway point. When he reached it he looked up at the moon, then down at the water several times, before selecting a rock to stand on. As soon as he did that, the wind blew a cover of clouds, blocking out the moon.

"Do you see anything?" she called out over the roar of the falls.

"Nothing yet," the young prince yelled back.

The breeze kicked up once more, sweeping the clouds along with them. The half-moon appeared overhead and cast a mirror image of itself on the water's surface. A moment later, the dark pond bubbled. A light rose up from the depths of the pond, illuminating the water from below.

"I see something!" Kauikeaouli yelled.

"What is it?" she hollered. She could see that the water was growing brighter as if someone were swimming to the surface with a lantern, but not much else.

"I will take a closer look!" He dove into the water and appeared seconds later at the base of the waterfall. He shouted something she couldn't hear before disappearing below the surface.

The glow from the water made it easier for her to see the rocks. She followed them along the edge of the pond, careful not to step on the slippery, green, algae-covered ones. She arrived at the spot and said aloud, "Wow."

A brilliant beam of light streamed from an underwater cave directly under the waterfall. It didn't look too far or too deep from where she stood, so she inhaled, plugged her nose, and jumped in. The icy mountain water pierced her to the bone as she plunged in, making her entire body feel like one giant brainfreeze.

She took a big gulp of air when she surfaced before plugging her nose once more and threaded her way into the hole. She came through on the other side, and burst through the surface. She was in a cavern right behind the waterfall.

"Kino!" Kauikeaouli limped over and helped her out.

"Thanks," she said, squeezing the water from the bottom of her t-shirt. "Did you find the plant?"

"No, not yet. There are two passageways on either side of this cave. I just went down one, which led to a dead end. I was on my way to the next one when I saw you."

"I'll go with you," Kino said.

The hair stood up on her arms as she followed him. The tunnel became darker and colder the deeper they went. It took a right-angle turn, leading them to a shorter passage with glowing light coming from it.

Kauikeaouli glanced at her before making the final turn into the room. As soon as he did so, she heard him gasp. She hurried to find out what was so breathtaking. When she turned the corner, she gasped as well.

In the very center of the circular room sat a giant shrub, at least ten feet tall, covered with small white flowers and clusters of small, black, round berries. The plant was illuminated by a brilliant light that shone from a hole in the wall, revealing a curtain of water pouring down in front of it. At the base of the wall under the hole was another open space, two feet high and rectangular in shape. The walls of the cave shimmered as if crystals were embedded in the rock. A tangle of vine-like plants lined the perimeter, yet none of them bore fruit.

"Wow," Kino said, walking around the bush. "That's so cool. Look at how the light…"

"Do you have the container?"

"Oh yeah, right." She pulled the grass-wrapped gourd from around her then lifted her right foot. Balancing on one leg, she placed it on her bent knee and opened its clasp before grabbing the vessel with both hands and putting her leg down. "Here, can you hold this?"

She handed it over and walked to the plant. Leaning over, she selected a thin branch with several stalks of berries attached, and pinched it, attempting to cut it with her fingernail. It didn't work. She pulled the stem out further, then pinched and twisted it several inches lower. Nothing. She let it go and picked up another vine. After several tries with the same results, she said, "It won't break."

"Try squeezing it with your fingernails."

"I've been trying. It's not working. You try." She took the container from him.

Kauikeaouli tried the same technique on several different branches. No matter how deep he dug his nail in, the plant just bounced back without even a dent.

"Try pulling the whole thing," she suggested, taking a step back to give him space.

He reached into the plant and took hold of a branch, pulling it hard toward him. The rest of it emerged, stretching out like a vine.

"Can you find a rock we can cut it with?" he asked.

Kino closed the lid and walked around, then stopped at the waterfall. "I don't see any loose ones, but there are some stones on the ground here that look pretty sharp." She placed the container down.

Kauikeaouli pulled the shoot toward her. It stopped three feet shy of where she stood. "Let me see if I can find a longer branch." He dropped the one in his hand and walked back to the plant. The unfurled vine coiled back into the shrub. He made several more attempts before finding one that reached her. "Here." He stretched out and handed her the long, green stem.

"Thanks." She pulled it to the opening of the waterfall. Digging her feet in, she yanked at the vine and tried to make it reach a large stone with a honed edge.

"Can you pull it more?" she asked. The top cluster of berries barely grazed the rock.

"One second," he braced himself and pulled at the vine. The plant bent toward them and the earth rumbled. A few loose rocks and debris fell from the ceiling. They both froze.

"Did I do that?" he asked, his eyes wide with alarm.

"I don't know, but pull more, I only need another inch," she said, tugging at the vine. A thin tendril emerged from the leaves, twisting its way up the stem toward her arm. Petrified, Kino froze and watched it wrap around her wrist.

"Hey!" she yelped and recoiled, banging her back against the wall as she pulled the tendril off with her free hand. The contents of her container fell out as the latch popped open. "Just great." She scooped up the items and put them back.

"Close it!" he yelled.

Ignoring him, she placed the container on the ground, and pulled out the black stone. Kauikeaouli pulled the vine taut between his hands and over the edge of the honed rock. Kino grabbed the black stone that they had found in Kipapa and sawed it along the sharp edge of the rock on the ground. The stem separated with a snap. She grabbed the loose cutting and dropped it into the container with the Kipapa stone, before securing the latch, just as the tendril withdrew the branch back a few inches. Then it lurched forward and coiled around Kauikeaouli's waist, pulling him to his feet. Berries, flowers and leaves fell from the tree and hit the ground. Gravel fell from the ceiling. The two looked at each other and Kino shouted, "It's a cave in! We've gotta go!"

The tendrils lashed out and wrapped around his ankles. "No, you go!"

"I'm not leaving you here!" She looped the vessel's cord around her neck, bent down and frantically pulled at the vine. Another branch shot out, wrapping around one of his wrists.

"I said go!" he yelled, and slammed into her, knocking her off her feet and through the hole behind the falls. She squeezed her eyes shut and gulped in a breath before plunging into the ice-cold water. Rocks the size of softballs tumbled around her. She swam toward the shallow end of the pond and turned around in chest-high water, just in time to see Kauikeaouli shoot out of the waterfall with a vine wrapped around his legs.

"Kalani!" she screamed. He disappeared below the surface. The tendril withdrew as soon as it touched the water.

The illuminated pond water grew murky, enveloping his form. His hand shot up, fingertips grazing the surface.

"Kalani!" she yelled and dove in. She swam in his direction until she felt his hand touch hers. Taking a firm grip of his upper arm, she kicked water as hard as she could. He didn't budge no matter how much she pulled.

Oh God, he's stuck.

She let go of his arm, swam to the top, and breathed in a gulp of air before diving back under, this time grabbing him under the arms and pulling. No matter how hard she struggled, she couldn't get him to move. He was trying too, treading water with his hands, when she tried to lift him. She rose to the surface once more, panicking.

"Help!" she screamed, scrambling out of the water and unhooking the container's cord from around her. "HELP!" she continued yelling as she searched the ground for the walking stick. She located it and dove back into the water. Paddling as hard as she could, she reached the struggling young prince. She put the stick in his hand. He grabbed it and pulled it underwater. She could see movement. The top of the stick swiveled one way, then another, then stopped. The wooden stick slowly bobbed to the surface.

"Kalani!" Kino cried, diving under and searching for him with her hands. Her fingertips brushed his palm. She grabbed it, expecting him to return her grip. Instead, his hand floated limp in hers. She screamed underwater.

A sudden froth of bubbles gushed next to her and she felt his hand get pulled away. She pushed up to the surface just as a dark head popped up, followed by another one. Lokela panted, holding his arm across Kauikeaouli's chest, while towing him backward through the water.

Kino helped the younger boy pull the prince to the shore. They placed him down and knelt on either side of him. She grabbed him by the shoulders and shook him.

"C'mon, get up, Kalani!"

He remained limp. She leaned forward and put her ear near his mouth. He wasn't breathing. She tried to feel for a pulse but couldn't find one. She had to find her own first to know where to put her two fingers. She found her jugular and matched the same area on him, but still didn't feel movement.

Oh God, I have to do CPR. Thoughts of self-doubt and "what if's" flooded her mind as she stared at his lifeless face. *What if I do it wrong? What if it doesn't work? What if it works and he wakes up with my mouth on his? What if...* Beads of perspiration prickled on her forehead. She wiped them away with a clammy hand. To open his windpipe, she tipped his head back. His lips parted open.

At the same time, Lokela put his head against the prince's chest.

Kino pinched Kauikeaouli's nose, leaned in, and hesitated, her face just inches away from his. She looked at his full lips that were turning blue. There was no other option. She took a deep breath, shut her eyes, and slowly lowered her open mouth to his.

Lokela leaned back on his heels, swung his hands up in the air and threw his body across the young prince's.

Kauikeaouli's eyes flew open as he lurched up and coughed out water, right into Kino's mouth. She gagged and recoiled, spitting the liquid out. He rolled to one side and kept on coughing until his lungs were clear.

She and Lokela helped him up to a sitting position.

"Are you okay?" Kino asked.

He went to say something but coughed again and cleared his throat.

"Take your time," she said.

"You saved me." He looked dazed.

"Actually, it was Lokela here who saved you. I just helped him pull you from the water."

Kauikeaouli gazed at the younger boy for a moment. Then he spoke to him in Hawaiian. Kino watched as the boy's expression went from concern to elation. She didn't understand exactly what was being said, but she recognized a few words, such as "mahalo" and "kōkua," and guessed that he was thanking Lokela for his help. He finished with a question.

The younger boy's smile faded. He looked down and answered, "Ua make ku'u makuahine."

Kauikeaouli thought for a minute then stated something in Hawaiian. The younger boy's happy expression returned. His eyes shone as he listened to the prince, slowly shaking his head to certain questions and nodding at others. At the end of the conversation, Lokela wiped away tears with his fists, then grinned. He sprang to his feet and ran off into the trees.

"That was weird. What did you say to him?" Kino asked.

"I thanked him for saving my life, and asked him about his family."

"Yeah, where's his mom?"

"She died shortly after giving birth to the baby. He has only his father and brother now."

"Wow," Kino looked in the direction the boy ran in. "That's sad. That must be really hard for their dad, especially with only one hand."

Kauikeaouli nodded. "That is why I told him that I want the three of them to come live at the palace when I become king. His courage will be well rewarded."

24

Iwakāluakūmāhā

The cascading waterfall masked the sound of hoofbeats until the riders were almost on top of Kauikeaouli, Kino, and Lokela, asleep near the pond.

"Ay! Aloha!" Pono called, as he and Nohea stopped their horses at the foot of the sleeping mats.

Kino and Lokela bolted upright, but Kauikeaouli continued dozing. Kino shook him awake. Lokela rose to his knees and put his hands on the ground, ready to push off. Fear filled his eyes as his gaze darted between the riders and the pair next to him.

"Ho'opau," the young prince said. Lokela froze.

Pono and Nohea dismounted as the other three stood up.

"Aloha kakahiaka," Nohea said, nodding at Kauikeaouli and Kino. Her gaze stopped at Lokela.

The young boy dropped and prostrated himself.

Looking down at him, she said, "Kū."

He stood up, but kept looking at the ground.

Eyeing him, Nohea asked, "'O wai 'oe?"

"He is my new kanaka hana. He saved my life. He and his family will live at the palace when I am king," the prince said. "What are you doing here?"

Pono said, "We are here to help get you across the island."

Kino lit up. "That's great!"

"How are we to do that without being caught?" Kauikeaouli asked.

"With this," Nohea said, as she held up two long, folded swatches of kapa, one purple, the other tan, with dark-brown geometric squares on one end.

"I don't think those will make very good hiding places," Kino said. "Are we supposed to wear that over our heads?"

Pono laughed.

"No," Nohea handed her the purple fabric. "You wear it as a kīkepa, like mine." She pulled at her dress.

Kino glanced at Kauikeaouli. "How is that supposed to help him? You can still tell it's Kala-, Kaui-, uh..." she wasn't sure what to call him in front of them.

"With this," Pono held up two thick scarves of gray Spanish moss. He walked over and placed one on Kauikeaouli's head and the other on Kino's.

"It itches," the young prince said, pulling it off.

Nohea stopped his hand and placed the dry, gray fronds back on his head. "This is the only way. No one will recognize you."

Kauikeaouli fidgeted with his impromptu wig.

"I don't know – he still looks like a kid up close," said Kino. "And why do I have to wear one of these, too?"

Nohea scrutinized her. "Perhaps you do not. Let me see your hair."

Kino pulled off the plant and undid her braid. She bent forward and shook her hair out from the roots, then flipped her head back as she stood up.

"You, aloalo," Nohea said to Lokela.

The young boy ran off into the jungle as Kino fiddled with her hair. A minute later, he returned with a red hibiscus.

"Put it behind your ear, and put on your dress," Nohea pointed at the purple cloth in Kino's arms.

Lokela handed the flower to Kino, who took it and tucked it behind her right ear. Gramma told her years ago that only women with boyfriends or husbands wore their flowers on the left.

Nohea walked over to Kauikeaouli. "I will help you with yours."

Kino hurried behind a tree and undressed. She wrapped the fabric around and tucked the end piece into the hem, but it kept slipping.

After several attempts, she gave up and peered around the tree. "Uhh, Nohea? I need some help."

The older girl came over, unwrapped and rewrapped the material, tying the ends into a knot over Kino's left shoulder.

"Here," Nohea said, as she reached behind her head and unfastened her necklace, "turn around." Kino did so, lifting her hair up in the process. "You will be easier to pass off as an ali'i if you wear this."

The whalebone pendant felt warm and heavy as it touched Kino's skin. When she felt Nohea's fingers let go of the tied end, she turned back to face her.

"Thank you. I mean, mahalo." Kino picked up her clothes.

They rejoined the group. Kauikeaouli had his back to her, adorned in a wig of gray. She burst out in laughter when he turned around.

Kauikeaouli placed his hands on his hips, scrunched up his face and said in a high-pitched, shaky trill, "Aloha, na keiki!"

"I wish I had a camera right now," Kino grinned.

He said in the same, old-lady voice, "What is a..."

She cut him off before he could finish, "I'll explain it later. We have to get going now."

Nohea said something to Lokela, who bowed and began rolling up the sleeping mats. "We will fill our ipus at the waterfall," she said to the others.

When they reached the water's edge, Pono asked, "What happened here?"

The fallen rocks at the waterfall had filled in most of the pool, turning it into a shallow pond, more than half a size smaller than its original form.

Kino and Kauikeaouli exchanged glances.

"Cave-in," the young prince shrugged, breezing by Pono and stepping into the water. "Kino, give me the ipus."

Pono's brows knitted, as he stared at the pond for a moment, before following Kauikeaouli and filling his own gourd under the falls.

Lokela rolled up two of the sleeping mats and was in the process of rolling up the last one when the boys returned. He finished and grabbed one of the other mats before standing up. Bowing, he held both out and offered them to the young prince.

As Kauikeaouli spoke Hawaiian to him, the boy straightened up and nodded, as his smile grew bigger by the minute. He picked up the third mat, clutched it across him and bowed twice, saying, "Mahalo nui, mahalo nui," each time. With a final nod to Kino, he ran off into the forest.

Pono guided the horses over and handed his sister her horse's rein.

"You ride with Pono," Nohea said to Kino.

Pono climbed into the saddle and Kino pulled herself up behind him. He was too tall for her to be able to see the trail over his shoulder, so she settled on looking at the sights on either side of her.

Rich green foliage and bird song surrounded them. Their descent was faster on horseback, but still scary in some spots. The steep angle of the slope made the horses slip and lose momentary footing in a few places, causing rocks to tumble. Kino held her breath and closed her eyes whenever she felt Pono's torso tense up and the horse hesitate.

Once out of the thicket, the land gave way to fields of grass. They walked the horses down the trail until they reached the main road.

"Be on the lookout for guards," said Nohea. "If we reach a checkpoint, let me do the talking."

The other three nodded in agreement.

They made it across the island with very little contact with anyone, aside from other travelers and workers in the fields. Kino loved how everyone they crossed paths with either waved, greeted them with "aloha," or did both.

At one point they stopped to eat the food that Nohea had packed. Back on the road, Kino's full belly, the heat, and the steady gait of the horse made her drowsy. She had to catch herself from leaning too much on one side. Her eyelids felt heavy.

Her eyes flew open when she heard Pono say, "Auwe! Look."

Up ahead, several guards with long spears blocked the intersection. Other guards walked along the line of carriages, and horseback riders lined up for inspection. Kino's heart pounded. "Maybe we should turn around."

A guard directed one of the carriages to another area to form a second lane then motioned other riders to queue up behind it. He spotted the four kids and motioned them into the new line. It was too late to turn back without arousing suspicion.

Kauikeaouli shot her a worried look. She tried to encourage him with a smile, but it felt insincere. Inside, she too was terrified.

"Pretend you are sleeping," Nohea said over her shoulder. She steered the horse toward the first lane, which had more carriages. A large and menacing hulk of a man with a square jaw gestured for them to pull into the second lane behind an enclosed carriage. The guards searched the carriage in front of them then waved the driver forward.

Two guards crossed their spears to block the group from traveling past a certain point. Square jaw walked up and asked a question. Nohea sat straight up and answered him in a calm and matter-of-fact tone. She said the word "kupuna," in her explanation.

The man studied Kauikeaouli, who was hunched forward with most of his head buried in Nohea's thick, wavy hair. The Spanish moss wig blocked both sides of his face. He coughed several times, snorted, and made loud, snoring sounds.

The guard continued past and fixed his eyes on Kino. He walked closer. Her heartbeat sped up with his intense gaze. She straightened her spine and tried her best to look stern, something she saw the aliʻi kids do when speaking to their subjects. He asked her a question she couldn't understand. Her heart galloped in her chest. A heat washed over her face. She prayed she wasn't turning red.

Nohea blurted a sentence with the word "kuli" which Kino knew meant "deaf," so Kino looked away, pretending to not know the guard was addressing her. His eyes lingered on her a moment longer. She held her breath.

Pono cleared his throat. Kino could feel the guard's attention shift. He eyed Pono then asked Nohea another question. Satisfied with her answer, he signaled, and the two guards lifted their spears to let them by.

It took several minutes before Kino's heart slowed to normal.

"You can stop snoring now. We are well past the checkpoint," Pono said.

Kauikeaouli sat back and grinned.

"Good job. High five!" Kino held her hand up.

Kauikeaouli smacked hers with his. She grinned back at him.

Pono and Nohea were highly skilled riders, switching between walking and trotting as they made their way across the island. Several hours later they reached an intersection, where the road crossed the trail leading to the heiau.

Nohea said, "It is getting late and we must return home. We will leave you a horse to take you the rest of the way." She leaned forward in the saddle. Kauikeaouli swung his leg over and jumped off. He winced when he landed, favoring his ankle.

Pono dismounted and handed over the reins.

Kauikeaouli pulled himself up into the saddle. Kino leaned back as far as she could to make room for him.

"Mahalo," Kauikeaouli said, first to Pono, then Nohea.

"Yes, mahalo nui loa." Kino unhooked the necklace and handed it back to Nohea. "It would have taken us forever to get here on foot."

"We will see you tomorrow, at the ceremony." Nohea leaned forward as Pono climbed into the saddle behind her. Looking directly at Kino, she said, "I hope the kahuna gives you what you need for your kupuna kāne."

25

Iwakāluakūmālima

The hair on Kino's arms stood on end as they trodded up the hill. All around this holy place, the energy felt powerful yet serene. There was no chanting, or eerie wind like the first heiau they visited. Instead, beautiful singing filled the air.

A handful of women in white kapa dresses were gathering plants and flowers outside the stonewall surrounding the compound. They all stopped working as the riders appeared. Kauikeaouli climbed down from the saddle and guided the horse toward them.

A beautiful, dark-skinned woman placed the basket she held, down on the ground, brushed herself off and walked toward them. She wore a purple kihei over her white dress and a yellow hibiscus in her long, black hair.

"Aloha," she bowed. "You must be Kauikeaouli and Kino."

The two kids nodded. It was Kino's turn to climb off the horse.

"My name is Hokulani. We have been expecting you." She took the reins from the young prince and handed them to a fellow keeper. "Please, follow me."

"Where is Kahu Pauo'le?" Kauikeaouli asked.

"He is inside, awaiting your arrival." She glanced at Kauikeaouli's wrapped foot and motioned to one of the attendants. An old woman with long, silver hair acknowledged with a bow and hurried through the gate.

As they approached the entrance, Kino stopped. "I thought women were not allowed in heiaus."

"In most cases that is true." Hokulani gestured for them to enter. "However, this is a different type of heiau. Here, we practice medicine and the art of healing. Wahines and kānes – women and men – work side by side to tend to the sick and injured."

They walked past women in clothing similar to Hokulani's. Men in earth-toned malos and kiheis tended to their patients, who were lying or sitting in the open-air pavilions.

Medicinal plants grew between each structure. Kino recognized the sweet-smelling white awapuhi flowers of the ginger plant, the small, yellow flowers of the uhaloa plant and the intoxicating, dark-green kawa kawa bushes. Gramma grew the same plants in her own garden.

"Kahuna Pauoʻle is there." Hokulani pointed to the back of the compound. Four twelve-foot-tall carved wooden posts with fierce expressions sat before the entrance of a thatched hut. These sacred totems still sent a chill down Kino's spine.

The silver-haired woman returned with a walking stick and bowed before presenting it to Kauikeaouli, who acknowledged her in Hawaiian.

Hokulani said to the prince, "A place has been readied to treat you. I will escort Kino to Kahu."

Kino exchanged glances with Kauikeaouli as he limped off with the old woman.

She ran her fingers down the cord of the ipu that held all the objects of her quest. When her hand reached the gourd connected to it, she shook it. The sound of the rock hitting the inside reassured her that the container wasn't empty. Her heart started beating faster as she ducked into the entrance.

The old, white-haired kahuna from the first heiau sat on a woven mat in the middle of the single room. He wore an elaborately patterned kapa garment that wrapped around his body and tied on one shoulder, with a ti-leaf wreath on his head. In front of him lay a large wooden bowl on a wooden tray. Next to the bowl sat a stone mortar and pestle.

"Aloha," he nodded, and gestured at the mat in front of him. "E komo mai."

"Aloha," Kino said as she sat down. She unhooked the cord and handed him the container.

"We did it."

"Well done," Kahu said, taking it from her.

"Does this mean I can go home now?"

"Not quite yet." He placed it next to the wooden bowl.

"But I got everything you said we needed to get, exactly where you told us to find it all." She frowned. "What else is there?"

"The items you have gathered will be made into an elixir." The kahuna unhooked the latch and flipped back the lid. He pulled out the compass and handed it to Kino. "I believe this is yours."

"Yes, thank you." She took it from him and looked at it. Memories of her grandfather came flooding back. It felt as though ages had passed since he had given her the compass. "How long will it take you to make it?"

"It will be ready tomorrow."

Those words sounded incredibly sweet to her. She was so close to going home.

Although the room's light was low, the golden fiddlehead of the fern glimmered. She suddenly remembered why it seemed familiar.

"My grandfather is ill and needs healing. Can you help him?"

"You both have already helped him," The kahuna gestured to the items laid out in front of them. "These elements will be used to create a healing potion for his skin."

Kino's heart sped up. "How did you know about my grandfather?"

"The spirits spoke about the descendant of a cursed one, a child from a different time. By saving the land, the child lifts the curse." The man removed the black rock.

"What does that mean? I don't know how to save the land. If I did, my family wouldn't have to worry about moving." She held her hands out to her sides and shrugged. "And how the heck am I supposed to lift a curse?"

"You will have done so by completing your journey and curing your grandfather. There is, however, still the matter of the third sign. You will not be able to go home until that occurs."

"But we've worked so hard and come so far, only to be told to wait? I need to go home. My family must be freaking out by now." A lump formed in her throat as she fought back tears of exhaustion and disappointment. She swallowed hard then asked, "If these items were gathered for the potion, what will I need to get home?"

"When it is time, you must take this sacred pōhaku," he picked the black stone up off the board, "and smash the shell that holds your blue stone. Then you must pass that blue stone to someone special to you."

"My grandma gave that to me. It was my birthday present. I can't give it to just anyone. What would I tell her?"

"It is the only way." He carefully removed each item and placed them into the wooden bowl. "I will give you the elixir tomorrow, before the ceremony. Now go. The palace guards have been looking for you both. You must get back."

*****

"Stop the horse. Something's weird." Kino looked down at the container on her left thigh. It seemed to be vibrating.

Kauikeaouli brought the horse to a standstill then twisted in his seat. "Why? What is going on?"

Kino brought out the compass. The marker rotated around the dial in a slow spin.

She tapped at the face. The needle spun even faster.

"Why is it doing that?"

"I have no idea. Maybe it broke, being in the container with everything." She held it up. The needle swiveled in the opposite direction before swinging back and pointing east.

"What the…" She shook it and held it back up. The needle pointed east once more. "I think it's broken." She held it in front of Kauikeaouli.

He took it and held it up.

"Hmm. How curious. Perhaps we should head in the direction of the arrow. If nothing awaits us, we can just turn around."

"Yes, let's do it."

Kauikeaouli snapped the reins and directed the horse uphill.

It was only a matter of minutes before she saw two palm trees crossed over a pointed rock.

The hut!

"Do you see those trees that looks like an X?" She pointed. "I'm pretty sure that's where the hale pili I arrived in is."

As they reached the markers, the rectangular house and adjacent triangular huts came into view. Kino recognized the decorative gourds hanging near the doorway. "That's it!"

He hurried the horse toward the houses. When they reached her hut, they both jumped off the horse and rushed inside.

Kino spotted the upturned shell the moment she entered. She knelt in front of it. When she lifted the conch up, the rattle of the rock inside made her heart beat faster.

"This is it!" She held up the shell up as if showing off an award. "This is how I got here!"

They peered into the dark-pink opening of the shell. Its deep crevice revealed nothing.

"The rock's way in there," she said, turning the shell over. A clattering noise followed from within.

"Wait!" He put his hand on her arm. "We should mark the location of this hale on the map, so we can find it again."

"Good idea. The map's in here." She looked down at the container on her hip.

He pulled out the map and opened it up.

"Here is the heiau, and here is the palace. Based on the road we are heading toward, I will say it is somewhere around... here." He pointed at a spot. "I just need something to mark it with."

"Kauikeaouli!" A male's deep voice boomed from outside.

Kino jumped. "Who's that? Who knows we're here?"

"It has just been a matter of time before Maleko found me. He always finds me. At least we have gathered everything."

"Now what?"

"Now we go to the palace and prepare for the ceremony."

26

Iwakāluakūmāono

"Wake up!"

Kino opened her eyes and jumped. Princess Nahienaena's face was just inches from hers. She wiped the drool off her chin and sat up. "Huh?"

"You have visitors." As the princess leaned back and gestured at the doorway, Sophie and Makani peeked through.

"Hi! Come in!" Kino stood up. The two women rushed through the door and threw their arms around her and each other in a group hug.

"You made it back!" Sophie gushed. "You have to tell us all about it!"

"There is no time," said the princess. "You slept too long. It is almost time for Kalani's coronation. Put those on." She pointed at a stack of clothes on a low table. On the floor next to it lay a clean pair of leather shoes. "A carriage awaits to take you all to the ceremony. Make haste." She exited before Kino could thank her.

"We'll turn around to give you privacy, dear, but you must tell us about your journey!"

Kino picked up a navy-blue cotton dress and pulled it over her sleeveless white undershirt. The dress had a round collar, with short, puffy sleeves, and it was tied at the waist. The hem hit just below her knees, an inch above the bottom of her white, cotton bloomers.

"I'll tell you everything on the ride to the Governor's house." She pulled on her shoes. "Can you button me?"

Sophie said, "Of course." She fastened Kino's dress and tied the white sash into a bow.

*****

"It felt so good to finally eat a real meal and sleep indoors." Kino glanced outside at the crowd lining the street. "Wow, there are a lot of people out there."

"It's not every day that a nation gets a new king," Sophie said, as the carriage came to a stop.

Kino looked out the window. A throng of people gathered around the yard of a large, wooden, two-story, dark-green, thatched-roof house. Posted at various sentry points were Hawaiian guards dressed in navy-blue tailcoats and black pants. Tall, black-leather helmets with metal buckles covered the tops of their heads, down to their eyes. Upstairs on the balcony, two soldiers stood along the railing observing the crowd.

One large, dark cloud loomed overhead. The humid air felt thick and heavy.

"Looks like a storm is coming." Sophie dabbed her forehead with the back of her gloved hand as she exited the coach.

"I think it's the new rain that I'm waiting for," said Kino.

Manu, Pono, and Nohea each touched their nose to hers as they greeted her with Aloha. Both boys wore long black pants with crisp, white, long-sleeved shirts. Nohea's full-length burgundy dress was that of an adult. In their western clothing, they seemed much older than they had the day before.

"Kauikeaouli is waiting for you," said Nohea. "This way."

Sophie and Makani accompanied Kino as they followed the aliʻi teens through a path in the garden that wrapped around the house and ended in the backyard. As soon as Kino made the turn, she saw her former traveling partner wearing a dark suit and white collared shirt. He ran up to her and gave her a bear hug, lifting her off the ground. She laughed as he set her back down.

"Mahalo nui loa, Kino," Kauikeaouli said.

"For what?"

"For taking me on your journey."

"What are you talking about? *You're* the one who helped *me.* There was no way I could have done any of it without you." She meant every word.

"I told myself I helped you because you needed me. Deep down, though, I joined you because I wanted to run away from my duties. But after seeing the beauty of the ʻaina and the people," the prince glanced at the squirming baby on Haoa's handless arm and the corners of his mouth turned upward. "I now know that it is my kuleana – my responsibility – to govern, which I accept."

Lokela, with a fresh haircut and wearing a clean, brown malo and a big smile, took a step away from his father and waved at Kino to follow him. The boy led her around the corner to a spacious courtyard, surrounded by flowering plants. She let out a gasp.

"The hut!"

"I had it moved here – they finished reassembling it this morning," Kauikeaouli said from behind her. "It will be easier for you to get to it now."

"Thanks!" Kino grinned. "Is the kahuna here?"

"I have not seen him yet." The prince glanced upward as the sound of thunder rolled across the sky.

Nahienaena and two of her lady servants emerged from the house. The two women stopped outside the double doors. The princess looked like a regal doll in her white silk dress and matching ribbons in her curly black hair.

"You are needed inside, dear brother. It is time."

Kauikeaouli faced Kino and said, "I will never forget you, and I will always watch over you." He cupped her face, pressed his nose to hers and breathed. She inhaled as he did and felt a rush of energy. He smelled like coconut oil and sweat. Her stomach felt as if she had just rode a dip on a roller coaster. The feeling was scary, yet exhilarating. "Aloha." He released her face and followed his sister to the house.

Kino muttered a delayed, "Aloha." She watched as the tall female servant tied a cape around his shoulders, enveloping him in shiny red, gold and black feathers. The shorter woman draped a thick cord of fragrant maile leaves around his neck. Nahienaena led the way back into the house.

"So, this is the hut that brought you here." Sophie crossed her arms and scanned it from door to rooftop. "I have to admit, your time-travel story made me wonder if you were touched in the head."

Kino laughed. "Yeah, it's still hard to believe myself. I keep waiting to wake up from this crazy dream." Thunder clapped, startling her.

"This is no dream," said a voice behind her. She turned to face the kahuna.

"You have fulfilled your destiny." The old man clutched his carved walking stick and hobbled toward her, holding up his fist as he approached. "Have your grandfather drink this. It will break the curse and he will be healed."

She held out her hand to meet his as she heard the crowd stir out front. People pressed closer toward the house. Hawaiian and Haole faces turned upward at the balcony where two muscular young Hawaiian men stepped forward and blew the conch shells they each held. They then walked to the side of the balcony they were nearest to and sounded the aquatic horns before exchanging sides and repeating the haunting, single note. They returned to the center of the balcony before stepping back into the small crowd on the landing. Thunder rumbled across the sky once more.

A gust of wind swooped down and wafted through the yard, right between Kino's fingers, before the kahuna pressed something into her palm. As he did so, a second, much stronger wind, picked up, blowing leaves off the trees. Men and women clutched at their hats, and pressed them onto their heads. As the breeze continued, growing and swirling, the crowd murmured and gasped, their umbrellas collapsed, and the moving air lifted skirts.

The dark, looming cloud above them slowly crept across the sky, revealing the bright sun. The thunder faded as the large cloud drifted further away, and the wind quieted as well.

Kino looked up. "Oh no!" Her heart sank. "How's it supposed to rain now?"

The crowd applauded and cheered. Kino turned to face the balcony. From her angle she could only see one half of it. A Hawaiian man in a dark suit stepped up to the front railing and stopped in the center. A red-and-yellow feather cape adorned the man's broad shoulders.

"Aloha!" The man called out to the crowd before breaking into a speech spoken only in Hawaiian. Kino could not understand the words, but based on everyone's reaction, whatever the man was saying pleased the crowd. He finished by introducing "Kuhina Nui Ka'ahumanu."

Applause erupted once more as a large Hawaiian woman in a white gown stepped out onto the balcony. The golden feather lei she wore around her head matched the two-foot-long ka'ili she held in her hand. She waited for the crowd noise to die down before speaking – first in Hawaiian, then in English. Kino found it difficult to hear what was being said and turned her attention to the kahuna.

"How long do I have to wait until it rains again?"

The crowd cheered. Kino glanced at the balcony. The man returned to the address the crowd as the woman departed. Again, he spoke in Hawaiian, and then again in English. Applause and cheering erupted before he finished speaking.

"Presenting, his royal highness, King Keaweawe'ula Kīwala' ō Kauikeaouli Kaleiopapa Kalani Waiakua Kalanikau Iokikilo Kīwala' ō i ke kapu Kamehameha." He almost had to shout the last half.

Kauikeaouli stepped up to the railing, waving at the people below. Atop his head was a bejeweled European-style crown of gold. He walked to the corner, turned and waved at Kino. She waved back and moved closer to the house.

"There he is – our new king!" Sophie clasped her hands together.

The boy returned to the center of the front rail and raised his arm, his palm facing up. Kino couldn't help but see the similarities between his posture and his father's that is commemorated in bronze.

"Where are you chiefs, guardians, commoners? I greet you. Hear I say! My kingdom I give to God. The righteous chief shall be my chief, the children of the commoners who do you right shall be my people, my kingdom shall be one of letters."

The crowd whooped and cheered, hats flung in the air.

"It is time." Kahu said in Kino's ear. He motioned toward the doorway of the hut. A light glowed from the conch shell inside.

"We're going to miss you." Sophie dabbed the corner of her eye with a gloved knuckle before opening her arms.

"I'll miss you both too." Kino hugged her back. "Thank you for everything."

Makani stepped forward and cradled Kino's face in her hands. She pressed their noses together as she inhaled, saying, "Aloha a hui hou."

"Aloha, Makani." Kino gave her a hug. She put the vial into the pocket of her dress, and glanced at the rest of the group. Lokela held the baby's fists in his hands, as the little one wobbled like a tightrope walker. "Mahalo, everyone, for all of your kōkua." She made sure to nod also at Nohea, Pono and Manu.

Entering the dark hut, Kino knelt in front of the shell. The black stone from Kipapa sat next to it.

Outside the hut, Kahu Pauo'le chanted.

Kino picked up the black rock and raised it over her head. Gritting her teeth, she brought it down hard. A pointy shard broke off, but the shell remained intact. "Ugh." Kino took a firmer grip on the rock and hit down on the conch. A crack appeared down the center. She sat up on her knees, raised the stone once more and slammed it hard. This time, the shell shattered. The blue-green rock lay in the center of the rubble. Remembering the kahuna's instructions, she threw the stone out the door. Makani caught it.

A blinding light filled the room.

27

Iwakāluakūmāhiku

Kino opened her eyes. In the dim room she recognized the wood rafters of the hale pili. Rolling to her side, she propped herself up on one arm, then scanned the floor. The shell and the rock were gone.

Was it all just a dream?

She crawled to the door and stuck her head out. Cool, conditioned air touched her face. Kino exhaled in relief. Seeing the familiar dark-paneled walls and glass displays made her heart leap with joy. There was no sign of Cyan or any of the other girls. Climbing out of the ancient exhibit, she wondered how long she had been gone.

Piercing sunlight blinded her when she walked out of the building. She held up her hand to shield her eyes then closed them to refocus. She jumped when a voice from behind her said, "There you are! I've been looking for you everywhere."

Kino opened her eyes.

Kawika walked toward her. "What are you wearing?" he asked.

Kino looked down at her navy-blue dress.

It wasn't a dream.

She threw her arms around him. "I'm so glad to see you! You won't believe where I've been."

"Um, I'm glad to see you too." He hugged her, then stepped back and stared at her clothes.

She grabbed his shoulders. "What is today's date?"

"May sixth."

"What year?"

"Uh, 2016." He narrowed his eyes. "Did you hit your head or something?"

"No, I traveled back in time. That's how I ended up in this dress."

He raised an eyebrow. "You must have hit your head. C'mon, your mom is waiting for us in the parking lot."

She didn't see their red Hyundai, just a white Mercedes Benz sedan at the curb. "I thought you said my mom was waiting?"

"She's right there." He pointed at the white car.

The glare off the windshield prevented Kino from seeing the driver. It wasn't until they were almost next to it that she could see into the side window. Mom sat at the wheel. A girl with thick glasses sat in the back.

Kawika grabbed the handle, opened the passenger door, and looked at Kino. She hesitated before climbing in. He shut the door behind her and took his place in the back seat.

"I was wondering what had happened to you." Mom leaned in to meet Kino's hello kiss.

Kino threw her arms around her mother's neck. "Mom! I'm so glad to see you!"

Her mom hugged her back and said, "I'm glad to see you too, honey."

Kino clung on and squeezed harder, breathing in the scent of hairspray. She noticed that Mom's hair was freshly styled and her dark roots were covered by honey-colored highlights. The way she had always worn it on the mainland.

"Ow, ow, ow." Mom patted Kino on the back. "Ease up, honey. You're hurting me."

Releasing her grip, Kino sat back with a sigh. Before she could ask whose car they were in, a familiar voice from the backseat said, "It's about time. We were waiting forever."

Kino twisted in her seat.

"Nalani?"

"What?"

Thoughts swirled through Kino's mind. Maylani was now Nalani again. How was that even possible?

"Where are Cyan, Tiffany, and Chanel?"

"How should I know?" Nalani shrugged. "Probably on their way home, I guess. It's not like they talk to me or anything."

"Whose car is this?" Kino asked.

Mom answered, "Ours, of course."

"What? How did we get this? Where's the red car?" Kino looked at the sleek dashboard and video screen on the console. It showed the station they listened to on satellite radio – an extreme upgrade from the AM/FM/cassette deck on the Hyundai.

"What red car? We only have this one." Mom frowned. "Are you okay?"

"I think she bumped her head on something," Kawika chimed in.

"I told you, I didn't bump my head – I travelled to the past," Kino said over her shoulder.

"She sounds like she hit her head," said Nalani.

Kino opened her mouth to say something but decided against it.

Mom glanced into the rear-view mirror before looking at Kino. "Buckle up. Let's get a move on."

As Kino latched the seat belt, her hand grazed her pocket. She reached in and pulled out the glass vial.

"We need to go to the hospital to see Grandpa."

Mom glimpsed both ways before pulling onto the street. "We'll go to see him after we drop everyone off."

"But I have to see him now. It's important." She clutched the vial tighter. "I have something that will cure him."

"What are you talking about? The doctors haven't even figured out what is wrong with him."

"Mom, you have to believe me. I traveled back to the past, met Kalani right before he became Kamehameha III, went on a crazy quest and got all these items that a kahuna used to make a cure for Grandpa." She held up the vial just as the light turned red at the intersection. "Please! We have to go right now."

Her mom glanced at the bottle and furrowed her brows, "Maybe we *should* go to the hospital. You might have a concussion."

"I didn't hit my head!" Kino dropped her hand on her lap. "We just need to get to the hospital. Please, Mom, it's important that I see Grandpa as soon as possible."

The light turned green, but Mom didn't go. She stared at Kino. "I don't understand what is going on."

The car behind them honked their horn. Mom glanced back before she stepped on the gas. "Well, I suppose we can head there first. Is that okay with you guys?" She waved an apology to the driver in her rearview mirror.

"Sure," said Kawika.

"Fine with me." Nalani sounded disinterested.

*****

The kahuna who had visited the first time she saw grandpa at the hospital was standing next to the bed. "Aloha," he said with a nod.

Kino and her mom returned the greeting.

"There she is, my favorite granddaughter." Grandpa's raspy voice wavered, contradicting his happy tone. He looked frail, and even weaker than the last time she saw him. The red sores now covered his neck.

"Hi, Grandpa!" She rushed to his side and pulled out the vial. "I have the cure! This should make all the sores disappear and make you well again." She offered him the container. "Here, drink it."

"What's in it?" He reached a shaky, blistered hand out toward her, and dropped it, as if his effort exhausted him.

She listed the items she gathered on her quest, "…And lastly, the fiddlehead of a golden hapuʻu fern."

Kahu's eyes lit up. "Those are the items that my great-kupuna said were needed for the cure. Where did you find all of these things?"

"In 1825."

"Is that a store?" Grandpa asked.

"No. I went back to the year 1825! Somehow, I found a way there through the grass hut at the museum, and I ended up in old Hawaii. I met a kid named Kalani, I mean Kauikeaouli, before he became King Kamehameha the Third. He helped me gather all the stuff to make this."

Both men glanced at each other, then at Mom.

"Don't look at me," Mom said, raising her hands up. "She's been acting strange ever since I picked her up."

"Look at what I'm wearing, Mom. You know I don't own anything like this, and I definitely didn't leave the house dressed this way." She fanned one side of her skirt. Looking into her grandfather's eyes, she pleaded, "You don't have to believe me – you just have to drink this. It really *is* the cure!"

She held the vial toward the kahuna.

"Kahu Pauoʻle made this."

The man's bushy brows rose in surprise and he met her gaze. "Who did you say gave this to you?"

"Kahu Pauoʻle. He said I was the chosen one or something."

He stared at her for a moment then cleared his throat. "That is the name of my ancestor. My great-great-kupuna." He directed his next sentence at Grandpa. "He is the one who made the medicine with the golden hapuʻu fern." He took the vial from Kino's hand. "It will surely cure you."

"You need to drink it, Grandpa." She gripped the side rail on his hospital bed. "Please."

Her grandfather looked at Kahu's hand, then into Kino's eyes. "Yes," he whispered.

The kahuna closed his fingers around the vial and said a prayer in Hawaiian. Although she didn't understand the words, Kino still felt the emotion of the blessing. When he was finished, he uncorked the container.

Mom pressed the button on the bed remote to elevate the upper half of the mattress. Kino stepped aside as the kahuna moved in closer to Grandpa. Mom propped pillows behind him to hold him more upright, then backed up and stood next to Kino.

Kahu held the vial up to her grandfather's pale lips and tilted the bottle. He gulped down the liquid, grimaced then swallowed hard. He groaned and lay back as the kahuna corked the empty bottle.

Kino stepped to the bed. Her mom joined her and held her hand. "Do you feel anything, Grandpa?"

"No." He looked at his arms. "Not yet. Maybe it takes a little – UPFFFF – GAH!" He clutched his abdomen. "Ughh…" He collapsed into the pillow, panting.

"Grandpa!"

"Dad!"

Kino and her mom called out at the same time.

"I'm calling the nurse." Mom grabbed the bed's remote and pressed the call button.

"Wait!" Grandpa's voice sounded different. "Look!" Her grandfather held out his hands. The flesh under his skin rippled and undulated from his fingertips up his arms. He sat up and looked down at his body. His eyes grew wider the lower his gaze traveled. He ripped back the bed sheets. The movement continued down his legs, the bandages rising and falling with each surge.

"I can feel it! I can feel something happening! It's tingling." He pulled at the gauze around his wrists, revealing his forearm.

Everyone gasped in unison as they watched his bare skin turn a bright bubblegum pink, then purple, and finally yellow, before fading back to his natural tone. Mom and the kahuna hurried to uncover the rest of his arm.

A blonde nurse rushed into the room.

"Stop! You can't do that!" She grabbed the end of the unwrapped bandage from Kahu's hands – then froze. "How is this possible?"

The kahuna, Mom, Grandpa, and Kino all exchanged glances and knowing smiles.

The nurse continued unwrapping Grandpa's biceps, while shaking her head and muttering to herself in wonder.

"I can't believe this. It has to be a miracle. I have to call the doctor." She dropped the roll of gauze into the trash and hurried out.

Kino approached the bed and looked at her grandfather's skin. No trace of the blisters remained – not even the slightest scar.

Grandpa pushed himself upright and took her hand. He squeezed it. "Thank you, Kino. Aloha wau iāʻoe."

"I love you too, Grandpa." She threw her arms around him and hugged him tight.

The nurse returned. "In here, doctor."

A gray-haired Asian man walked in behind her. He wore a white lab coat over a set of blue scrubs. A stethoscope hung between his lapels. The photo badge clipped to his pocket read, "Andrew Kim, M.D."

"Hello," he said with a nod. Opening the medical file in his hands, Dr. Kim approached the bed as he read, closed the folder and handed it to the nurse.

Pushing his wire-framed glasses further up his nose, the doctor gently lifted one of Grandpa's wrists. He scrunched up his face as he carefully examined each side of Grandpa's hand, then the rest of his arm. He gave Grandpa's other arm a quick once-over too. Laying a hand on her grandfather's thigh, he asked, "Does this hurt?"

Grandpa gazed down and chuckled. "No. Not at all!" He smiled at Kino.

She beamed as she watched the physician take a pair of medical scissors and cut the bandages down the front of Grandpa's legs. When the white cotton fell away, everyone gasped in unison. His legs were blemish free. Not a mark appeared on his dark skin. Her grandfather gave each leg a kick to release them from their gauze cocoons.

Mom laid a hand on his shoulder. "Take it easy, Dad. You might hurt yourself."

"No way. I've been taking it easy for months! Now I feel better than I have in years." He looked at Dr. Kim. "I'm ready to go home now."

Kino clapped her hands. "Yes! We'll just wait for you!"

"It might be better if you stay one more night, just for observation," said the doctor.

"I'm cured – nothing is wrong with me anymore." Grandpa held up his arms. "See? All gone. I'm ready to go."

Mom looked at the doctor. "I don't think he'll let you keep him another night."

Dr. Kim smiled. "Well, I'd like to run a few tests," he said to her, "just to make sure. If everything comes back normal, you can pick him up in a couple hours."

28

Iwakāluakūmāwalu

Mom put her arm around Kino's shoulders as they walked back to the car. "I don't know where you got that vial, but I'm really glad Grandpa's better." Before Kino could reiterate her journey back in time, Mom's phone rang. She fished around in her purse, and answered it as she opened the car door.

"Hello? Oh, hi, Eileen..." Mom climbed into the car and started the engine. The car's Bluetooth picked up the call. "You're on speaker. Can you hear me?"

"Yes. I'm still at the school, and I won't make it home for another hour. I need to finish correcting these tests so I can turn grades in today. Can Nalani come home with you for awhile?"

Nalani leaned forward and yelled, "Hi, Mom!"

"Hi, sweetie," said the woman's voice on the speaker.

"No worries – of course she can." Mom pulled out of the parking lot and onto the main road.

"Thanks. I'll pick her up as soon as possible."

"Take your time. I'll be taking Kawika home later, so I can drop Nalani off at your house."

Kino gazed out the window. The neighborhoods of wood houses and cement buildings they passed seemed so foreign. She longed for the vast stretches of open greenery and grass huts. Feeling a strange tug at her heart, she realized that she missed Kauikeaouli. She wished he were there too.

Mom's voice interrupted her thoughts of the far-gone past.

"How's it look on your side, sweetie?

"Huh? Oh." Kino looked in her side mirror then glanced over her shoulder. "It's all clear."

Mom flicked on her blinker and steered toward the exit marked Punahou Street.

"Where are we going?" Kino asked.

"Home. At least until they release Grandpa from the hospital." Mom maneuvered with ease up the winding hill.

"Why are we heading this way? Isn't Kalihi back there?" Kino threw her thumb over her shoulder.

"Yes, but we're going home first. You heard the call – we'll drop everyone off before we pick up Grandpa."

"What do you mean – don't we live in Kalihi?"

Mom frowned and glanced at her. "No. You know we live in Tantalus."

That made no sense to Kino. As far as she remembered, they lived in a much lower-rent district, several cities away. "I thought we lived in Kalihi."

Kawika leaned forward and said, "There she goes again, sounding crazy. Maybe she has a concussion."

"Stop saying that. I don't…" Kino's eyes widened as their car pulled into a wide, tree-lined driveway that led to a sprawling white house with black trim. Across the manicured yard lay a smaller house with a similar exterior, and a rectangular pool filled with shimmering water. Colorful flowers and shrubs in planters accented the pool's edge.

"Gramma's here." Mom eased into the open garage past a dark-blue SUV.

"How do you know?" Kino's eyes darted around the unfamiliar surroundings.

"We just passed her car."

Kino twisted toward the driveway behind her.

"That's Gramma's car?"

"Yes." Mom climbed out, frowned and shut her door. "Maybe we should take your temperature when we get inside."

Kino followed her mom up the stairs to the front. "What happened to her red Hyundai and the house in Kalihi?"

"What house in Kalihi? What are you talking about?" Mom unlocked the door and pushed it open, kicked off her sandals and stepped into the house. "We have land there, but no houses of our own."

A voice from behind Kino said, "Go in!"

She took a step forward and Nalani pushed past her.

"The one Gramma and Grandpa bought when they were first..." Kino removed her shoes and followed her mom inside. She sucked in a breath when she entered.

Standing in the rich, wood-floored foyer, she gazed out at the uninterrupted view through the floor-to-ceiling windows lining the walls of a living room filled with leather furniture and a big, flat-screen TV that hung from the ceiling. In the distance, Diamond Head bathed in the afternoon sun.

"First what?" Mom placed her purse and keys on the table in the entryway.

Kino stood motionless, staring at the koi fishes in the pond that ran from the living room to the outside.

"Hello? Earth to Kino?" Kawika waved a hand in front of her face.

"Huh?"

"Your mom's talking to you."

Kino blinked and looked at her mom. "What did you say?" Her feet sank into the soft, plush carpet as she stepped into the living room. She wiggled her toes.

"I was asking what you said." Mom walked toward her. "About grandma and grandpa buying something?"

"Oh yeah," Kino replied. "Didn't they buy their first house in Kalihi? You know, the one you grew up in?"

Her mom frowned and felt Kino's forehead.

Kino took a step backward and said, "I'm not coming down with anything. Didn't you grow up in a small house in Kalihi?"

"You mean Kahala. And I wouldn't call Gramma and Grandpa's place small. It's the same size if you combined this one with our guest house."

Kino rubbed her temples. Kahala was known for its affluent homes and high-end shopping mall. "I swear, before I went to 1825, we lived in Kalihi across from Kawika. And GRANDAGRA was kicking everyone out of their homes."

"What are you talking about?" Nalani said. "*I* live across the street from Kawika in Kalihi."

Again, thoughts tumbled through Kino's head. Nalani had never become Maylani; if they'd never moved, her mom must not have married the CEO of GRANDAGRA. No wonder she was grading papers at school. She still had her old teaching job.

Mom picked up a remote from one of the end tables and pressed a button. The glass panes slid open, letting in a fresh, cool breeze. "Of course, we'll never consider selling that area, no matter how much money anyone offers us. Kamehameha the Third himself gave the land to your great-great-great-grandfather Haoa when your great-great-great-uncle Lokela saved his life." Mom walked outside onto the stone-paved deck and stopped at the edge of the small pool that the koi stream emptied into. "Look out there." Her hand swept the horizon.

Kino gazed out at the panoramic view. Below them lay the many buildings and houses of Honolulu that stretched out to the ocean.

"The king was very generous and gave us parcels of land throughout Oahu, as well as many acres on the outer islands."

Kino's mind spun. She couldn't believe her ears. She put her hand on the back of a wooden deck chair to steady herself. She missed Kauikeaouli even more, and wished she could thank him.

A big, beautiful, gold-and-black moth with red spots fluttered in front of her, then landed near her hand on the back of the chair.

A woman's voice from behind her said, "A spirit is among us." Her grandmother wrapped an arm around Kino's shoulders and gazed at the insect.

"Gramma!" Kino squeezed her tight.

"Hi kitten, I like your outfit."

"You won't believe where I got it!" Kino gushed.

Kawika jogged out to them. "Your phone is ringing, Ms. Kahele."

"Maybe that's the hospital." Mom hurried into the house.

"Where did you get it?" Gramma felt the material on Kino's sleeve. "It's beautiful."

Before Kino could answer, her mom walked out, cell phone in hand. "Great news – we can pick up Grandpa in an hour. If we leave now, we can stop off for shave ice before we drop off Kawika and Nalani."

"Awesome!" Kino glanced at the deck chair. The moth was gone. She followed her mom toward the house.

"Kitten, I have something to give you," said Gramma.

Kino stopped and turned around. Her grandmother held out a closed, wrinkled hand. Kino opened her palm. When Gramma let go of the object, Kino's eyes widened.

"I could have sworn that I gave this to you already," Gramma said. "This is a special pōhaku filled with mana, the lifeblood of the islands. Always keep it with you. It will help you find your destiny."

Kino made a fist around the familiar blue-green stone with ribbons of gold throughout, before hugging her grandmother.

"Thank you, Gramma." Kino glanced over her grandmother's shoulder, and smiled as the moth returned to its perch. "It already has."

THE END

Made in United States
North Haven, CT
01 February 2024

48191667R00134